Praise for: The Cold War of Kitty Pentecost

"In fact it's a large novel, large in style and large in scope, and the illusion of size is only due to the small size of the print. No sooner is one into the book even a little way than one realizes that the novel is large in intention.

—William Davey, novelist

"Alexander Blackburn's first novel should be required reading. Although his cold war is more personal than political, it is nonetheless as dangerous as the global one, and it provides sharp insights into the personalities that thrive on frozen relationships...

—Jerry Bradley, Editor, New Mexico Humanities Review

"There is in it an extreme and genuine romantic sensibility that is almost entirely missing in other contemporary writing. And Cold War reminds me—sadly—of how much we are missing now. There is in it discernibly the influence of Faullkner and even of Wolfe, but these voices are quite amiably absorbed. This is a tough, sweet, and classy book."

—Fred Chappell, Poet Laureate of North Carolina

"The people aren't just variations on a single personality, and they don't all melt together, and the range of voice and mind is impressive . . . A hell of a book"

—Clark Brown, novelist

THE COLD WAR
OF
KITTY PENTECOST

Alexander Blackburn's

Twentieth Century Quartet

The Door of the Sad People

The Voice of the Children in the Apple Tree

The Cold War of Kitty Pentecost

Suddenly a Mortal Splendor

Books by Alexander Blackburn

Author

Novels: ***The Twentieth Century Quartet***

The Door of the Sad People
The Voice of the Children in the Apple Tree
The Cold War of Kitty Pentecost
Suddenly a Mortal Splendor

Literary Criticism

The Myth of the Picaro

A Sunrise Brighter Still: The Visionary Novels of Frank Waters

Autobiography/Biography

Meeting the Professor: Growing up in the William Blackburn Family

Essays

Creative Spirit: Toward a Better World

Editor

Anthologies & a Collection

The Interior Country: Stories of the Modern West (with Craig Lesley)

Higher Elevations: Stories from the West

Gifts from the Heart: Stories, Memories, & Chronicles of Lucille Gonzales Oller

Literary Magazine

Writers' Forum, 21 vols. (with Craig Lesley, Bret Lott, and Victoria McCabe)

THE COLD WAR OF KITTY PENTECOST

A NOVEL

BY

ALEXANDER BLACKBURN

RHYOLITE PRESS LLC
Colorado Springs, Colorado

This is a work of fiction. All the names, places and events are fictional and are products of the author's imagination or are used fictitiously. Any similarity to an actual person, whether living or dead, is coincidence and entirely unintentional.

Published in the United States of America by
Rhyolite Press, LLC
P.O. Box 2406
Colorado Springs, Colorado 80901

www.rhyolitepress.com

Blackburn, Alexander

The Cold War of Kitty Pentecost / Alexander Blackburn

Revised Edition, January 2017

Originally published 1979 by Swallow Press

Quoted by permission: "I'll get by (As Long As I Have You"), Cromwell Music, Inc., and The Richmond Organization; "When the Swallows Come Back to Capistrano,"Leon Rene Publications.

Library of Congress Control Number: 2016952477

Print book ISBN 978-1-943829-07-1

eBook ISBN 978-1-943829-08-8

PRINTED AND BOUND IN THE UNITED STATES OF AMERICA

Cover design, book design, illustrations & typographical layout
by Donald R. Kallaus

For Inés with love

PART I

Chapter One **Chris**

Plunk!

The first stone sinks. Chris aims and throws the next away from a dragonfly. This stone skips low across the river. "That was a good one," Chris tells himself. One by one he throws the rest of his stones. They plunk or skip away. The dragonfly remains hovering over the water.

"Wish I had a dog." At the sound of his voice an imaginary golden retriever appears at his side.

Down by the river, Chris picks up more stones. On mudbanks of the river there are his useful stones, flat and smooth,but there are bigger ones where water is shallow, still bigger ones where the river turns dark golden getting deep. Where water is deepest there are boulders, big round rocks like gingersnap-colored cows sleeping in summer pastures. From these rocks come the sounds of rushing, whispering water. Where willows let down into the river their long green hair, in pines sundappled, in trembling leaves, birds and squirrels have suddenly vanished. Clouds, racing across the sun, have transformed it into a poppy-strange gold. It will rain.

Down by the river, Chris looks for sticks. Finding a stick that's short and smooth, he slips it in a pocket of his corduroy knickers. Down by the river are his useful sticks, pale and green in the mud, and down by the river, in trees around, things feel sad filling up with breezes. Chris and his dog are listening.

"Awright, Pharaoh . . . fetch!"

One by one the sticks are thrown so that the dog he does not see can retrieve them.

After school there is not that much to do.

Christopher Stebbins heard from nearby an old man's laughter. Whirling around, he spied a pair of skinny brown legs poking from frazzled dungarees and rolled-down lady's silk stockings. A fishing rod appeared. Then, popped out from behind an uprooted tree lolling branches in the river came a wizened face gleaming. It was the little old Indian's face. Wagging a surprise finger at Chris, he said, "Look a-yonder, bigger ever time."

When was the last time?

Not here by the river. It was . . . waving from the car window, Chris waving and the Indian shuffling with hat on and fishing-gear slung, limping down the red clay road to the farm which he and Mommy were leaving to drive to Poe's Hill to see Daddy at the university and Mommy saying *It's Mr. Jackson wave to Mr. Jackson* and Mr. Jackson waving back smiling in a lips-sucked-in way. After he smiled he just had a fed-up expression like a mud turtle's before you tortured him. There was a time Mr. Jackson helped Daddy with ploughing and Chris said–*Can I?* and Daddy leaned and rinsed and filled the dipper and brought and gulped, and cisternwater slicked his adamsapple and he wiped his face with his old Army Air Corps shirt and said–*Hot work*, and Chris said–*Can I, Daddy? –Can you what?* he said–*Ride the mule*, and in the distance where goldenrod edged the woods toward the river Mr. Jackson was leaning back and jerking forward as the mule dragged the red earth out from under him and Daddy said—*Jesus that mule*, and went running shouting *whoa-theres*.

"I'll be eight," Chris said. "In November."

"Uh huh." Mr. Jackson studied the river, then, with a smile, Chris. "Know how old I is?"

"No, sir."

"Guess."

Chris also studied, thinking *Daddy's forty-one Mommy's thirty-two Miss Huff at school's most dead so Mr. Jackson must be.* "Sixty," he blurted out.

Mr. Jackson burst out sputter-laughing like a let-go balloon. "Guess again, boy."

Chris shook his head. "Eighty-nine?" Daddy said his grandma in Tennessee lived to be eighty-nine by telling everybody she had heart murmurs so they did chores for her and felt awful sorry for her and she outlived them all. "How old are you?"

"I don't rightly know," said Mr. Jackson, then looking surprised-funny because it was a funny-clown joke. "I is two quarters Cheyenne Indian and two quarters cullud man and fo quarters damn fool."

Mr. Jackson was squinting at the river, Chris, too, trying to locate the dragonfly which had been so beautiful. After a while he wet lips and said, "Some day my daddy's getting me a dog."

"Had me a dawg oncet."

"What kind you have, Mr. Jackson?"

"Just dawg."

"What you doing? Fishing?"

Mr. Jackson shushed him . . . reeled in line . . . cast deftly across the water. "They got golden fish down there. I gonna get some!" He laughed his words with wheezes afterwards.

"Catch any ? Bass? Catch any smallmouth bass?"

Mr. Jackson pointed at an enamel pail by the tree. Chris saw in the pail a bloody string with one whiskery fish on it. "Coo. Looks like a cat."

Mr. Jackson worked his gums and spat. "Catfish." He spoke the word as if it were bad. "Daddy catches bass yonder."

"Ain't no bass in this river, boy!" Mr. Jackson said hotly, a wild look in his eyes. Chris's legs wanted to run but didn't.

"My daddy says so."

Mr. Jackson swiped at the air, closed his fist until veins bulged. When he opened his hand, he blew a crushed bug off his pink palm. "Nothin but catfish in this here river," he said, again with scornful emphasis, "but one day I'll catch Old Red-Eye . . . Don't mind, reckon. Good eats."

Chris pointed to the pail and asked with his own accent of distaste, "You eat *them?*" He was thinking of Mommy's serving dinner to him and Daddy, her countenance beaming upon them as she said, "That'll hold you."

"We don't eat them," Chris said.

Mr. Jackson, bloodshot eyes wide open, looked surprised again. "What you-alls eat then?"

Mr. Jackson's skin had changed color. It had gone gray like a cup of cold cocoa. Clouds had blanketed the poppy-sun. Distantly, thunder rumbled like a ball bouncing on a giant's drum. Mr. Jackson played his line into eddies and muttered to himself. "You set with the chains on where you's at . . . They brings the tin pannikin. Toes frostbit, legs swole. They brings this bucket. Mush and fatback, sometime bake beans or cabbage smell like the shithouse. Smells good when you's hongry. You set there and you et and that mean Mr. Burgess watching with the shotgun."

Mr. Jackson squinted, wrinkled skin under eyes rolled up, but then he again expressed a big startled look like a clown's on TV, surprised by something wonderful. Backing away a few paces, Chris picked up a stick. Finding a bunch of wild violets at his feet, he battered them with the stick until Mr. Jackson, pretending like he was waking up and yawning like one of the Seven Dwarfs, beckoned with a secretive finger-sign, "Com'ere, boy, show your sumpin."

Feeling as if a hand were caressing his heart, Chris picked up a crushed violet. "I got to go," he said, eyes on the ground until he flicked them up.

"You don't mind I have a look-see by myself?" Mr. Jackson shrugged thin shoulders, looked sad, glanced away.

Now that the wind was rising, the river was rippling like golden tinfoil shaken. On the slopes slender saplings shook until foghued undersides of leaves swayed up and back, to and fro. The air began to cool. Chris, seeing Mr. Jackson slipping off boot and lady's silk stocking from his right foot, saw at once that there were several toes missing, the foot like a goat's, a "V" between big toe and stumps, saw, too, that the ankle turned inward at a gross angle and was a jellyfish color peppered with sores. Mr. Jackson rubbed his sad foot.

"Do it hurt?"

Mr. Jackson nodded. "They had gret big old chains, that's what. I hep a lady and they put me away like I dead. I ain't done nothin. Lord's truth." Rolling the stocking back over his foot, like Mommy after a bath, Mr. Jackson turned to Chris and said with a gummy grin, "You, me friends now . . ."

It began to rain, drizzle bits then leaves splattered. Chris had the sensation of raindrops clamped to his skin. His legs wouldn't run yet even though Mr. Jackson had heaved himself up and was coming toward him at a stiff gait, the good leg bending at the knee. When he was close, he stopped. Chris smelled a spicy sweat on him and kerosene. Mr. Jackson spoke toward the river. "I had me that little dawg down in the camp," he said. "That Mr. Burgess used to kick him. He always come right up to me his tail awaggin. He stick his nose down and lick my sores. Always saved him sumpin t'eat. Et that slop right out the pannikin. Wes Jackson was his *friend*! Lord's *truth*!" Mr. Jackson had swung around. His eyes were wild again. "Run, boy!" he suddenly cried, "run befo Mr. Burgess cotch you!"

Chris ran. Where the path rose abruptly toward bluffs, he stopped and waved. Sure enough, the crazy old Indian waved back. He had been joshing about Mr. Burgess. Then Chris was running again—to the bluffs, through the pinewoods and across the fields, weed-patchy and unplowed, to the house. From the half-shelter of the doorway he watched Noah's-Flood-like waters rain down. He was just in time as thunderrumblings exploded CRACK! Fields and woods looked steamy as they cooled. Between house and barn the liveoak's leafed-out branches writhed and hissed trying to reach out, catch and devour him.

He did not hear the whine of the motor until the Chevy had splashed over ruts by the barn. By then it was the sheet-tearing sound of tires and the *whoosh-snip whoosh-snip* of windshield wipers and finally the no-motor doorslam that he heard. Then it was Daddy breaking into crouching run, the tall man with horned-rim glasses, clutching his briefcase in one hand, with the other hand keeping his wet hat from blowing away.

Chris ran to him.

"Hello, sweetheart," Daddy said and removed his hat. Chris hugged his father's middle and gazed up at rainshiny, dripping gray hair. The magic of this was vast. "Son, let's get the pluperfect bejesus out of the rain."

Chris swam his gaze over the termite-rotted railfence at the field's edge and into the wilderness toward Tuscarora River.

"Anything the matter, son?"

"I saw a catfish," Chris tried to explain. "It wasn't no smallmouth bass."

"It wasn't *a* bass," Daddy corrected him. "What makes you

think there are bass in the river? "

"You said."

"Oh? I did?" Daddy looked puzzled. "I must have been thinking of a river in Tennessee, when I was a boy like you . . . Let's get out of the rain."

Chris wanted to ask about chains but didn't.

"You've been down by the river?"

Chris said nothing.

"Good day at school?"

Daddy climbed the steps to the porch, opened the screen door and the oak door. Chris followed him into the living room where Mommy already had a log fire blazing by the brick hearth.

"I'm home, honey," Daddy said in a raised voice toward the kitchen. He went there to see Mommy while Chris peered out a pane-glass window in the direction of the river. It was sad, old Mr. Jackson all alone out in the rain.

Chapter Two **Max**

It had stopped raining.

Don't think about it.

Smoking his pipe, trying to relax in a Morris chair by the fireside, Professor Max Stebbins remembered how he used to tell himself not to think whenever he had to fly another mission across the English Channel. It, this command to put his mind on automatic pilot, was a kind of amulet with the illusory power of invincibility. If he didn't *think*, he might be able to disengage himself from consequences. Others would then be responsible for *his* decisions. If, in fact, he allowed himself to *think*—absurdly, his conscience refused to obey such commands—he would forever remain at the RAF base when he was holding Captain Sculley's severed head under his arm like a jack-ó-lantern from Hell.

During the past week he had felt too anxious to begin thinking. So now, thinking wishfully in spite of himself, he conjured up today's scene, saw those emissaries from Stanford University arriving in black funereal limousines outside Henry Memorial Building, wondered why Californians were dressing in dark suits, black neckties, pork-pie hats and sunglasses like F.B.I. agents and then was terrified when they marched into his office and, without beating around the bush, offered him the Chairmanship of their Department of English, a tenured full professorship at three times the salary bestowed upon him by South Atlantic University in benighted Poe's Hill, North Carolina. Of course, he had gingered up enough of the old martial process to tell these clowns that he would consider this offer after consulting with Ginny, who might well want a position in the Drama Department thrown into the deal. After the departure of the ridiculous Search Committee, Max must have reflected upon the unsought, indeed unimaginable honor dumped in his lap and had to suppose it had something to do with his book on the Spanish origins of the modern novel. Of course, following favorable reviews of his book in *PMLA, The New York Times*, and the infallible *London Times Literary Supplement*, word about the incredible Dr. Max Stebbins must have swamped the corridors of power.

The only problem was, once Ginny discovered California Gold, he would have not only to think but also to make a commitment to drive her and Chris in his private jet Out West.

Miles over the city thunder crumped its bombs.

The war defied time, being always inside you with, beside him, Captain Sculley's headless torso spouting blood like a monstrous Roman candle, Max steering their plane through exploding flak over Belgium.

Firelight flicked golden fingers against plastered walls. Every now and then windowpanes rattled from explosions in Poe's Hill of the usual cluster of atomic bombs.

He had been reading the local newspaper when he told himself not to think, for there in bold letters on the front page was the story of a fellow professor's suicide, that of Carlos Brodie, a man his own age, a professor on a windowledge of the fifteenth floor of Bright Leaf Hotel in the middle of glittering downtown Poe's Hill, and down he goes in a shabby place in a time of shabby emotions.

He tossed the newspaper aside and in spite of himself thought about the dead man. Carlos, a neurophysiologist, left his wife and went to live with a young woman, said to be one of his students. Wifey telephoned everyone that her husband was paranoid-schizophrenic, a drunkard, and a sex fiend depraved by student orgies. The lunatic inventions of Mrs. Brodie had been campus gossip all winter and had led certain waggish professors to remark that perhaps they were missing something. Last week General Scroggs, President, and Dean Blacklaw had called Brodie before a faculty committee and fired him for moral turpitude . . . Carlos Brodie, *mon semblable*, the tribal spirit of denial dissipates the energy that affirms connections between humanity and the humane. If the second law of thermo-dynamics is morally true, the human will goes into a trance and creative lifeforce is driven to ever lower potentials. Pompous nonsense. He had never even met Carlos Brodie.

A glass was shattered in the kitchen. Ginny. Still angry? "Let it go," Max said aloud to himself, rose, and went into the kitchen where Ginny was drying her hands on jeans. Her dark hair, pale blue eyes, and lovely, really lovely body were not a hell of a strain to look at. Ginny, focusing attention upon herself, was indeed an actress, her hand upon brow even now a kind of tragic gesture. "Look at this bloody place!" Her favorite word. Must have picked it up from English showbiz types in New York at the Lamb's Club.

"May I help?" Tiny fragments of broken glass glittered on the linoleum floor under the newly installed floodlights. When he squatted to collect pieces of glass, groaning from the effort, he suffered from his increasingly frequent embarrassment, the fact that he'd been letting himself go, not only to what Scott Fitzgerald had called emotional bankruptcy, but also to fat, not enough of it yet to change his waistline size but enough to inflate him into a

Falstaffian caricature in the eyes of his young wife.

"Leave it," Ginny said. "It's your old sherry glass. Sorry."

"Don't worry about it," he tossed off matter-of-factly to show he couldn't care less, though he did.

It was indeed the last of six sherry glasses presented to him in the Stone Age of a dozen years ago by the professor who had supervised his doctoral thesis in New York, Erlich, Professor Erlich. The recollection threw a stone in the shallow waters of his life. After the war he had treaded water as a research assistant in a life insurance company, New York home office, before he sickened of its ghoulishly hackneyed ads about widow's tears and its heartless practice of paying fortunes to lawyers in order to disallow legal claims from impoverished, grieving immigrant families. When, in addition to funds from the G.I. Bill, he won a scholarship to attend graduate school to work toward a Ph.D in English, he flourished. Moreover, Erlich, a veteran of the First World War, understood the insidious after-effects of "shell shock." While some of Max's professors expected their indoctrinated pupils to publish specialized research at prestigious Ivy League universities where, he was advised, as if it were a blessing, "teaching wouldn't count," as if undergraduates were literally "under," Professor Erlich had proposed a less stressful approach to the profession, one in which teaching *did* count, at least until Max felt ready to revise and publish his groundbreaking thesis on the origin of modern fiction. Max brought his bride, Ginny, to an institution devoted to fraternity parties and football, the arts being, as so often in Puritan cultures, a leisurely pursuit devoid of divinity and dollars. Ginny, he knew, felt about as welcome in the South as Darwin's monkey.

She was half giggling. "What's so funny?" he asked, crawling about on the floor.

Observing himself through her eyes, he deserved derision.

"You look like you're auditioning for *Waiting for Godot*," she said.

Max rose, moaning, to his feet, dumped glass fragments into a garbage pail, bowed theatrically and said, "You think I'm Lucky the slave? As I remember the second act, Lucky lies prone on the stage and doesn't say a word . . . Well, I'm crazy enough for the part . . . Chris tucked in?"

"He cried himself to sleep."

"Whatever for?"

"Poor lamb, he's sad."

"Did he talk to you?"

"Yes," Ginny said. "He's upset because you apparently told him there are bass in the river, then denied it."

Blood rushed to Max's temples. The accusation, though based upon his simple mistake in memory, carried an implied stereotype of "Senior Moment."

"Your ex-con friend, Wesley Jackson, from our local Harlem, Vinegar Hill," Ginny pressed on, "has been showing Chris foot and ankle wounds from the good old Southern chain gang. Sure, I've posed in the nude for a photographer in order to earn a few lousy bucks, but when an old half-black Indian man starts exposing the flesh to a little boy, I think you ought to call the police. It's not as if he were giving dimes to little girls to perform somersaults."

After a long pause to cool down his own anger, Max contrived to say evenly, "Wesley has been imprisoned so long he's unsure how to make friends. As for whatever crime he may have been charged with, I believe he was innocent."

"He was convicted for life and only recently paroled. It's a fact. I didn't imagine it. I am not the storyteller in this family. I want you to tell Mr. Jackson not to come around here anymore."

"I can't do that," Max said quickly. "Telling him he can't do as he pleases in his golden years would be cruel." Max stopped there. He didn't want to reveal that Jackson's daughter, Mrs. Mary Branch, had been part of his life in Poe's Hill during the war. He liked to keep quiet about those days.

Ginny glared, he thought, at him. Gradually her tight lips curled into a smile. "Fix me a drink, sweetie, something fizzy, like sex."

"Ecstasy coming up," Max said. "Jack Daniels, in case you haven't heard, is distilled in Tennessee by us culturally challenged hillbillies."

"We'll sit by the fire," she said. He could tell by her tone of voice that she wasn't really angry with him anymore. He could guess why she had been upset: early that afternoon she had interrupted him in his office and drawn out of him his deliberately vague hint that he would leave the university and Poe's Hill for employment elsewhere. He hadn't said a word about California, though he had a real offer from there in writing, the letter now tucked into the breast pocket of his damp Harris tweed jacket.

He fixed two strong bourbon highballs and followed Ginny to seats by the fireside.

"Don't be angry with me, honey," he said, tilting his glass to hers in salute.

"I'm not angry with you," Ginny sighed, lifting gaze to ceiling. "I'm angry at the world." Max met her gaze when she lowered it. "I'm with you there," he said.

"Max," she resumed, "you know this afternoon in your office? What have you planned about Chris?"

He put his tumbler on the hearth. "Well," he began, "it strikes me that giving up my job and our home here, to go somewhere else . . . well, Poe's Hill has the same bourgeois charm that nowadays stretches from San Francisco to Moscow."

"Well?"

"Well, what the hell!"

"Darling, I asked you calmly what you plan to do about Chris.

The farm is no place for us."

"I thought you liked the farm."

"Shush. You'll wake Chris."

"So what's wrong with it?"

Ginny replied to his lowered voice. "It's phony as hell and sentimental, this bloody nonsense about trying to become self-sufficient peasants. You're not a farmer, sorry to tell you. Still, if you ignore your precious hillbillies, the smug born-agains, the Ku Klux Klan, and the absurd belief that every human embryo is entitled to own a machine gun, nothing is *wrong*, dear, except . . ."

"Except," Max interrupted, "me and the South I love, all her madness notwithstanding." "Oh," Ginny said, "I'm having a ball, alone all day. I love having hominy grits and hush puppies to prepare and Dixieland sweat to launder. Now that ex-cons are roaming our woods and saying, like Mark Twain's slave, 'Come to the raft, Huck, honey,' I guess there is nothing wrong. Only, we have a little boy who's so imaginative he invents stories about things that don't exist. Is there nothing wrong? You're always right."

"Look." Max pumped hands for professorial emphasis. "I'm not forgetting that you gave up your career in the theater to marry me."

"Career?" Ginny pounced. "I learned the showtime trade all right. I was quite a glamorous ingénue in summer stock in wonderful Ogunquit, Maine. I once earned $500 for a TV commercial about toilet paper. I had a one-liner in which I exclaimed with a look of radiant gratitude to heaven, 'What a bummer!' If I'd had train fare, I would have tried my luck in Hollywood, but I was starving, so I picked you up like a half- smoked cigarette and blew you away, you big jerk."

"Hollywood?" Max made the word sound sarcastic even though he intended to put the city of Los Angeles within easy future reach for her. He paused to drink, letting the ice slither to his lips. Ginny's thighs left his emotions sprawling. "I've been selfish to stay here. I like my job, I have tenure and health benefits, the climate is good, the government here, whatever you Yankees say, is usually progressive. In other words, I try not to think about change. Forty-one wants peace, your thirty-two wants Cinderella's prince, entertainment, attention. I understand." He let a sly grin spread over his face. "How pompous is that?"

Ginny observed him with raised eyebrows. "Are you changing your mind from what you promised this afternoon? Are we staying here until you retire and the envious faculty, no longer feeling threatened by you in their little power games, regard you as a used Kleenex? Your hippie co-ed students have flattered you into thinking you *matter* to this riotous little retirement home for mediocrities."

"I'm a mediocrity," Max said.

"No, you're *not*!" Ginny exclaimed. Much to his surprise, he hadn't expected his real, though not abundant, inadequacies to be vehemently defended.

"You've written a book, a beautiful book," Ginny went on, "and that's more than the mediocrities have done. You've proven that English and American scholars have been wrong about the origins of modern fiction."

"Thanks very much," Max replied, shaking his head in an author's rejection-misery. "Three university presses have turned the book down."

"Well," said Ginny, "you've upset a few applecarts. The English believe *they* invented the novel. The French believe *they* invented it. The editors at university presses, Northern as well as Southern, associate Spanish literature with Mexican peasants, faces covered with *sombreros*, bodies leaning against cactus plants for a perpetual siesta . . . You'll publish your book when you find an editor who has actually *read* one." Ginny paused, then said, "Chris is lonely here."

"The kid has a mind of his own," Max said. "When I was a boy,

I *valued* being alone."

Ginny held her tumbler in her lap. She did understand the difference between solitude and loneliness, didn't she?

"Did you? Did you value being alone? You told me once you did exactly what your father wanted, except to become a doctor. You were a pilot in the war, dropping bombs."

"Jesus," Max said. "I didn't drop bombs, I dropped parachutists, and the thing that keeps me going is that I love teaching, I love my students, I love literature, I love nature, and I love you."

"Exactly, and you're ready to move on," Ginny snapped back but in a sympathetic tone.

"I'm going the right way to work," Max said, unable to dodge the guilt he felt about waiting so long to pull up stakes. However, in his own defense, procrastination notwithstanding, he had actually learned something from military service, namely, a cooperatively caring society trumped unbridled liberty—his father's obsolete love for the cult of individual freedom without requirement.

His father had tried to instill in Max the logic of invulnerable convictions about honest faith and hard work, about knowing your place and keeping it. His father, still in touch with an old order of life, would read his favorite Emerson aloud, pausing to repeat wise saws . . . *So much only of life as I know by experience, so much of the wilderness have I vanquished and planted, or so far have I extended my being, my dominion* . . . Max had learned that one by heart. It had seemed true once to many of the people. His father had thought it was true, even though his father should have seen enough evidence of human suffering to know that the ego-centered self, when solid, separate, and alone, actually depended upon the gifts and restraints of society. But there they were, words, words as seductive as stories about cowboys fast on the draw with guns, words that finally fell soundlessly from the air like dandelion seeds, words from a father, the countryman's love of platitudes, his father telling him *Take it easy, the accelerator is a glandular disease*, telling him, too, how Clayton, Tennessee, was expecting another Stebbins to make a fortune off of its simple poor. Max had listened, but the war changed his way of listening until the struggle for Success and for the so-called Dream, which had been his father's and his grandfather's struggle, seemed undermined by compassion. Before the war Max was no rebel to the faith of fathers. Afternoons after school he dawdled around his father's clinic doing odd jobs, sterilizing instruments or emptying wastes. He accepted with piety odors of frailty and decay. Crisp antiseptic and whitewashed walls contributed to a romantic idea of honor. Nor would he have anticipated, then, amid the keening of undernourished babes and bewilderments of pregnant mountain girls, the growth of some answering cry of his own. He would hear hushed voices somehow loud behind the big oak door to his father's office, would hear a deepthroated mutter like an echo in a long tunnel, rising, and would go at last when he was seventeen, about to take the longest trip of his life, north to college, into his father's office, there to sit in a corner out of the light and to watch people, his people, shuffle in to sit bolt upright and to bless unintelligible prescriptions signed by Clayton's Doctor Stebbins, physician, capitalist, and Emersonian Self-Reliant Man. It made a tableau, his father's son outwardly correct and conventional, inwardly withdrawn into his own dream of a better world, breathing in solidarity with others under the same sky.

Ginny was waiting for his agreement to, as she might put it in the popular reject-the-past-and-remorse idiom, "move on."

The irony was, by moving the family to California, he was exposing them all not to his make-believe Stanford, not to a new life in the fast lane but to the real prospect of joblessness, homelessness, and the skids.

"I need time," he said.

He watched her quizzical expression change into a frown. "So we remain here while you have lots of bloody soul-searching?" She finished her drink and handed him the tumbler. "Fix me another, sweetie. I think I'll become an alcoholic."

He found his drink and finished it. The fire, the very idea of hearth and home, was going out. How sweet was the sound of rain pattering on the roof before, when the rain stopped, he would be left with a hollow feeling in the belly as if he had been the pilot responsible for nuking 100,000 innocent civilians whose emperor was defeated and ready to surrender, make-believe justification of mass murder to the contrary. It was true, he had cocooned himself in a dream above the world. It was true, he was not a farmer. If he didn't think about California Gold, he could once more find in himself the resolve that had enabled him to scramble for his twin-engine aircraft at any time, day or night, taking off into skies buried in human misery.

He removed the letter from his jacket, rose with a groan, and started for the kitchen. Then he heard Ginny's raised voice distinctly say, "I forgot to tell you, Kitty Hasbrouck has been taken to the hospital."

Max was thunderstruck. For several moments there was a sensation of burning in his chest as if his nerves had been drawn to extreme tension, like a bow, and left without release.

Kitty's name opened the door locked against the world. How much had Ginny guessed? Had Kitty been talking? Not to a living soul had he uttered the secret truth of his heart: Kitty had been the mystical Other whom one met once in life! . . . Of course this was romantic nonsense. He knew it. Nevertheless romantic nonsense was probably what had compelled him to return to Poe's Hill—in order to exorcize it, to, if possible, recover from Kitty what he had given away too completely, himself. This much he had clarified about his quest before. Now here they were again, all those feelings of failure and rejection, residue of the lost estate of passion. Why, he even met Kitty every now and then by accident, accompanying her big bald husband, Adam Hasbrouck, the university psychiatrist, at faculty cocktail parties. They had some agreeably safe conversations, and, physically, though in her mid-thirties she was more remarkably beautiful than ever, she no longer aroused his interest. In fact, she was not his type. Had they married—and time was when marriage to Kitty Pentecost had been the most powerful intention of his life—they would surely have fallen flat on their faces. Thank the gods she had turned him down! He was persuaded that he ought to be grateful to her for destroying what they had together. And of course he pitied her with that devastating pity reserved for former lovers who marry someone else. In sum, he had honestly come to believe that she meant nothing to him. Now in a matter of seconds he remembered her all too well.

He pulled himself together, went into the kitchen. "Oh? What's the matter with Kitty?"

"She's having a baby at last."

"Oh."

"Aren't you even interested, Max? You knew her long before I did."

"Say that one had met her once," he declared with a self-minimizing shrug. "We met twenty years ago in forty-two. In a moment of imbecility I joined the Army Air Corps, and they sent me, a raw prig of twenty-two, to a pre-flight school in Poe's Hill. Kitty Pentecost would have been about sixteen then. You must imagine the scene."

"I do," said Ginny. "You are probably a man who cannot form relationships except with teenage girls."

"Probably," Max said coldly. "And you were nineteen when we married. A little mature for me, but still—"

"The Hasbroucks haven't much time. Adam's over sixty. Kitty's taking a big risk. Apart from being diabetic, she has trouble with her kidneys and . . . Anyway, the doctors warned her that, if she becomes pregnant, there is a fifty-fifty chance she and the child may not live. She decided to take the risk. That gal has guts."

"Yes," Max nodded and said without irony, "and I'm glad for her. She used to be terrified of her mother. She had to find the courage to be herself."

"Max," said Ginny.

"Hm?"

"Did you like her better than me? . . . Max, I'm teasing! Don't look so woebegone. Now, just suppose little Gin-Gins wanted to give acting one more try, you'd understand if she went to New York, wouldn't you, sweetie?"

He said nothing and went outdoors where his Weltschmerz would be a nuisance to no one but himself. The air was cool and fragrant. About him, palpable in moonlight, were tangible possessions, the house, barn, and ten acres of farmland and timber—once the homestead of Kitty Pentecost's family on her father's side. Destiny? Oh, he had gone to war and returned unscathed. Five years had passed since he had met Kitty. She, psychologically damaged, otherwise had not answered his letters. Although he could not forget her, he assumed that he was forgotten. And then she looked for him in New York and found him. And found her courage for the first time. She was twenty-one and just asserting herself against her mother. She was still terrified: some as-yet nameless misfortune would pursue them and fall at last upon their love. And so they fled together, fled to the High Rockies where they lived cocooned in a dream above the world a little while until one day she was gone like a *belle dame* in a myth, and the flower of passion had been eaten and had disappeared. Then he had turned eastwards to the cities of leftover life and had tried to forget her and could not, and came back to Poe's Hill, not to corner her, not to woo, but to be near enough to her to find his heart at home, knowing even before he arrived with his wife and baby that he would find Bermuda Farm boarded up and untenanted exactly as Kitty had first shown it to him in the early days of their desire. It was as if the place had been reserved for him, unchanged in the motion of time and not even changed by a bill of sale and the signing of deeds or the sound of voices once more invading. One look at the farm and he had telephoned the Pentecosts, given his name, said that he had a job at South Atlantic University and would like to buy the farm. And all Kitty had said was, *Oh, that would be all right.*

Some years he ploughed and planted, other years he felt too apathetic to work the farm. Sometimes, as now, a metaphysical loneliness settled down with moonlit mists and drew his dreaming soul toward the stars. He felt as if he were proffered happiness only in another sphere of existence.

Chapter Three **Ginny**

Ginny woke. The bedroom curtains fluttered their fuzzy sheen. Everything was very still, hardly a sound to break the monotonous droning of crickets. The bloody crickets, how she hated them! It had been different in the early years of her marriage when life in the country was a new experience. Yet nine years had passed! She had rediscovered something about herself—she felt it most strongly when the crickets droned. She had always feared confinement.

Max breathed heavily beside her. Until yesterday he had seemed remote to her, someone not *there* for her, perhaps a stranger in the back row with another world to go to. She had entertained a horrid idea: leave Max and take Chris with her to New York!

This notion of making a dramatic change in her life had its appeal as a phenomenon of the times, like shopping for new cars, new lovers, new homes, new jobs. Perhaps her dread of confinement was really a narcissistic rebellion. There was a redbrick mock-Tudor apartment house in Forest Hills, Long Island, just up the street from the railroad station. She had lived there with two silent sisters, three brooding brothers, a mother whose only reading was *Lives of the Saints*, and a father who dreamed of riches and drank.

Although the family had barely survived the Depression, it did not seem to occur to Mother McBride to stop having babies after Ginny was born. As a girl, she was known to kick in the shins anyone who criticized her. Once at convent school she kicked the nun who had caned her for refusing to bow her head in prayer, and when she was marched to the Mother Superior, who told her she was a devil, she screamed the worst blasphemy she could think of, which was, *Jesus was a smelly old faggot like you*! Although priests were her natural enemies, she studied their craft. As she grew older, she realized that she could deceive others into thinking Ginny McBride was willing to heed their demands: but, lying on the floor under the second-hand grand piano (it was her mother's second solace: she would spend hours playing weepy ballads from Ireland, singing how her heart longed to go back to this place and that) Ginny had heard over the Philco radio ravencroaky war correspondents and had gained the child's sense of universal hypocrisy, peering into the abysm between the impious world and the one for which others prepared her. *You're the slyboots, Virginia, here's the back of me hand to you*, her father said. She, too, dreamed of life on the grand scale—the McBride dream was infectious—of living on Park Avenue or, better, in Hollywood. She needed clothes and she needed freedom. She worked after school in the popcorn reek of a local five-and-dime store, and later, weekends, posed in the nude for an odious freelance photographer. Her father said, *It's hooring she's after, the vain piece of perdition.* One day her father found where she had hidden her savings, went on a three-day binge, and came home wailing like the Bean-Sighe, beating his breast and proclaiming himself, like a Dostoyevskian character, a louse. She left home. Soon she was living in a coldwater flat in the Village and working as a waitress to pay for drama lessons. Through Equity she picked up occasional work off-Broadway and in summer stock. Eventually she caught the eye of a director who was casting for a skin-flick. She read for the big part and, lo, she was chosen for it—but there was a catch, the sleeping-with-the-director bit. If he had been a jot less truculent, she might have satisfied the bastard and justified everything on the usual professional grounds. But Ginny turned him down, lost the part, and found herself virtually cut off from employment in her profession. She felt as if she had let everybody down, including her father, moral write-off though he was.

It was at this time that she met Max. It was a Sunday. Deciding to spend the day reading and strolling in the park near the Museum of Natural History, she took the bus uptown to 72nd Street and on the way began to read her book—Kafka's *Trial* which a friend who feared Senator Joe McCarthy had recommended. She had scarcely read two pages when a tall man with thick wavy dark hair and bright gray eyes (softly twinkling as if amused by the world) entered the bus, sat down beside her, and at once pointing to the book asked, "Do you feel guilty about something?" She liked his voice, his looks, his freshness and said, "Doesn't everybody?" He chuckled in his throat and said, "Whenever I feel buried in a landslide of guilt, I dumb-down conscience and still keep my index finger stiffened upwards toward my invisible assailants." They looked fully at each other. When later they alighted from the bus, she had determined not to lose him.

Was he hers? As a casualty of war he was almost too much for her to cope with, and she was not coping with life in Poe's Hill. Some of the faculty wives spoke of "tithing for God" when they baked cupcakes for one another and, once a year, prepared baskets of goodies for distribution among black families in Vinegar Hill, the ghetto whose name was uttered with supercilious condescension. The wife of President Scroggs had even warned the ladies against including raisins in these parcels. When Ginny inquired why, Mrs. Scroggs had explained that raisins, my dear, could be fermented.

Ginny smiled, acted a part for Max's sake, held her tongue even on the occasion when Dean Angus Blacklaw's wife, a gargoyle-faced moron from Tidewater, Virginia, informed her that the Catholic church of her youth was "the Ho of Babylon."

She had slept little, so stunning had been Max's news that the family, after all, would be moving to California. A Disneyfied vision opened up for her, literally. Mesa Vista Community College, wherever that was, would be within leapfrogging distance of Hollywood.

When Max had entered the kitchen where she had been washing dishes in the stained enamel sink, she had listened resentfully to the familiar sounds of the male hegemony in the process of making highballs, the *whuff* of the refrigerator door, the cracking of ice and its clinking into tumblers, the faint slurping noise of Jack Daniels being poured, the little hiss of Canada Dry. Max, nearby, said nothing. When she finished the kitchen chores and dried her hands, she found him at the kitchen table, waving an envelope at her, motioning for her to join him and read it—a bit of theater she liked.

Addressed to "Professor Max Stebbins," the envelope looked intriguing, "Dr. Billy Bob Bass, Office of the Dean, College of Letters, Arts & Sciences," the "Mesa Community College" bit followed by the name of a California town she'd never heard of. She removed from the envelope an official letter with the same addresses, and from the opening sentence it appeared that Max had been applying for a Full Professorship recently advertised through the Modern Language Association—except that Max have failed to make the cut, the position having been opened "for qualified applicants under forty." Well, that was a piece of academic skullduggery, age discrimination blatantly announced, so Ginny was happy to see that the second paragraph began with the old standby of blah-blah,"However." The connective introduced an available job, a shitty job but a job. For one whole academic year at an unspeakably insulting salary, Professor Stebbins was invited to replace an Assistant Professor on leave of absence. Apparently, the Ass Prof Eng was ill. Should, "unfortunately," he retire, quoth Dean Billy Bob, the visiting professorship would become a "tenure-track" one, and Max would certainly be eligible, if not actually "overqualified," to apply, though the Search Committee would have to do its blah blah. "Unfortunately"—there was another cover-the-ass bit—"unfortunately, your salary will not be sufficient to match our cost of living, but we would be delighted to offer your wife an adjunct position in our Speech & Drama Department."

Ginny knew enough about academic politics to put little faith in a Search Committee even if a teacher were to be another Socrates. For any tenure-track position there would be at least 300 applicants, most of them still attached to their mother's umbilical cords, one paw scratching the millimetric brow, the other clutching a Ph. D. or lesser degree. As for the "adjunct position," the words carried subliminal suggestions of intercourse pilfered from Hindu sex manuals. Would she have to assume the "adjunct position" with a harassment-entitled dean in order to match the cost of living?

Max stirred in his sleep. The scented aroma of his warm body aroused her. The thought of his still surprisingly slender body flowered in her like the stem of an exotic plant. Tracing with a finger the sterno-mastoid muscle flaring from his collarbone, she snuggled herself against him and slipped her hand around his penis. It was like a warm bean burrito until it stiffened on its tenure-track.

"Hey," Max said huskily.

"Thank you for finding us a way out of Occupied God's Country," she said. "Kiss me, kiss my breasts."

Love was made.

. . .

AFTERWARDS SHE LAY AWAKE, THINKING. Life in California might be as confining as, or even worse than, life in North Carolina.

Mornings would, Poe's Hill or Hollywood, just keep on coming. Like yesterday morning. Waking Max and Chris. Cooking breakfast. Seeing Max off to his eight o'clock class. Like getting Chris ready for school, driving him in her pickup to Poe's Hill and the Green Street Elementary. Thinking about Chris and that awful Miss Huff. Returning home, washing dishes, cleaning, reading, eating without appetite, wanting to talk to Max, to someone. Gathering sheets for the laundromat. Like, finally, driving to Max's office to talk about Chris and his, Max's, wife, about Forest Hills and the misbegotten, yet knowing that when she saw him she would forget most of what needed saying . . .

That afternoon she had parked at Henry Memorial Building and walked upstairs to Max's office. She liked going there, crowded as it was with deskboard chairs. Max's office was personal, part of what he had to give. Originally but a storeroom adjacent to a gloomy, old-fashioned amphitheater or lecture hall, but with spacious, pigeon-cluttered windowsills and a view of green lawns and antebellum, *Gone with the Wind* magnolias, it had been transformed by Max, its walls replastered, painted Botticellian blue and decorated with brassrubbings of Crusader knights and with foxhunter prints he had collected in England during the war. She entered the office as though walking on stage, knowing she would forget her lines. Max was typing.

"Hope I'm not interrupting?"

He stood up nervously, still in mid-paragraph. "It's O.K.," he said, "come in."He made a fuss to find her a seat.

"Oh." Her gaze settled on an unfamiliar painting on the wall near his desk. "What's that?"

"Present from one of my students, Helen Wade."

The "Helen Wade" demolished Ginny's tolerance for modern

art. "It looks like an enema tube."

"It's a banjo," Max said, "being crushed like the artist in Picasso's *Guernica*."

"What are we writing? Are we published or perishing?"

"We are, both," Max half-smiled, turned his back to her. "I'm requesting from Chicago a photostat from an obscure learned journal."

"Max, you're not going to Chicago, are you?" She had a dread of Chicago based upon nothing more than her reading of Dreiser's *Sister Carrie*. She identified strongly with that heroine's struggle to exist in her own right as a person and actress. All the same, she was distressed by the way Carrie and Hurstwood fell victim to economic and social forces beyond their control. Since she associated these forces with Chicago, she had determined never to go there.

"No," Max said. "They say it's a great city, though."

"Good, darling. We'll go north. You'll be at Harvard, summers I can do stock in Maine. And Chris can be a dayboy at a prep school and study Latin and . . . I'm worried about Chris."

"What's wrong?" Max paused to pick up and light his pipe. "It's Miss Huff at school."

"Oh, her," Max nodded, puffed. "The one with a big wart on her face? "

"It's not her face I'm worried about."

"Nor she either, apparently."

"Max, don't make jokes! Do you know what she has told Chris' class now?" She told Max how Miss Huff informed the class that God puts seeds into mothers' tummies and that a child who didn't learn geography would go to hell. "Maybe," Ginny went on, "maybe she doesn't actually say these things, but that's what Chris *thinks* she says. Oh, I could choke that stupid woman! I don't propose to sit back while a sick society poisons my child's mind!"

"Agreed," Max said after another pause. "But who are we to say what goes on in that mind? Falsity stacks high the corpses by the tens of millions, and no one can afford complacency, but that doesn't mean we are all deceived by the lies." Max paused to place the pipe in an ashtray. Happening to glance at the letter he had been typing, she wondered why its address appeared to be California, not Illinois, but, since she wasn't wearing her glasses, she could have been wrong. Max put his arms behind his neck, stretched his legs, and spoke as if he had a message of great importance. "Human beings," he said to the ceiling, " like to believe in things that aren't literally true, myths, illusions, delusions. We wouldn't be human without this desire to surpass ourselves. Now, for me, literature is a liar's craft, magical. For you, actors impersonate imaginary people in order to create evidence of things unseen. I don't know why we create imaginatively as we do. We absolutely must have stories to live by. Stories are a drive, like food and sex, necessary for survival . . . Very well, honey," Max, sitting up and folding arms, went on in another voice. "When the time comes, we'll bug out of here. Promise."

Ginny wondered where Max was going with his lecture followed by an apparent commitment, so accustomed had she become to believing whatever he said. "Oh," she said in a teasing tone, rising from a desktop chair like an intimidated student after the ringing of a bell, "go to hell." At the door, hearing the typewriter clicking again, she felt as if she were once again in convent-school uniform listening to her mother's thin whimpering, hearing a door slam, and seeing her father drunk and sneering on the other side of her cage.

Now the crickets outside the bedroom window droned like a chorus of a million muffled baby rattles, high-pitched. Or were they cicadas? She didn't know the difference between crickets and cicadas, if there was one. Unheard and unseen by day, they surrounded the house by night with a presence that could easily be more than a billion years old. The choking wilderness certainly put human life in perspective. Why had she become so obsessed with making a change? The only thing changed by uprooting the family to California would be the weather, the crickets, and a real possibility of disaster. Everyone, as Max had said, his pontificating actually convincing, not pompous, needed stories to live by. But what had happened? He had, out of his true compassionate nature, offered to sacrifice himself before the altar of her nagging complaints and resentments, mistaking these as evidence of her unfulfilled dreams. In truth, she had already fulfilled one essential part of herself through marriage and motherhood, whereas he, as Man biologically traduced as dominant when in fact he was a wombless wanderer, could fulfill himself only through a struggle to identify and pursue *his* dreams, bringing his bacon home. It was too much, what he was selflessly surrendering to Woman so generously.

Rolling over in bed, she touched Max on the shoulder. "Are you awake?"

"What is it, honey?"

"You were writing a letter to that dumb dean in California, weren't you, not to Chicago? You were accepting that crappy job for my sake? Did you mail that letter?"

"You got me," he said, clutching his chest like a bad guy shot in a mythical "Western" duel. "No, I haven't mailed it."

"Destroy it, she said. "It's not a good story for us. I have what I want right here. Listen! The bloody crickets have stopped singing!"

Chapter Four **Chris**

"Christopher Stebbins!" roared old Huff next day. "Yes, ma'am?"

"Tell the class what we learned yesterday."

"Yes, ma'am. You said the Nile was a dirty old river in Egypt. It's full of crocodiles. The Nile flows past the pyramids. They buried Pharaoh in his mummy"—giggles erupted in the classroom, but Miss Huff's eyes were like slate so everyone shut up and Chris continued—"and they put this mummy and his treasure in a boat inside a pyramid. You said the Nile is not as nice as the Tigris."

"Anything else?"

"Yes, ma'am. The Tigris has a twin river, Euphrates. On the map the Tigris and Euphrates look like a wishbone. There's this swamp in the middle of the wishbone where there's this Cradle called Civilization. Noah found the animals there before this flood."

"*The* Flood," Miss Huff corrected him. "Approximately 3,765 B.C. That will do. *Hoo*-rah for you."

Chris raised his hand. "Miss?"

"Yes, Mr. Stebbins?"

"Do they have catfish in the Nile?"

"No, Mr. Stebbins, they do not have catfish in the Nile."

"Well, ma'am, what about the Tigris and Euphrates? They have catfish there, don't they?"

"Mr. Stebbins, the class does not care whether they have catfish in the Tigris and Euphrates."

Someone tittered. Miss Huff puffed out her lower, pencil-blackened lip. The noise stopped as though sheared off by invisible scissors.

"What kind of fish do they have there? Bass?"

"Yes, they have bass. The best kind of fish only. They have bass and they have the whale that swallowed Jonah."

Chris frowned. "A whale ain't a fish, ma'am."

"That will do, Mr. Stebbins."

Chris kept his hand raised. "But, ma'am, do they have catfish in the Jordan we studied about."

"Mr. Stebbins. They do not have catfish in the Nile and the Tigris and the Euphrates. Certainly such an ugly fish would not be found in the blessed River Jordan. Now, Mr. Long, you have your hand up?"

"Please, ma'am," said the small boy in a dry voice, "can I be scused? I got to."

The Huff-Puff stood slowly, brushing creases from her black dress. She stepped off her platform and stationed herself, arms folded, before the door. "Well, *hoo*-rah for you, Mr. Long. We did not hear from you yesterday. We shall hear from you now."

"I got to, ma'am, please."

No one giggled. "Mr. Long," growled Miss Huff the way she did when she wanted to scare in Daddy's funny words, the *pluperfect bejesus* out of you, "what shall we do with you? The only thing you *got to* is tell us where the Pharos Lighthouse was located."

The last hour always dragged. Chris stared down at Miss Huff's legs. On one of them were two meandering stripes of purplish blue. Joined where her ankle was, they looked like the wishbone of the

Tigris and Euphrates. . . . After a while he seemed to hear, very faintly, sounds of near-motionless water, the whispering water. If he shut his eyes, he could listen to the sweet close sounds of yesterday—sweet and big. For when he played in the woods after school and down by the river or had little to do, he was aware of something in life just *there*, making leaves fall and always about to tear open the sky like the sharp cry of a bird in its grief. Mr. Jackson knew about this feeling. There was that faraway sadness behind the funny old Indian's eyes. Maybe that was why the Pharaoh wanted to lie down in a mountain of stone, in a little boat lie down in the dark, and, when the last stone was fitted in place and the golden treasure had ceased to glitter, then the Pharaoh's boat began gently to take him to a beautiful new home, sweetly to ease and drift away . . .

His eyes were closed it seemed but an instant when his name was called again. "Christopher Stebbins!"

"Yes, ma'am?"

"You may wipe the blackboard after class. Good afternoon, children."

"Good afternoon, ma'am."

"Good afternoon, Betty."

"Good afternoon, ma'am."

They were all gone, all but Chris. He picked up an eraser and stroked the blackboard with it. When he had smeared the yellow chalk of the pyramids into the yellow chalk of Mesopotamia, a golden river flowed from one end of the blackboard to the other except for one gap—the golden river of chalk had parted in the middle so that the black of the board showed through. Two golden men, one of them lame, crossed the river. One wore an Army Air Corps shirt, the other a feather headdress. They were followed by a golden woman whose countenance beamed upon him. Every now and then the three of them stooped to pick up things and put them in a pail.

What could be in the pail, Chris wondered. And then he saw clearly right into the pail. There were fish there that looked like cats and they were golden, too, and very beautiful.

"WHAT'S DADDY DOING HOME SO EARLY?" his mother exclaimed as the pickup bumped around the bend and they saw the Chevy parked along the slant between the house and barn.

"Don't tell me he's going to plant this year!"

There might be a mule and Mr. Jackson or there might be the planting Chris recalled from the time he was five. There were tractor men and stump-burnings and his father killed a copperhead and the men smelled of damp clay and one had a blue dog that chased the tractor all day.

Then they saw him. His father wore a white shirt and tie and stood by the farmhouse door. He looked at first as if he had just woken up, but as they got out of the pickup, they saw that his eyes focused shinily on things faraway as though mirrored in a cistern.

"What is it, Max?"

"Kitty died."

"Kitty?" His mother stared ahead. His father glanced at Chris, who saw the eyes, shellac-bright. "Mary Branch, old Jackson's daughter, I meant to tell you," his father was saying to his mother, "phoned me at the office. It seems Kitty's whole metabolism. . . exploded."

"The baby?"

"No."

"Bloody hell."

Chris went to his room. The sun slanted through dustmotes at his window. There was small careless birdsong in the eaves. The room seemed small. Presently he ran downstairs to the kitchen, arranged two slabs of bread, smeared peanut butter on one and yellow mustard on the other, squashed the slabs together, nutty oil oozing like wet cement between bricks, and went munching into the yard. His mother was having one of her fits. One moment his father looked at his feet, the next moment at the sky.

"You mean *I'll* do the bloody work! I cook your meals, I wash your socks, now I'm kennel-girl as well! As if I didn't have enough to worry about already. In future you can wash your own bloody socks!" His mother glared at his father before going on in cold voice. "No wonder Kitty couldn't stand you. You don't love anybody. You *think* you do. Now that you can't indulge in sexual fantasies about a pre-war teenager anymore, you suddenly remember you have a family and bring home a *bribe*!"

His father glanced about. When his shellacked eyes rested on Chris, the brows knit.

"Ginny, I think you've said enough. What you say is cruel and untrue."

"Oh, you're so bloody superior!" His mother turned, swept past him. The screendoor slapped behind her.

His father looked down at him and half smiled. "Chris," he began, "your mother and I… a good friend of mine died today."

Chris nodded.

"Good sandwich?"

"Peanabudderanmustud."

His father made a face. "Come on down the barn, son, help me decide something, will you?"

Chris kept his eyes open for snakes as they went under the dying liveoak to crosscut. A squirrel skittered into the branches. Toward the barn where rain had cut ruts of red clay, birds feasted on worms. His father unhooked the half door. Chris breathed the barn, dusty haywarmth and dungdaubed beams. A shadow moved in gray, mewling light.

"How is he now, Mr. Jackson?" his father said.

Mr. Jackson straightened up slowly. His gummy grin caught the light. "Oh, he be fine. Had him some milk. Got you a good little dawgy, it's truth."

The pup in the old man's arms was quivering inside its tan delight.

His father explained that he had fetched the dog from the pound where it was about to be put down. If Chris would be responsible for the dog, then it was his. "We can kennel him here in the barn where the snakes and rats don't get to him. Shall I take him back?"

Chris worked his mouth against the collapse of his throat. "You got to talk to him," said Mr. Jackson, placing the pup in Chris's arms. Pink tongue tickled his neck. He pressed his nose into kennel-foul fur. Chris giggled, "He purrs you all over." He talked to the pup. When he looked up, his father's eyes were softer.

"You'll take care of him?"

Chris nodded.

"Perhaps Mr. Jackson could use your help to build a kennel. He won't be any trouble, sir?"

"Him and me is friends. Ain't no trouble."

He placed the pup down and ran a few steps and the pup followed. "Come on, boy," he called.

"Got a name for him, son?"

He would have to say a name forever, not just the pretend-named dog who fetched sticks. He looked at his father's eyes. They caught a golden ray of light. They had seen Death. "Pharaoh," Chris said.

"That's a nice names," said Mr. Jackson.

"Pharaoh," Chris called. He lifted Pharaoh and looked at his father. A smile rippled across his father's face. "Fine," Daddy said. "Don't mind your mother. She just gets moods."

"You can wash your own bloody socks," Chris said.

Chapter Five **Max**

Evidently, Mother Pentecost had cut herself off from Kitty and Adam Hasbrouck. Up to the time of the marriage Kitty and her mother had managed to live together in the family home, a big rambling white clapboard structure on Cornwallis Street. Then the marriage. Mother Pentecost protested that Kitty was living in sin. The old woman packed a few things—white kid gloves, for instance, and the masonjars in which she concocted vile-smelling yoghurt—with a few reminders of the imminent destruction of the world and of hellfire everlasting for those fallen from grace, stormed out of the house, and arrived five minutes later at the Confederate Daughters Home where she had been ever since. Evidently, there had been no response to her daughter's communications. At the same time the old woman was kept remarkably well-informed about Kitty, perhaps by Mary Branch, who had once been the Pentecost's housekeeper and was known to be devoted to both mother and daughter. At least Mother Pentecost learned of Kitty's death within an hour of its occurrence. She did an unheard-of thing: she telephoned Dr. Hasbrouck.

"I want her buried, do you hear?" No preliminaries, just, "I want her buried, do you hear." Evidently, the astonished Hasbrouck knew the voice instantly, imagining, as he told Max, that Queen Victoria would have spoken with the same unmistakable inflection if Queen Victoria had had a South Carolina accent. Kitty had expressly stated that she wished to be cremated, her ashes scattered in the Tuscarora River. Hasbrouck approved this poetical fancy, having himself spent years in India where similar whims were custom. But he felt so taken back by Mother Pentecost's demand, coming as it did and when and where—he was in his office at the hospital, his head buried in his hands—that he gave in at once. "Buried? Yes, if that's what you want. We'll bury the ashes. It will be comforting to think she has a little place of her own . . ." Hasbrouck heard the telephone click.

Katherine Pentecost Hasbrouck, 1926-1962, was buried at Eternal Rest Cemetery one bright afternoon.

Driving back toward Poe's Hill from the cemetery, Max and Ginny were silent. His tears were barely under control. He kept thinking of Kitty in sugary terms, of her courage, her profound desire for life, the struggle against the current, the triumph of the leaf in the storm . . . He thought of Hasbrouck, too. He had misjudged Hasbrouck, had thought of him as the comical psychiatrist, overbearing, pompous, bitter and crafty. This was but the appearance, perhaps: that huge 6'5" frame, that massive bald head, that mouth thin-lipped as Bellini's Doge. But Hasbrouck must have really understood his young wife and been worthy of her, which was more than Max could say for himself in his own marriage. Indefatigably, the aging doctor had arranged proceedings much as Kitty would have wished, a correct and simple service now to be followed by a wake. There had been no eulogy, no extravagant praise. The university chaplain read Psalm Forty-Six about the river which makes glad the city of God. There were vibrant hymns such as *Eternal Father Strong to Save* sung before family and friends drove to the cemetery.

"Look!" Max cried as he spotted Mrs. Pentecost walking alone along the highway near the sign that read POE'S HILL CITY LIMITS. Transcontinental eighteen-wheelers were expresstraining past this figure in black mourning clothes of a bygone era, head and shoulders almost as stiff as a waxwork at Madame Tussaud's, sounding horns at her, raking her with cyclones of diesel exhaust, yet there she was walking, a scarecrow in black whose flesh, he remembered, sagged off high gaunt cheekbones like drippings of candlewax and was of that pallid hue—a figure fragile, indomitable, ludicrous, haughty, and mad.

They passed her.

"How utterly alone she must feel," said Ginny.

"Alone with God. She and God have everything under control. 'Ever the fiery Pentecost girds with one flame the countless host.' Ralph Waldo Emerson. Ralph Waldo EgoTrip."

"That's in bad taste," Ginny said.

"Well," Max said, "I admit I have a score to settle with old Mother Pentecost. She almost succeeded in thwarting Kitty's happiness. Even her going to live at the Confederate Daughters Home was punishment designed to make Kitty feel guilty for having married. Mother Pentecost, like the Ancient Mariner, has grabbed hold of strangers and told them her daughter is damned. Now death is the triumph of the God of herself."

Ginny lit a cigarette and said, "Don't talk about God so much. You make me nervous."

"I don't suppose she's going to Hasbrouck's party," he wondered aloud when he no longer saw Mrs. Pentecost in the rear view mirror. "Shall I turn back?"

"She doesn't want help," Ginny said. She wasn't smoking her cigarette. "I begin to realize what Kitty was up against. Unlike me, she couldn't run away."

. . .

HIGHBALL CLINCHED IN FIST, Max disengaged himself from a group of professors heatedly discussing the Carlos Brodie affair. The suicide leap, the unspeakable wrongness of being made to feel so insignificant, the man his own age, his youthful feelings still intact, experiences much the same, sharing a world much the same, yet going to it of his own volition, which was not the same: to think of Brodie and then to think of Kitty, her victory in death, her rage for life, her recent long-striven-for emancipation from other people's arrangements of her reality: this was not the same, this was surely not the same.

"It was murder," one of the professors was saying, his voice gravelly yet pitched to a kind of girlish hysteria. Max half turned and identified the speaker as Archibald Leary of Political Science, the intense Yankee liberal. "Just plain simple murder. Scroggs and Blacklaw ruin a man's life for what? For shacking up. Jesus H. Christ, in this day and age . . . No. It was a witch hunt, Brodie smeared as a commie."

"Hell, Archie," someone else drawled, "they didn't fire him for adultery. They fired him for living with one of his students. There's a difference."

"What's the difference? I don't see any difference."

"Corrupting the young, Archie," the other said.

"What has screwing the young got to do with corruption? It's stupefying, sickening, and infuriating for us to sit back and let a couple of over-the-hill fascists like General Scroggs and Dean Blacklaw get away with this!"

"Hell, Archie, don't talk so loud. You'll get us all into trouble."

Max moved away.

The livingroom, diningroom, and downstairs vestibule of Kitty's house on Cornwallis Street were crowded with at least a hundred people, many of whom he knew by sight, quite a few who were complete strangers. Voices were loud, animated by Hasbrouck's liquor, and yet, remote to Max's thought and need, unreal.

I'll get by
As long as Aye-ee
Have you. . .

In a corner nearby a tape kept playing with baleful persistence tawdrily dolorous songs of the thirties and forties. He would hear snatches of a song and in a moment he would be thinking of Kitty, the eyes of a laughing girl, the ravenglossy hair, the courage and sacrifice and beauty of her being, and tears, tears of a mingled grief and joy, would spring into his eyes.

Though we mayee
Be far awayee. . .

A big beefy man lurched heavily against him, spilling the contents of an icy highball on Max's necktie and suit. "Sorry, bud," the man said.

"Let it go," Max said, his tone of voice insincere.

"I said I'm sorry," the man repeated, inexplicably aggressive. Max lifted his gaze and took in the flushed-red visage of a middleaged person of about his own height but powerfully built, brutish with a thick red neck, the collar of shirt opened to expose a slate-blue tattoo.

"O.K.," Max said.

The man was glaring at him and swaying. "I said I'm sorry, and if you don't like my apology you can go screw yourself."

"Jesus," Max said with awed inflection.

"What's wrong with you, mister?"

"I was about to ask you the same thing," Max said. He's going to hit me, Max thought. "You knew Kitty?" he asked with a deliberately disarming smile, as if conducting an interview.

The question seemed to give the man pause. He passed a beefy hand over his face, looking sunk, done-in. He shook his head several times, eyes half shut before he said, "She was my sweet little girl, know whatta mean?" The man gripped Max's arm tightly and said, "I'd get stuff for her anytime . . . *any* time daynight she come to my store . . . say, 'Mason, y'all got to get it for me,' I did that little thing. I don't do that for just these college kids. She was my sweet little girl."

Since there was a small grocery store called Mason's just across the street, Max made a deduction. If this were that Mr. Mason, then Kitty might well have known him since the time she was a girl, and since Kitty had been a friendly person, it would follow that this big drunk was another devotee, with feeling. Here at any rate was feeling. Max was a little envious of a man who only needed alcohol to vent it. On the other hand, a cloud of suspicion had drifted across his thought. What sort of *stuff* was meant if not a drug, and if Mason pushed drugs other than the insulin she required as a diabetic, how could one square the fact with her late magnificent fortitude?

A woman's party laughter, piercing the mind like the shriek of a seagull: it fell back to a sea of murmurous voices and he heard

Though there be rain
And darkness too
Aye'll not complain
Aye'll see it thuh-roo

and said to Mr. Mason, "Excuse me, I'm going to get a drink. Care for a refill?"

Mr. Mason released his arm, pawed the air, shook his head

with eyes half-shut and said, "She was my sweet little girl." Half treadmilling backwards, his tongue an exclamation mark in his open mouth, he careened across the room, shook himself, and studiously concentrating upon his footsteps, pitched and rolled toward the door to the street.

Max went up to the bar which was being tended by a high school kid whom he could identify as Mary Branch's son, Manny —tall, slender, brighteyed.

"Another bourbon and Seven, Mr. Stebbins?" Manny's movements as he mixed the drink were graceful, quick.

"So what are you doing nowadays, Manny?"

He had not expected Manny's eyes to come up, just for an instant, with voltage.

"Go to school, play ball."

Max thanked him for the drink and remained where he was, sipping the drink, watching Manny mix other drinks, the hands and long arms making every move rhythmic, precise, an aesthetically-pleasing thing. Muscles released upon hair-triggers. Glistening forehead frowning upon the work in hand, lips curling in disdain of that work, but the work of the hands ritualized with subtle shifts of tempo and gesture.

Max during the war had not thought much about death. He felt as if he'd been placed in a glass dome, that there was a normal life on the other side but that he himself had had experiences that sucked him out of the rest of humanity. Death was unreal because life was unreal. Then Kitty had seemed immortal. Immortal the beauty of her face, lost and on the other side of time. Now indeed she was lost, not just lost to him, because he had faced that loss a thousand times and ways over a period of many years, but lost to the world, and the world so full of terror and magnificence was lost to her.

Stepping to a window, he turned his back. Tears were in

his eyes again. If only he and Kitty had been allowed one final, fateful interview. If only he could have heard her speaking once more in passionate intimacy to him, clearing the debris of misunderstandings and of shattered dreams. He would not have interfered with the life she had chosen, but he yearned to be at one with her. Now he was cut off forever from her. He was alone, his body busy digesting food and growing cells, his lungs sucking in and expelling air, his heart coolly pulsing at sixty-four beats to the minute, all toiling without conscience or reason, solemn as doom.

He had his tears under control when Ginny appeared, looking cross. "You'll have to speak to Dr. Hasbrouck before we leave. Do it now before you've had too much to drink."

He looked at his wife and saw a stranger, pent-up lines about her eyes and in those blue eyes the depthless and predatory bitch. He felt her humiliation, but she was going too far this time. He made an effort to refrain from comment.

"Where is he?"

"In the other room with a student named Tom Driver who is from this neighborhood, just back from Viet-Nam, engaged to your co-ed sweetie Helen Wade. He was invited by Kitty herself to make his home here in this house, *and*, if you ask me, looks enough like Kitty to be her son," said Ginny all in one breath. "If you ask me, my dear, there was some hanky-panky going on under the magnolia trees back yonder when—" She paused and fluttered her eyes.

When you whispered farewell
In Capistrano

Max listened, shame passing through his heart.

You promised to
Come back to me. . .

He was experiencing Ginny's insinuations as if there might be some truth to them, whereas common sense told him that Ginny was merely putting down Kitty in order to claw him. He gave Ginny what he fancied was a hard look and went.

"Dear Max, how kind of you to come!"

Big bald Adam Hasbrouck had the tonsured look and hearty manner of an archbishop. The look he had acquired naturally, the manner he had picked up as a Rhodes Scholar at Oxford in the twenties and later as a physician attached to the Imperial Army in India. Max had just read a dust-cover description of the psychiatrist from one of Hasbrouck's books.

"This is young Driver. He's one of us. Going to move in, we hope. Max. Tom."

Tom Driver was of medium height with slightly drooping shoulders, nineteen, perhaps twenty years of age. He seemed to hold his head to one side, the chin tucked in and dark nervous eyes distrustfully a-squint. It was possible that he had been trained as a boxer—the nose was a little flattened—yet it was a pale, sensitive face on the whole, one that imagination might have stretched to a ghostly resemblance to Kitty's.

"Pleased to meet you, sir," said Tom Driver as they shook hands.

Hasbrouck hooted. "Never say 'pleased to meet you,' my boy. Crikey, what's the world coming to! On the other hand, the formality of the English was an attempt to make imperialism look respectable, wouldn't you say so, Max? How would you describe a gentleman?"

Answer the question.

"As a misfit," Max said.

Hasbrouck guffawed. "No, no, no! A gentleman—you must listen to this, Driver—a gentleman is like Stebbins here, high moral seriousness, that sort of thing. He's a war hero! Flew against the Hun, I tell you . . . I suppose we all have times when we like to indulge in a little sensual entertainment far from the madding puritans. Eh?"

Hasbrouck continued in this vein for several minutes. Max was conscious of Tom Driver's embarrassment. As for himself, he couldn't understand why Hasbrouck, whom he scarcely knew, was so maladroit. The affair with Kitty? Yes, must know. But what? How? And what did it matter now? Max wondered, only half-listening. Abruptly, Hasbrouck changed subject: "Tell me, old man, why did you buy the Pentecost farm from Kitty?"

"What if I did?"

Hasbrouck peered over the rims of his glasses and said, "Nothing, old boy."

"You meant something."

"I protest!"

"What's bothering you about me, Adam?"

Hasbrouck lifted both hands and let them open limply. "My dear boy."

This was almost intolerable. Max had almost felt twinges of guilt about that time years ago when he reappeared in Kitty's life and held her, perhaps against her will, to a sentimental promise made in the summer of forty-two that he should live at the farm when the war was over.

"The Pentecosts themselves . . ." Max began, groping for an explanation more tactful than precise. He cleared his throat. "The farm belonged to Reverend Pentecost. He was a friend of mine, a generous man. He knew what war was like before I did. He wanted me to know of a place I could come back to after . . . after."

Hasbrouck nodded approval—like a damned psychiatrist. "After the war. I see. But you didn't come back after the war, did you? I mean, not immediately."

"No."

"You were in New York?"

"That's right."

"Then you lived in, let me see, was it Colorado?"

Colorado, no one had known about Colorado but Kitty, yet Hasbrouck knew! Mother Pentecost might have known, though Max had never been sure. So it was Kitty who had desecrated the sacred. Yet nothing mattered now. Max said in an even tone, "Visited. Never lived there."

"I see," Hasbrouck resumed with supercilious stare. "Eventually you were hired by South Atlantic and you remembered Reverend Pentecost's extraordinary offer of a place with—sentimental associations?"

"Why, Max, you never told me that before," said Ginny. She had approached unnoticed. "You men are so romantic in your attachments . . . Poor Adam, you must be absolutely jiggered. You've handled everything superbly. An Irish wake in the Bible Belt, faith and begob!"

"My dear Ginny. How lovely we look."

Presently Max was left alone with Tom Driver while Hasbrouck took Ginny on a tour of the house. What Ginny had said earlier about Tom Driver's getting married to Helen Wade and moving in downstairs, with Hasbrouck converting the upstairs into an apartment and private consulting office, had been confirmed. The other bit, that about Tom Driver's being Kitty's son, had the quality of slander. Max began a brief interrogation. "Well, Tom," he said as affably as he could, "it seems we have something in common: both of us go to wars and return to Poe's Hill."

Tom returned him a sympathetic look. "That Dr. Hasbrouck was sure getting the needle in! I wonder why."

"Don't worry about it. We're all having a bad day," Max said and, after a pause, asked, "Do you mind if I ask who you are?"

"I don't mind. I've been asking myself who I am for as long as I can remember . . . I grew up just a few blocks from here. When my parents were drowned in a sailboat accident, I lied about my age and joined the army. They shipped my ass to 'Nam where I completed high school through a correspondence course, and that was about all I got out of the army except an ulcer and boredom and a discovery. I discovered I wasn't cut out for a soldier." Tom grinned. His teeth were crooked. Max liked him.

"Did you know Kitty Hasbrouck?"

"Not much," Tom replied. "I mean, I used to see her around when I was a boy. I didn't really know her. The woman who worked for my parents knew Mrs. Hasbrouck way back when. She used to work for Mrs. Pentecost, here in this house, before I was born. A neighborhood connection."

Max considered carefully. "Mary Branch?"

"Yes, Mary Branch. That's her son tending bar. She raised us both."

"Small Worldsville," Max said. "Can I get you another drink?"

"Thank you, sir. Double scotch on the rocks. For the ulcer."

The mention of Mary Branch in the context of the Pentecost family—it was really the only context in which Max had been acquainted with her—brought an image vividly to consciousness. Twenty years ago almost to the day one Lieutenant Max Stebbins in Army Air Corps pinks and greens was standing talking to Reverend and Mrs. Pentecost *there* where the temporary bar was set up, there by the long window the same amber light filtering through lace curtains, and he turned and saw Kitty entering the room, seeing her for the first time, Mary Branch just behind: laughter in Kitty's eyes, in the eyes of a girl of sixteen, your heart breaking loose, breaking back, in turmoil of the excited heart and the thought, the young man's thought, he must not get involved with a woman when he was gong to war: yet as Chance blew across that spring and summer he had not known how war would compel clarity and regret.

"Tell me," he asked Manny Branch when the latter had mixed two drinks in that rhythmic way which was such a pleasure to observe, "what you know about Tom Driver."

Manny Branch glanced away as if to say, in effect, he was not in the habit of conversing. Presently, however, Manny spoke without voltage in his eyes: "Mama worked for the Drivers from the time they got their boy to when they died a couple of years ago. They paid her good. They even left her money in their will. I got nothing against them. I really don't know anything about Tom Driver except, wherever he came from, he got himself well looked after."

"What do you mean, 'wherever he came from'? Was he adopted?"

"That's what Mama said."

"Thanks, Manny. You've told me what I need to know." Max added, "You'd be a welcome guest at the farm any time you care to come. Your grandfather will tell you how to get there."

Manny's eyes flashed. "That crazy old con? Man, I don't want nothing to do with him!... But I might could see you sometime, professor."

"DR. HASBROUCK WANTS TO SEE YOU PRIVATELY UPSTAIRS." This from Ginny a quarter hour later. "He said it was important."

"He employs you to fetch me. Who the hell does he think he is?"

The day had proved too much. His nerves were on edge. The pain of being in a crowd of people, all the talk, so many inside themselves in private encounters, chance revelations and insinuations, everything running away now . . . but perhaps he was too analytical of others, too vulnerable to their ways and passions. Pondering this, his isolato feeling, had a curiously calming effect because others felt the same way. He went upstairs and, as directed, knocked upon a door in the hallway.

The door was opened by Hasbrouck, who wordlessly ushered him in. The room was spare and gray and looked as if it had not been occupied for many years. A single lightbulb cast its glare upon a table on one side of which sat several men, their chairs somewhat pushed back so that their faces, catching the light aslant, appeared grotesque, color drained away and shadowy pits for eyes. They sat very still. They had been waiting for him.

"Gentlemen," Hasbrouck said in a faked deferential tone, "this is Stebbins about whom you know, and before we proceed I would like to have his word of honor that he will discuss with no one, at any time, what is said in this room." Guiding Max toward the table, he went on in another, commanding tone: "I want your solemn promise, you will not under any circumstances—"

"Cut the crap," interrupted one of the others. It was Archibald Leary, the ardent Yankee. Max also recognized Wee Willie Koontz, vice-provost of the university, a small man who smoked a small pipe. The others he didn't know. "Jesus H. Christ, you old radical," said Leary, addressing Hasbrouck with a grin, "a man's word of honor nowadays isn't worth a tinker's damn. Sit down, Professor Stebbins, we're just going to ask you a question. You don't have to answer, but we'd like your honest opinion."

Max did not sit down, though Hasbrouck brought a chair. The men relaxed their postures. Their faces caught more of the light and became faces of men who felt, reasoned about things, even reasoned about chairs.

It was Wee Willie Koontz who removed his pipe and spoke next. "Professor Stebbins," he said in small voice, "in your opinion did the administration's firing of Carlos Brodie for alleged moral misconduct conform to your idea of what is just and right for our community?"

"Of course not," Max replied without a pause. "Every man should have a right to work according to qualifications and competence. As far as I know, Carlos Brodie was fully qualified and competent—in fact, one of the few persons apart from Dr. Hasbrouck here widely known in the scholarly world outside South Atlantic University. His continuance in his profession was, I would have thought, assured. It is true, this unhappy man's private life seems to have become irregular. He left his wife and went to live with a student. Again, as far as I know, he did not *advocate* adultery, and, as to whether co-habitation with a consenting adult who happens to be a student constitutes grounds for saying he is corrupting the young, I would say that the burden of proof lies with the administration, to prove that a corrupt practice exists. For example, if Carlos Brodie's friend was, at the time of the affair, still performing tasks, in her capacity as a student, which it was his responsibility to assess according to truth and intrinsic worth, then their private business could be judged to have an effect contrary to the interests of the academic community and inconsistent with our institution's function in society. However, it is my belief that General Scroggs and his committee proved nothing of the kind. They seem to have been conducting a kangaroo court, concerned not with justice but with political hysteria. In this sense I would say that the case resembled that of Socrates whose ideal of academic freedom the Athenian majority condemned to death over two and one half millennia ago. That is my opinion. I could be wrong."

His mind raced as he spoke. Should he have held his tongue? What possessed him to give a lecture? What, after all, did his opinion matter? Why was he trusting these men? Their conspiratorial air, their silly solemn air of self-importance: why was he allowing himself to drift into involvement with what was unmistakably a power game? But suddenly stonger than usual, he was taking delight in exposing his thoughts, and not because he stood to gain an advantage: it seemed to Max that he was speaking from an internal sense of form and moral obligation and that this was important for its own sake.

Meanwhile the others had exchanged glances of an approving kind. There was some indication that Max was to be taken into their confidence. Archibald Leary was now spokesman. "We like what you say," he began in a cordial tone. "Carlos Brodie was indeed a scholar of international repute. His scientific research required extensive travel, to England, Germany, Japan and the Soviet Union. Unlike our distinguished colleague here—" Leary motioned with his head toward Hasbrouck—"Brodie had no socialist sympathies, in fact, no politics. Science was his life. Nevertheless, thanks to the Cold War, he was constantly under surveillance by the authorities, with whom, I need scarcely add, our boys, Scroggs and Blacklaw, are eagerly cooperating. At the risk of stretching your credulity, professor, I will inform you that Dean Blacklaw has a special fund for which he is not accountable to the university and the purpose of which is to pay informers. The vice-provost can confirm this."

Wee Willie Koontz took his pipe from his teeth and said, "We suspect that the girl with whom Carlos Brodie became involved was hired to compromise him."

"In other words," Dr. Hasbrouck broke in matter-of-factly, "the administration is busy pruning out members of the faculty whom the government looks upon with disfavor. I need hardly point out, that would include all present."

"That is why we have formed an action committee to get our faculty unionized as soon as possible." This was from Leary. Max studied him, the ardent Yankee as he thought of him, and concluded that Leary's idealism masked a yearning for self-glorification, thrusting himself to the forefront of attention. A young man in his mid-thirties, he was possibly being used by the others. Max felt a little sorry for him.

"What do you want with me?" Max asked the others, ignoring

Leary.

Again it was the small man, Koontz, who seemed to speak as leader. "Nothing for the time being," said Koontz in his small, bored voice. "Our aim is to get the faculty to rise to a vote of no confidence in President Scroggs. I take it you would not be opposed to such a vote?"

"MY DEAR MAX," Hasbrouck was saying sotto-voce to Max at the front door fifteen minutes later, "not a word or we all get the ax." Hasbrouck pressed Ginny's hand with theatrical effusiveness. "My dear young lady, if you should change your mind, do give me a tinkle, won't you?"

"What was *that* all about?" Max asked her in the car.

She wrinkled her nose at him. "I have talent, my *dear*. He thinks I'm wasted on you."

"He said *that*?"

"No, grumpy. But he did say, if I want to try the stage again, he has useful connections in New York." She met his gaze with one of her swift, impertinent flashings of the eyes. "Max, I want to feel important again."

"What's got into you?"

Her smile was cool. "I want to be cherished. If I am not cherished, then it is immoral our living together, and I shall leave you like a shot."

"That sounds rehearsed," Max said. "Say what you really mean."

She found a cigarette, lit it and said, "Very well. I think we should work out a mature relationship. I'll be in New York part of the year, you can stay on that woman's farm."

That woman's farm, his lips repeated soundlessly while wheels of thought seemed to clank through a revolution. It was not all over, but suddenly, he thought, the marriage is doomed. In mottled twilight, Cornwallis Street seemed appropriately named for a defeated general. He felt as if he were trapped inside a bottle. It smelled of old car, crusty layers of oils and dust. He did not take care of what he loved. Perhaps he could not love again, perhaps his capacity for love had been filled once and for all on a spring afternoon twenty years ago when the eyes of a laughing girl possessed his heart. "Why don't we all go north this summer?" he heard himself saying. "You act in summer stock, I'll work on a book, Chris can go to camp . . . Let's celebrate. Dinner at the Bright Leaf Hotel in glittering downtown Poe's Hill, city of exciting stoplights."

"I'll wear my new necklace," Ginny said, brightening. She removed a necklace from her purse and fastened it. "Guess who gave it to me." He said nothing. She said, "Adam. Wasn't that sweet?"

"Jesus," Max said.

"It was Kitty's."

The ornament pendent from the necklace had already caught his eye. It was a golden fish, both eyes bored on a flat dimension and its mouth an egg-like oval. This was turquois. The ornament, though odd, reminded Max of Indian jewelry he had once seen in Colorado, and he said so.

"Adam thinks it comes from Kurdistan where the Pentecosts were missionaries. Oh," Ginny said as he caressed her neck.

"What's all this about cherishing?"

"Adam was sweet. He said I remind him of Kitty. Do I remind you of her?"

"I've treated you rottenly, haven't I," he said gently. "I'm sorry." The end of their marriage was nobody's fault, really. Although he wanted to give Ginny all of his attention, he could only give part of it. Sooner or later she would, not having all, prefer nothing. All this was in the nature of things but not inevitable. No, not inevitable. He would resist. He would put his mind and will to work for the benefit of others, his wife and child most of all.

Chapter Six **Chorus of Old Women, Mrs. St. George, Billy Raven**

The mock-colonial veranda of the Confederate Daughters Home faced toward the setting sun. In the distance rose plumes of smoke from the factories of Mill Mile. Nearer, pines of South Atlantic University's campus pointed their shadows at the old ladies who sat in rocking chairs. Pigeons bobbed and cooed among chairs and pairs of black orthopedic shoes. Diamondy blue hands flung crusts left over from supper. From within the three-story brick building came clatter of dishes and the shrill caterwaul of television tuned high for the hard of hearing.

By now everyone at the Home had learned of Kate Pentecost's madness. Some time in the later afternoon she had stumbled in, mourning clothes covered with dust, hearing-aid disconnected, glasses so caked with mucus that she had not seen the veranda step, had tripped and fallen. When Betty Chick and Miss Bessie Lee Gooch (of Goochland, Virginia) tried to help her to her feet, Kate Pentecost (formerly Katherine Coligny Ball of Old Charleston, South Carolina) had screamed at them, "*The lord is my shepherd, I shall not want! The Lord is my shepherd, I shall not want!*" and, wailing strangely, had crawled to a rockingchair, hauled herself up by that (by a prodigious exertion of muscle taut as pianowires), and shuffled, bent forward, her long irongray hair falling over her face, toward her room. An hour later, just before supper, Kate Pentecost (daughter of Major Ball, C.S.A.) reappeared on the veranda. This time almost everyone saw her—the rockingchairs were occupied, all twenty of them—and she was not a pretty sight. She had dressed herself in a white robe stitched together from bedlinen, but this ragged appearance was not what distressed the women. It was what she had done to that long iron-gray hair heretofore combed and braided and clasped into a bun until it had achieved a correct austerity. Now she had hacked it off. The scalp bled from lacerations.

Horrified at ninety, Mrs. Hampton St. George (of Old Charleston, South Carolina) had cried, "Kate, poor child, what, I do declare, have you gone and done to yourself!"

Miss Bessie Lee Gooch, a small brittle woman who wore a cloche hat, shook her finger like a metronome and screeched, "Somebody stop her! She gonna do somethin' crazy, Lord ha' mercy 'pon my soul!"

Nobody stopped her. She was a great walker, old Kate Pentecost, and was made, they said, out of whalebone. She couldn't be stopped once she got pointed in a certain direction.

The ladies watched her scurry up Atlantic Boulevard toward Mill Mile and out of sight. Someone finally thought to inform the superintendent. He went out in his car to search for her, but after a while he returned, running fingers nervously through his hair. He telephoned the police.

In rocking chairs rocked and rocked before the setting of the dark red sun, the women talked in excited, sibilant voices. Memories were stirred. It was agreed that poor Kate Pentecost had been a very odd person from the time of her arrival at the Home three years ago. When her daughter married, she refused to speak to her and moved out of the house, the one just around the corner of the block on Cornwallis Street. Everyone agreed, her mind was already crazed by religion and had been so, perhaps, since before the turn of the century. How else explain why a lady of her breeding would go as a missionary to Kurdistan, few white Christian women within a thousand miles?

"Crazy blood!" screeched Miss Bessie Lee Gooch (of Goochland, Virginia) with a finger-wagging. "Was her folks in Charleston crazy too, Mrs. St. George?"

Ninety-year-old Mrs. Hampton St. George worked her mouth, shook her head sadly, and said, "I've known Kate Ball to look at since she was knee-high to a grasshopper. I can tell you something. She was the wild one, but she had more *sand* than all of us put together . . . I stayed to home and raised my young on East Battery. I wish now I'd struck out like Kate Ball and done the work of the Lord in the dark places of this earth." Perhaps moved by her own thought, Mrs. Hampton St. George slowly stood up and, leaning on a stick, stared into the dusk.

"Well," said Betty Chick after a pause. "Lightning bugs is out." Pinpricks winked in gloom. "Brother made me catch one when I was little. Scared me most to death, I declare."

Long-memoried Mrs. Hampton St. George stared into the dusk. What she saw interpreted itself on the near side of consciousness as familiar iconography illuminated by a raying light: whirling and turning the dancers swoop motionlessly, and soundlessly churchbells of Old Charleston drown their lamentations in the sine wave light: and her native city looked in perilous twilight like a graying woman down on her luck and innocence: the guns on the Battery had been silent for a generation, Fort Sumter was the grim and blinded pupil of the harbor eye, and along Tradd Street and King and Legare a few mansions had been restored to elegance without grandeur, and elsewhere Palladian houses had ceased to be used as brothels for the Yankee troops and carpetbaggers: and young Caroline Duval (not yet Mrs. St. George) strolls along East Battery, her brother Fitzhugh beside her swaggering in the white pride of a naval officer back from Manila, and a horsewoman clatters by, a mere girl in pink and white, already her eyes shining, torso upright, head lifted as though she hears voices like Joan of Arc, and Fitzhugh laughs, and his laughter ends abruptly as for the first time Miss Katherine Coligny Ball pins him with a glance: and the kind young mother Mrs. St. George observes Fitzhugh bedazzled, losing his Miss Kate to the glittering ballroom, then stepping forward with her by his side as they lead the Grand March, but she had already refused him and will do so again and yet a third time, even in the presence of syphilitic Major Ball, widower and father who is black to the brim with anger, and Fitzhugh will falter and die long before he yellows into death in Panama: and voices hushed in church whisper *despotic imperious capricious*, and amid voices at teatime someone cites the Goncourt on Countess Castiglione, on moods precipitate and fleeting as the pulse of Folly: and Mrs. St. George, her older son already parading at the Citadel beneath an aroused and righteous eagle, sees the aging maiden sitting stonily apart from spectators but being attended by the tender-eyed Indian halfbreed (whom, it was said, Major Ball had saved just an infant from massacre in the Far West and brought home and had raised among the negroes, his mother, it was said, having been a fugitive slave among the Indians) they called Jackson who will unintentionally reveal in court what the smart people have already guessed about the perfidious and degenerate character of Major Ball, C.S.A., and will be sent to state prison for assuming the guilt of others: and Mrs. St. George goes with her sole surviving son and ailing husband to the sixth Armistice Day service and someone nudges and snickers and there beside Major Ball are the rigid couple, the one with the fierce glittering eyes, with skeletal bones already pressing the bridal gloss of her cheeks, the other with eyes bulging like ivory billiard balls from the effects of mustard gas and with a nervous fidget of his brick-red hands, and someone says, *They go like lambs to be slaughtered among the heathen*: and the widow Mrs. St. George rocks to sleep her grandson Fitzhugh while her gossips gather and wait at the Yacht Club for the end of the boat race and the beginning of cocktails, and someone says *after her daughter was born in Kurdistan* telling how Kate Pentecost gave her milk to a Moslem child whose mother wanted it to have the mystical Christian milk and then the other village mothers brought their sucklings and the poor naive fool who had lived ignorant most of her life in that motherless house with only that sulking brute Major Ball, his mulatto mistress and Jackson the halfbreed factotum for companions and who didn't know or didn't want to know about breastfeeding once having melted to womanhood continued to nurse and nurse because the milk not only refused to dry up but replenished itself to bursting until for a while she was giving suck to goats and lambs and puppydogs converting them to Christianity too as she lived surprised at last to give and share in love: and Mrs. St. George in the wheelchair that her grandson Fitzhugh's pregnant wife thrusts in the breeze along the Battery tries to comprehend the Yankee admiral's letter of condolence concerning the honor and gallantry of the late captain her son at Pearl Harbor when she recognizes a passerby as the ivoryeyed apostle Pentecost and knows to be his and Kate's daughter the black-haired blueeyed beauty by his side as though no time passes and the dancers whirl and turn and swoop motionlessly and pitilessly, and by nightfall everyone is prattling again of the man's simplicity, of his futile quest for light in the house of iniquity, of the waste of valor, and of the long death of pride: and churchbells chime in the echoing sea, and the light is fading upon the waters . . .

PENITENTIAL MADWOMAN IN A WHITE ROBE crosses the tracks glinting in blue glitter reflected from the tobacco factories of Mill Mile. Piercing millwhistles announce the shift. Crowds of workers are in the night streets. There is comfortable raillery among them. Young and old men women black white work together and are not alone. Some hear the madwoman say, "The Lord is my shepherd." Some see the black blood on her scalp and robe. She strides past, into the dark again. It is time.

THE END OF TIME WAS FAST APPROACHING, no doubt of it. The Kingdom of Saints was nearer though smaller due to back-slidings and apostasies: the work of Satan.

When will Billy Raven see God face to face? The Reverend Billy Raven was pondering, was pondering.

Carnival brilliance of his Gospel Tent lit the field of dog-fennel where he stood pondering the significance of himself. And had not his soul hungered and had not the Angel appeared and put him in a trend?

Fiery tip of his cigar made a dignified parabola. He allowed himself one cigar during intervals between performances. He had a golden voice to hoard, incantatory and hypnotic in effect, its natural timbre like a choirboy's whose testicles had not dropped. Behind him in the tent Mrs. Pooley on the Estey organ was playing the last hymn before the sermon; he ground the cigar beneath the heel of his cowboy boot.

A white figure at the far end of the field caught his eye momentarily just before he went into the tent. He felt the brightness of a hundred light bulbs upon him, felt the eyes upon him, felt the eyes.

Billy Raven underwent a transformation when the moment arrived for live contact with his people. Then he became not the possessor but the instrument of powers. These seemed to flow through him magnetically, completing their circuit in other people. Then he did not have to ponder his own words; they seemed to spring from his throat of their own volition, nor did he always need them. He was transformed by contact with others into a man of tenderness and compassion. He appealed to the poor, the dumb, the debased, the afflicted. He loved them, they him. He touched them with his hands. His words were a form of touch, leaping toward others to create a luminous arc of the spirit. The sound of his words, much more than the pondered content of them, aroused and soothed people with their caress. With sound and touch he drew sinners from their devotion to loneliness and despair. They found the Holy Ghost together. Such were his powers, though he scarcely understood them. *There is a river*, saith the gospelmaker. It flowed through Billy Raven. He was the lightning-rod man of the Lord!

As Billy Raven felt the eyes upon him and was speaking words that the Lord Jesus Christ placed upon his tongue and was rejoicing in the early ecstasies sighing up to him murmurously, lo, an old woman of his people entered the tent and slowly came toward him up the aisle of trampled grass. She wore the white robe of repentance but had laid violent hands upon herself. She was sore afflicted by Satan.

He ceased preachments and cried with the tongue of Jeremiah, "*See O Lord, and consider, for I am become vile!*"

Then approached he this old woman even as Satan contended there for her soul, and Billy Raven did bless her, and then he placed his hands upon her head which was torn and bleeding, and even so began the healing of her woe. He embraced this old woman and felt the strange heart beating against his.

Thus he did comfort her.

And he said to his people, "Fear not, my friends, for even the lowliest of sinners shall repent and be exalted."

And Billy Raven embraced the old woman until she fell upon her knees and wept piteously for her daughter who was the fruit of her womb and whom the Lord in His wisdom had taken away.

PART II

Chapter Seven **Tom**

When the faculty rebellion of sixty-two had by the summer of nineteen sixty-four succeeded in forcing the resignation of General Elbert C. Scroggs as president and Angus Blacklaw as dean and in replacing these with the liberal administration of President William Koontz and Dean Archibald Leary, Dr. Adam Hasbrouck emerged as a dominant behind-the-scenes power in the affairs of South Atlantic University. He was wealthy—a solid New York fortune accumulated over five generations was, it now appeared, his—and by the standards of Poe's Hill he would have to be accounted a tycoon, albeit an eccentric one because he made little show of his wealth and lived in his modest apartment upstairs in the old Pentecost house on Cornwallis Street and continued to practice medicine and to write books of philosophical cast, obscure, prolix, dull, nonconformist, idealistic, mildly pornographic and sentimental. He seemed to have the best of both worlds: on the one hand he operated as a capitalist and on the other he removed objections to great wealth by serving as a philanthropist. Already the Katherine Hasbrouck Memorial Hospital was rising in the pinewoods a mile west of the campus. He gave advice, too, heeded because he was assumed to be disinterested and impartial, a man already too rich, old, and respected to be involved in petty scrambles after status. Hasbrouck's books, reissued in paperback, had achieved wide circulation, especially the inscrutable *Psychoeroticism of Culture*. It had attracted favorable notice in the United States and abroad, its author puffed as a social saint and a prophet of psychic revolution because, he proved, Eros, though denied, found release in spectacles like professional wrestling. By the spring of nineteen sixty-five, Dr. Hasbrouck, though nearing retirement age, and though little known to the public at large, was a force to be reckoned with, an influence, an important personage. When he was called out of town to New York or Washington, his was one of the voices that was heard, one that was shaping policies that would affect the lives of hundreds of millions of people. At South Atlantic it was said that his word was virtually law.

However, there was another side to Hasbrouck, the one that was least suspected because least known, least understood because least observed. This other Hasbrouck was a nervous, envious, insecure little man who would lock himself into his apartment for days and be heard trampling, trampling late into the night and giving vent to sudden inexplicable howls of rage and other sounds that might, through the floorboards, be interpreted either as the laughter of a lunatic or the half-choked sobbings of someone in the throes of a breakdown.

This was the Hasbrouck whom Tom and Helen Driver had been coming to know and to wonder about during their three years' residence in the apartment below. It was Tom Driver who had gradually come to suspect Dr. Hasbrouck of being peculiarly possessed, in particular, by hatred of one man—Max Stebbins.

Of course, in the final analysis the old gasbag was entitled to hate anyone he wished. It was so *like* a man of Hasbrouck's age and generation to get hung up on a fixed standard of conduct to a point where he might hate that person who deviated from it, even though it no longer existed except in his imagination! But lately Tom had discovered that he himself, via a process over which he had no control and for which he was not responsible, was involved in Hasbrouck's feud. He did not wish to be involved, to take sides. Neither Hasbrouck nor Stebbins mattered to him, and the spectacle of two professors locking horns over an incident obscure and almost completely buried was altogether unpleasant to anticipate. Yet he could see, he was drawn in, and about the only thing that he could do to protect himself was to keep Hasbrouck's character under surveillance, scrutinizing the minutiae of appearances for whatever real purposes these might conceal.

ONE MORNING IN NINETEEN SIXTY-FIVE Tom woke feeling feverish and depressed. His stomach ulcer, which had remained fairly quiet for three years, the years of happiness with Helen, had recently begun to erupt like a half-forgotten volcano. At moments the pain was almost unbearable. It was as if hot coals were being poured upon the roots of well-being. This morning he was in agony, which no doubt accounted for the other symptoms. In addition he had a really rotten hangover. As soon as he swung out of bed (this was about six o'clock judging by the brightening stillness of the street outside), his head swam with dizziness, his eyeballs smarted as if scratched by diabolic cats, and the bilious residue of last night's, and the past week's equally infernal libations of gin and whiskey visited his gorge with nausea and his brain with remorse. Nevertheless he managed to get up and dress without waking Helen, whose belly, mountainous with child, heaved quietly against the topsheet: parenthood would claim him at any hour. What if the baby had been born in the night while he was still writhing about in drunken stupefaction? Helen would have organized something. She usually did. But it was rotten to be drunk when your first child was being born. Come to think of it, it was rotten to be drunk at any time, period.

He had never been more or less drunk for a whole week before. He had achieved something, a college degree of Fine Arts in three rather than four years. No vacations, no letups. He stayed out of trouble, did what was asked of him, and built up a modest but satisfactory record, a kind of official identity that, taking in his real though unspectacular performance in the military, gave the name Tom Driver a history and a place in the sun—thus leaving the young man of that name unassailable and free and keeping the world at a distance. The best way to do this, he had found, was to convince the world that he was already wound up and driven like a shiny new car off the assembly line, fit at the touch of a button to cover the main traveled roads. This confidence game, he knew well. Sometimes it left him feeling weary and lonely and angry, angry at the world for failing to see through, even to take an interest in, his transparency and to expose him as an imposter. To his relief, he had learned to share himself with Helen. But, again, their intimacy would probably not survive the birth of their child. They would drift away from one another, perhaps diverting themselves by a struggle to possess the child. In the end everything would collapse and he would be driven in on himself for good, unneeded, unwanted. O he *knew!* During final examinations, he promised himself to get drunk, pissed drunk. Since he didn't drink or use drugs, he would do the unexpected. He would surprise everybody by the degrees of torture he could invent and inflict upon himself without complaint. For a week, he had done that.

He navigated his way to the kitchen pantry and breakfasted upon two triple whiskeys, straight up. Presently, when his head and ulcer seemed to feel better, he remembered that he was forcing himself to read Dr. Hasbrouck's *Psychoeroticism of Culture*. The book on the kitchen table lay open to a passage Tom had been reading the night before without making much sense out of it. Now with a look of bleary concentration, slowly he read again:

> A paternalistic culture-concept, central to psychic stability, falls apart. Subsequently the mind, bereft of old absolutes, yearns for a new totalism. It finds it now in images of cataclysm. Whether the image is of earthly life annihilated by nuclear activity, by bacteriological takeover, or by depletion of resources, the psychological manifestation is clear: man must have a god, for his psyche cannot tolerate infinite solitudes, cosmoswise. And yet if the only gods are gods of destruction, then, for our survival, it is necessary that his mind be changed. Why? The first assumption of ethics is that life is good. It follows, therefore, that life is worth preserving and that psychic energy should be directed to the purpose of preservation. But this purposive directivity has always been thwarted by the Ego's belief in its own superiority in the evolutionary schema. It is this belief which must now be altered by new, if necessary enforced, social tolerances. Society in the future can then be conceptualized as an electro-magnetic field, that is, as a world infrastructure of related beings. However, to create such a society, we cannot afford violence. To achieve the very revolution necessary to survival, by violent means, would increase guilt and accelerate processes of terrorism. On the other hand, by acknowledging the reality of our common humanity, a redemptive Gestalt is possible. Then we see that the discovery of electro-magnetic waves represents a prodigious psychoerotic event . . .

"Eureka!" Tom whispered hoarsely to the morning light slanting from the window. Although the passage remained obscure, he was not unfamiliar with some of its fashionable content about world destruction, non-violent revolution, and common humanity. What struck him was that Adam Hasbrouck had nothing of his own to say beyond sinister implication of *enforcing* "social tolerances." Didn't that sound like dictatorship masquerading as a utopia? The passage was a pastiche of commonplaces. The mind that conceived it and the will that exhibited it in public for recognition and profit were staring at their own impotence. Tom formulated his reaction: *Sanctimonious impotence.*

He read for a while, had another triple whiskey. About seven-thirty, he went out for a walk.

IT WAS MONDAY, JUNE THE SEVENTH. His graduation day. For some, Parents' Day.

Seventeen he had been when his foster-parents died and he had enlisted in the Army. It was a stupid thing to do, to volunteer, but that was what he had done: nobody expected it of him, that was why. The Army made him a clerk-typist. It was in its way quite a humane occupation, but it failed to put his manhood to the test. He tried to take up boxing and became runnerup lightweight of his outfit, a distinction up to the usual standard of absurdity. He had "artist's hands," lacked a punch and disliked having phony managers feeling up his body between rounds. He quit boxing. His body, like everything else, seemed destined to fail him. In Viet-Nam he developed his ulcer. After honorable discharge, he brought it home to Poe's Hill along with some memories that were either cheap and boring or else nauseating—memories that chose you when you weren't looking. That was another thing: they should let you choose your own past. If you didn't want a Dr. Hasbrouck to go and tell you one day, with his concerned it's-for-your-own-good look on his face, that once upon a wartime the semen of Max Stebbins fertilized the egg of Kitty Pentecost and that that fertilized egg was *you*, bud, you could try for a new deal.

At the corner of Cornwallis Street and Atlantic Boulevard he stopped to look at the Confederate Daughters Home. On the top story behind little boxlike windows edged with black palings like metallic flowers, shadows quavered. Pigeons bobbed on the slate roof, one dropping sheerly and rising again as if worked by strings of an invisible yoyo. Dangled out of the past: Mother Pentecost whom Hasbrouck had revealed as his grandmother: until recently, though, not even Hasbrouck had known about how she had used Mary Branch to prevent letters going between Stebbins and Kitty, but the effect of that conspiracy was clear: he, Tom, was no sooner born than bundled off to an adoption agency . . . He began to walk again. Sun-gritty foliage struck the fire of a redbird down and across the street into a garden where it cooled among roses and lilies, honeysuckle and bee-hatted clover. A watercolor formed in imagination: against a swift wash of semi-tropical light, full of the shifting, melting, diaphanous effects that gave Carolina its drowsy charm, he would try rich hues in abstract suggesting the tameless energy of the land and, for the strangers come over the ocean and lost, slabs of zinc whiteness as here in clapboard houses over whose trellised porches wisteria cascaded lavender waves, and contrasting slabs of gray, the ambiguity and receding future of all dreams.

At the corner of Cornwallis and Greene he saw a barefooted boy scamper into Mason's store. So Tom himself had done a dozen or more years ago, gone running ahead of Mary Branch along the blocks from the Drivers' house, come thinking perhaps of the Lady. Mary Branch, she had believed: he saw that now. He saw the beauty of a long and unrewarded determination, saw how she had tried to anchor him in the world he was to know, not that he had known then of her long devotion, but he knew now about his birth in the Pentecost house, about Mary's tracing him from the adoption agency to the Drivers' house and presenting herself to his foster parents as a providential nurse, cook and housekeeper and serving for seventeen years because she had not come as a servant. It would have been Mary Branch who arranged for the Lady to meet him. How far back the meetings went, he did not recall. As he grew older, Kitty might have felt compelled to avoid him. Nonetheless he had seen enough of the Lady to be conscious of her. (Once in Mason's store—was he six? seven?—they met the Lady and she smiled and stroked his hair and said he was a fine-looking boy and she hoped a good one too, and had left, quickly; and afterwards when he asked Mary Branch about the Lady, Mary would hug him and rock him and say nothing. Memory blurred like an over-exposed photograph or else for a long time he did not meet the Lady, yet one day he had a bicycle and as he entered the store found Mason bending over someone who lay motionless upon the sawdust floor: it was she. Mason told him what to get and he had gone like a shot, on the run, not waiting to cycle, and the name over the doorbell said *D.D. Pentecost* and the old woman came and listened and went and came and then he was running and then Mason stabbed in the needle and the Lady fluttered alive, soft blue eyes upon a terrified boy. Mason said, "The boy run for your insulin." "He is kind," she said. And Mrs. Pentecost came and took her away and the Lady kept looking back at him as time closed around the wound of that look she gave him). He dreamed of the Lady, knowing no more of her than this and the dream itself which quickened in him until he was trying to paint landscapes out of his feeling for her. His painting went well when he dreamed of her. She became part of the whole visceral yearning that the land created in him: ploughed fields streaky with clay, pines mixed with bleached flames of dogwood, strongtimbered wattled tobacco barns their corrugated tin roofs prevailing against skies, the winding rutted roads where black men hunched over mule-drawn wagons.

And he had known all along, perhaps. He had been in the hospital, summoned with Helen, to meet a Mrs. Hasbrouck who was to die the same day and met her and knew that the Lady was a real part of his life. Always coming back to him were those words, how vehemently Kitty Hasbrouck, dying, gripped his hands and spoke the two words that would be benediction and valediction: *My son.*

Outside Mason's store were exuberant yams and golden corn in pale green shucks and perspiring watermelons and Virginia apples assaulted by tippling wasps. Tom hesitated before going in. Mason, too, he thought. *All that world of the past turned upside-down and beyond invention but true: a thousand perhaps a hundred thousand friendly hardworking childloving taxpaying fatherfigures weak and rotten: not just why but how does the jolly old neighborhood storekeeper turn out to be someone who supplies illegal drugs?*

He went in. The store felt cool. Sawdusted floor and tin-can-stacked shelves. Delicious aroma of freshbaked bread.

"Mornin', Mr. Driver." Tom recognized Mason's tattooed arms akimbo on a bloodsmeared butcher's apron. He was not looking at Tom. He said, "Be right with you, sir."

They waited for the barefoot boy to buy a popsicle. The screendoor hawinged and slapped. There was then this beefy redfaced man who, incredibly, read books and made shrewd observations about life and people, who was worth cultivating for his knowledge of Kitty and her family, and who, one evening in early spring, while Tom was present, supplied Widge, a fellow student, in exchange for a big wad of cash, with a carton of cocaine. "What'll it be this fine mornin'?" Mason came up beaming.

"Weed," said Tom. "For the baby."

Mason's smile froze. "So your missus had the baby?"

"Any time."

"It'll all end in tears," said Mason. This was one of his favorite expressions, about everything ending in tears. Mason stopped smiling, his look quizzical. "Has there been any new developments, son?"

It took him a moment's pause to recover the context of Mason's familiarity. It was true, in a time of contemptible self-pity a few weeks ago, Tom had taken Mason into confidence, just gone and spilled everything about himself and Hasbrouck's plans: this to Mason, of all people, Friendly Neighborhood Death-Merchant. Mason had been, of course, genuinely fond of Kitty.

Tom reasoned that there was no harm in further candor. "Yes," he replied. "Mary Branch is bringing my mother's—" He stopped, his cheeks aflame with embarrassment. "—Kitty's letters to Stebbins. That is, bringing them to give to Dr. Hasbrouck who is going to use them, probably later, to humiliate Stebbins with what you might call the facts of paternity."

Mason seemed to reflect. Then, "Why?"

"You mean, why is Hasbrouck going to see Stebbins? Ask him. If I could stop him, I would."

"No. Why is Mrs. Branch giving the letters to Dr. Hasbrouck?"

"They made a deal," Tom said. There was enough silence to hear a fly buzz. Mason wanted more explanation. It was impossible to stop talking, impossible. "She wants her son Manny to go to the university. Dr. Hasbrouck has promised a full four-year basketball scholarship in return for the letters."

Mason met his gaze in a way that was clearly meant to lend import to his words. "We all have to make a living, Mr. Driver. Business has taught me two things: never pay bills before they're due and don't trust anybody who offers quid pro quo."

The screendoor hawinged and a woman came in. It was some minutes before she was gone. By then Mason seemed to have mulled things over. He began to scurry about the store and to talk at the same time, without pause. "Suppose Stebbins refuses to acknowledge you. Suppose, in fact, he is not your father. Suppose the letters prove nothing. I was going to tell you . . . Some years after the Second World War, I drove your dear mother fifty miles to the train station in Raleigh. She said she had to go to New York for the weekend. She disappeared. The old lady told the police Kitty was kidnapped . . . The police found her—way up ayonder in the Colorado Rockies, a couple of thousand miles from here. She wasn't alone, I heard . . . Now, think about it. She wasn't kidnapped, no harm come to her, she was of legal age, needn't have had to come back to Poe's Hill but of her own free will, but back she come—and she was unhappy for the rest of her life. I don't know what it shows, Mr. Driver, except that she wanted to get shut of things at home and then decided she couldn't escape. I mean you, she couldn't escape *you*. My guess is, the man she went to Colorado with was the man she wanted. Whether he was your father I wouldn't know, but I kind of feel you was just a mistake when she was a girl and she sacrificed her happiness as a way of payment for that mistake. By the way, here's your man in the morning paper."

Mason plopped a newspaper down on the counter.

WHEN HE ARRIVED HOME, Tom's ulcer was fanging his stomach lining. Hot resentment of Max Stebbins passed and repassed through his thought—felt at the temples. He was quick to recognize symptoms of a familiar panic: other people were bearing down upon him, he was going to be exposed.

He found his own copy of the morning paper on the front porch and took it to the bedroom to show Helen. She was sitting up in bed, combing her hair, when he came in.

"Hi." Her look betrayed no sign of disapproval of him.

Returning her greeting with a kiss, he gave her the paper with the bottom-left-column photograph of Stebbins and asked her opinion of the short article beneath it. While she read, he looked over her shoulder, scanning phrases here and there: SEX ORGY WEEKEND CHARGE FACED BY SAU PROFESSOR: "Dr. Max Stebbins, 45, professor of English at South Atlantic University, faces possible dismissal . . . Administration sources announced a 7-man faculty committee headed by Dr. Adam Hasbrouck, noted psychiatrist and author . . . three students, unnamed, are involved in what is described as a 'sex orgy weekend' . . . alleged incident at a private beachhouse at Nag's Head . . . Contacted at his home on Old River Road, Dr. Stebbins labeled the charge as 'bizarre' and 'ludicrous' and asserted that it 'had about as much in common with a sex orgy as the Mad Hatter's tea party' (a reference to Lewis Carroll's immortal children's classic) . . . first case of its kind since 1962 when Dr. Carlos Brodie was dismissed from SAU for moral misconduct. Dr. Brodie later committed suicide."

"Oh," said Helen. It was beautiful to Tom, the way she reacted. It was as if the world were going to go on and on replenishing itself through the wombs of good, strong, compassionate women in spite of all the banalities, all the treacheries. "I don't believe it," she said in an even tone.

"Well," Tom said, "he must have done something."

"No, he didn't."

When he waited for her to explain why she was positive in her attitude about a teacher for whom she once had what she called "a silent crush," he found her eyes twinkling at him in self-amusement. It was a moment of pure pleasure to be interpreter of such mood and thought as passed serenely behind her eyes. Still, it was clear, neither he nor Helen *knew* Max Stebbins very well. "What was he like in class?" Tom asked.

She combed her hair that had lost its sheen and said, "Sometimes he would wear turtleneck sweaters and blue jeans. His hair would be tousled, and his eyes would look sunken in some faraway sorrow, and he would gaze at you intensely as if peering into your soul. Naturally, we all fell madly in love with him."

"Naturally," Tom said.

"And then," Helen went on, "he would read aloud. He had a harsh, rather strident voice as people from the mountains sometimes do, yet he contrived to speak very softly, gently, and made us listen. Most of us had never heard poetry before and didn't care for it. But when he read a poem, it had meaning for you. The poem took you on a journey into yourself, and you realized he had greatheartedness in him."

The sound of her voice fell upon a roomful of shadows. Here and there solid black walnut furniture brooded like a Puritan jury. Walls were papered with Mississippi steamboats, pink, and a myriad of belles with parasols and gentlemen with stovepipe hats promenaded past cotton-carrying slaves who were not pink: motionless, nerveless, bloodless phantoms.

"We speak of him as if he were dead," Tom said at last.

"Yes," she said. "We watched him dying a kind of death just after your mother died." Helen paused. He turned to find her gaze upon him. "Something went out of him. When he tried to read a poem aloud, his eyes would be filled with big tears that would suddenly roll down his cheeks and drop upon the book in his hand. The readings stopped altogether. He just shook his head silently, then seemed almost to forget that we were there."

Tom considered and said, "A minute ago I was angry at him."

"Don't be," Helen said.

"That bitch of a wife left him last year."

"Maybe he's a casualty of war. Maybe he gave her no choice."

"Hasbrouck's down on him. All of a sudden he's on the skids. They're going to kick him out. He'll be lucky to work ever again. That's hard."

"Tom?"

"Huh?"

"I think the baby will be soon. You'll be with me, won't you?"

"Sure," he said. "Sure I will."

SOME WHILE LATER HE WAS IN THE KITCHEN PANTRY basting his ulcer with whiskey and working up courage to go tell Hasbrouck to lay off Stebbins if only for Kitty's sake. Over and over the same question kept repeating itself until finally he spoke it aloud: "What difference does it make if I *am* Stebbins's son? It's nobody's goddam business but my own." He noticed that his fists were clenched as he was walking up the banistered stairway. He rapped on Hasbrouck's door. Hasbrouck presently appeared in dressing-gown and slippers in the half-open doorway. "Ah," he said, looking sleepy-eyed and cross, "it's the *bahstud*."

Tom explained that he wanted to talk. Hasbrouck tried to put him off, saying he was tired after a weekend in New York, had caught a late jet home, and had an outrageously busy day ahead of him.

"It's the outrage I wanted to talk to you about."

"Very well," Hasbrouck with ill-concealed displeasure. "Come in. I'll perc the coffee and put on my glad rags."

PARP THRUPP WEE GUHGUHGUH GUTTERROOM. *Puff of blue exhaust from propellers. First one wing vibrates then the next. Flagman leans into the airblast arms spreadeagled. Love me daddymachine.*

Kitty intended to tell you. That's why she invited you and Helen to share our house.

Pack of jackals.

You've had a trauma, dear boy.

A what?

Here. Use my handkerchief.

I don't want your snotrag.

Good. Express your aggression.

NOW BOARDING FOR NEW YORK

You didn't have to tell me. I don't want to know about it. Shut up shut up shut up.

You can't escape the truth, my boy. Time for me to go.

Next time you can get somebody else to drive you to the airport. Don't expect anything from me. If you have any decency, you'll destroy Mary Branch's letters as soon as you receive them. I don't care what they prove.

We're all together, Thomas. That's ancient Sufi wisdom.

I have rights to privacy. That's common sense.

***PARP THRUPP SWISH*. PERCOLATOR.**

Hasbrouck emerged from the bedroom in a Palm Beach suit and white buckskins. Tom closed his eyes. When he opened them, Hasbrouck was slouched in a Morris chair opposite to him doing something peculiar: drinking coffee by means of moving cup and saucer together with one beefy hand, tilting, slurping and meanwhile peering through hornrimmed glasses like an advertisement for nearsighted owls. Hasbrouck's voice, drifting as if from a late-night radio station: "I called on Ginny Stebbins this weekend in New York. If there's to be any reconciliation, Max must acknowledge you. She has agreed to that."

"Actress type," Tom muttered. Lifting his coffee cup with two hands, he drank. "Sanctimonious impotence," Tom said. "Dr. Hasbrouck, people are people, not . . . prodigious psycho-erotic events in culture. Just wanna make that clear."

Hasbrouck whipped off his glasses. His voice came with sharp inflection:

"You've had a bourgeois upbringing, education, money, women with soft skin, and you have nothing better to do with your life than dabble in the arts, grow your hair like a girl, and swill your guts with booze until you reek of it. The insolence, the gutless insolence of you and Stebbins and your kind . . . I know you all. I've seen you easing your way through existence on the basis of some trifling accident of birth and good fortune. There's a certain romantic aura, a kind of exotic emanation from the heart of decay. Your disdain, young man, is odious because it lacks a moral basis."

Hasbrouck sipped coffee, stared at the ceiling, and resumed. "Individualism is dead—five hundred years of it—a system of natural and social exploitation that disguises its real motives in a fog of rhetoric about liberty and justice, about the nobility of the private consciousness and the genius of the exquisite mind that perceives a higher truth and beauty than ordinary, humble people, to the credit of their humanity, may comprehend . . . This—all this individualism founded upon anything but science, which sees real life as a process, a biological and economic process, no more—all this is but the glow of decay on a dungheap composed of all the hundreds of millions of people who got trampled during the insane scramble for wealth and position! My gorge rises at the spectacle! Let these individuals who share the air we breathe, but presume to be gods, get down and wallow in the muck for awhile! Let them go hungry till their bellies are bloated, let them learn to curse the day they were born, and then—then let them fall down and bless the earth for nourishing existence, then let them acknowledge their fellows! Let them stand in the sun and see the shadows they have made, let them be horrified and confess their crimes against mankind! Ach!"

Tom had closed his eyes. Behind Hasbrouck's bullshit, he knew, was a Marxist attack on capitalism, fair enough, but the implied solution was totalitarianism, which was disgusting. He wanted to pull his thoughts together, to persuade Hasbrouck at the eleventh hour to stop using him as a means for humiliating Max Stebbins.

But Hasbrouck had taken the initiative. His words had the power and quality of hysteria. Perhaps madness spun its web in him, perhaps it dangled already, a firefoul kettle of a spider, out of the towered hold of volition. Multi-colored disks kaleidoscoped, collapsed. In sudden inner vision Tom saw a barracks room in Georgia where he and others just returned from Viet-Nam were looking down at the body of the soldier who had been showing you a grubby snapshot of the pretty wife and baby whom soon he would be seeing, the soldier's brains splattered over the new linoleum floor. The mailorder pistol had blown a hole the size of a chestnut through his skull. The gum-chewing captain came and said, *The son of a bitch has ruined my new floor.*

"You're going to destroy Max, aren't you?" A woman's voice made this weary declaration. Tom opened his eyes wide and turned. There, dressed in a slip, dark hair tumbling voluptuously to bare shoulders and standing where Hasbrouck's bedroom door was ajar, was Ginny Stebbins.

Chapter Eight **Tom**

"Do you want Hasbrouck to destroy him?" Tom was asking Ginny about an hour after excusing himself from the upstairs apartment. For a while he had taken his bottle to the back yard where vapor steamed from roses and privet hedges, from scruffy tasseled clover-spotted grass. He had felt as if his ulcer were the receiving end of an umbilical cord fed with broken glass. Oozing sweat from every pore, he sat and contemplated his insoluble existence. Then he had gone into the kitchen only to find Ginny there, her eyes a glazed and depthless blue peering from her jungle, studying him.

"I hope you don't think—" she held her hand limply over breast. "I can't imagine what possessed me to say such a silly thing. Adam is so sweet. He told me that Max needs help. I've come. Isn't that nice?"

"I thought you were getting a divorce," Tom said.

"But I love him. We shall always be good friends." She fumbled cigarette and lighter from purse, clicked lighter, inhaled a lovely lung barbecue. Blue smoke jetting from nostrils, scumbling the black stove: Ginny dropped the cigarette and ground it out on the kitchen floor with the raised heel of an elegant black shoe.

"Tom, I've got to be firm with Max. I want him to feel whole and happy again, to make him feel wanted and loved. You see, the terrible truth is, no one has ever made him feel anything but rejected. Kitty rejected him. Even I." Ginny sighed and gazed out of the window, squinting as though threading a needle.

"How's life in the fast lane?"

"Oh," Ginny replied in a rhapsodic tone. "Great." Cocking her head at him, she laughed just a little tinkly-winkly laugh.

"Lots of work?"

"Lots. Adam has done so much for my career. It's amazing the number of important people he knows—wonderful people, keen, dedicated artists."

"Chris?"

"Ohhh, just fine. He goes to boarding school in New England."

"He loves it, I bet."

"Yes," Ginny said. "He loves it."

"Does Max ever see him?"

"He's free to visit any time. He came at Christmas. They went to the zoo."

"And had a wunnerful time."

"Yes." Ginny laughed on her vacuous note. "Of course." Strolling to the window, she half-turned as if he were a camera. "I hear that Max has a young girl friend."

"He has dozens of girl friends."

"Really?"

"Haven't you heard about the sex orgies?"

"I don't think that's funny," Ginny snapped.

"I didn't realize you were so sensitive, betraying your husband for a mess of pottage," Tom retorted. His skin still felt wet with perspiration. He would have to change clothes before going to the graduation ceremony. Leaving, he, too, half-turned and said with a look of Hamlet-like intrigue, "The play's the thing to catch a conscience—and get a rich man's ring."

Backing out of the kitchen, he formed his arms into a submachine gun and sprayed Ginny Stebbins with invisible bullets.

HE WAS BEING SWEPT OVER A CATARACT. There seemed no beginning, no end to it. He was choking yet unresisting. He seemed to come up for air. Now he was alone in a forest. Deep snow lay all around. The snow was melting, baring fleshtinted roots. Golden grasses sprang from thawing patches and were a woman's hair. There was light in the forest. Fast and secret buds began to open to a caressing flame, the roots and grasses to stir . . .

"Time to go."

Helen's voice. He opened his eyes, saw her bending over him where he sprawled on the bed. He remembered now that, after leaving Ginny and shaving and dressing—he had even put on his hired academic gown—he had felt sleepy . . . The pain was gone. The sight of Helen filled him with tenderness . . . "I've had such a good dream!" he exclaimed as he sat up and put his arms around her.

She stroked his hair. "What did you dream about?"

"Spring," he said. "How, no matter what happens, she always wakes from her winter sleep."

"She?"

He laughed at her in his heart and cried, "She is you and you are Venus!"

"Come on," she urged. "Dr. Hasbrouck's having a fit."

"Goody," he said.

"Mary Branch has arrived. They're in the car waiting for you. Guess what happened?"

"Is it good?"

"You know Mary's son, Manny? Well, she says Manny stole Kitty's letters when he went to work this morning. Mary doesn't have them to give to Dr. Hasbrouck."

Tom began to dance the Highland Fling, but the walls of the room tilted until he pitched on the floor to recover his bearings. He noticed that he was laughing.

Even when he zigzagged to the street where the others were already waiting in Hasbrouck's snazzy British car, he was conscious of enjoying himself. No one, not Hasbrouck or Ginny or Mary or Helen, would guess that underneath his absurd black gown he was clutching a bottle of bourbon.

In the back seat a handsome olive-skinned woman in black Sunday dress was shaking her head and making a sound like *tsk-tsk-tsk.* He put one arm about her shoulders and gave her a big kiss. "Mary, I love you," he declared. "You're my *real* mama."

"Well," said Mary, lowering her gaze but smiling at him out of the corner of her eye, "you tell it like it is."

AN HOUR PASSED.

He had gone too far. He was drowning.

He had survived most of the ceremony held outdoors on the campus lawn. He had filed with hundred of others in their absurd caps and gowns and had shaken hands with President Koontz and Dean Leary and even with Dr. Hasbrouck, who was on the platform with officials and celebrities and looking extremely important in his academic robes which were trimmed with fur and overlaid with the gorgeous colors of Oxford University. Somewhere out where sibilant murmurings ebbed and flowed among a thousand spectators, Helen and Mary were sitting, and this was good.

Someone was gargling metallically over a microphone, someone who, one arm uplifted and one hand shielding his eyes, seemed to be contemplating a leap from a very high diving platform: the Chaplain.

Tom lowered head to hands. Between his feet a spider waited as an ant toiled past a grassblade. A sudden rush and the spider was performing its spindly dance of death, about, around the ant.

You volunteered for the search party. When you found the gash in the jungle carpet where the missing helicopter had crashed, you knew there was no need to search for survivors, so great was the stench. You went in, retrieved bodies. Everyone was sick to the stomach, many times.

"Scuse me." He stood up and stumbled past row on row of people who scarcely noticed him because their heads were bowed in prayer.

THE TASTE OF BILE WAS STILL ON HIS LIPS. He was in the garden near Henry Memorial Building where Hasbrouck had parked the car. Squirrels skittered up treetrunks; a fountain splashed upon a vertigrised bronze cherub, pitterpattered on lilypads. Leaning over the fishpond, Tom filled his mortarboard cap with water and splashed his face with it. He had a sensation that someone was watching him. A moment later he wheeled around. Not ten feet away there was a pair of sunglasses with a smirk beneath: Tom's fraternity brother, Widge, the class bore.

Tom had not seen him since the night about six weeks ago when Widge bought from Mason a carton of cocaine. Afterwards, Widge had pulled out a flickknife and told him to keep his mouth shut. Widge had this wonderful fantasy-life about being a gangster.

"You look loaded, kiddo," said Widge.

Tom tried to think of something equally brilliant to say. Widge, a real dude, wore a checkered sports shirt, white navy slacks with starched creases, and white tennis shoes. "Are they holding a special graduation for you, Widge?"

"They won't let me graduate, Tombo."

"Integrity lives again," Tom said. Having risen and begun to walk toward the parking lot, he was alarmed to find Widge materializing in front of him again. Widge was waving an arm toward Henry Memorial Building, saying something about Professor Stebbins. "What are you talking about, Widge?"

"I said he flunked me in English and won't change my grade so I can graduate. I offered him a deal. I said, 'Look, prof, change the grade and you got nothing to worry about from that committee tonight.' I got him on the hook, see? He wasn't buying it. Can you imagine?"

Widge's voice was excited and inflected by the peevish solemnity of small American towns. "I tell you, Tombo, I fixed Stebbins up with this chick that puts out. We drove down to my folks' house at the beach. He was all over her."

Tom closed his eyes and said, "You're a real stupid bastard, did you know that?"

"O.K., if you don't believe me, have a look for yourself."

Tom opened his eyes just as an old Chevrolet was being driven around a bend in the parking lot. Max Stebbins, who was driving, did not seem to recognize him, but the redheaded woman in the passenger seat looked at Widge, her lips parted in surprise.

"Jeez, she's another piece of cheesecake!" Widge said when the car was gone. "I guess I'm not as smart as some of you guys, but—"

"Piss off," said Tom. He walked swiftly and did not look back. On reaching Hasbrouck's Jaguar, he climbed into the back seat, found the bourbon where he had left it, and took several gulps before he sank against hot leather. Everything was reeling, collapsing. A cold slime of sick sweat, soldier sweat, clung to his skin . . . That was the womb-like helicopter strewn with charred and dismembered corpses: the cold cathedral smell . . . Widge's face swam, focused, swam outside the window so peaceful: the skindiver looks through the window of an aquarium tank: all is airless, still, festooned with brilliant light: there is the smell of smoldering rain on bright silent air: a wet warmth spreads and, deep down, the diver tears off his mask in ecstasy . . .

Chapter Nine **Mary**

The windup grandfather clock in the antebellum Pentecost house *pings* once and stops instead of *pinging* four times. It is four o'clock, though, Mary can see.

As if no time. Room bed wallpapers same now as when Miss Kitty know her precious babby taken away for adoption, her heart going to have miseries: the sea-feelings of things.

Miss Helen has said, "Contractions started." She has wanted Mary to go on sitting bedside, watching Miss Kitty's growedup Tom who, once that adopted babby, has had dry heaves without waking and could die. "It ain't no trouble," Mary Branch has said, thinking, *Jesus, family is trouble.*

She sits where the sun slants in as it used to afternoons when the room was Miss Kitty's . . . Troubles, the troubles she has known and the signs she has known them by: this June morning she has seen a crow fly by her house on Watauga Street. More'n twenty years ago in this very bedroom she was watching that mean-looking out-of-town doctor while Miss Kitty is having her precious babby that was taken from her on two accounts, no husband and Mrs. Pentecost fearing babbies like King Herod. Mary has been hearing rats squeaking behind baseboards and the plaster crumbling behind that stained wallpaper got pink steamboats and happy slaves, stuff like that revealing Time at work, bringing troubles. Still there is time, plenty of time. Hour ago she has said to Miss Kitty's Tom's wife, Miss Helen, "You time your pains, honey. There's plenty of time to have you-all a nice little babby." Miss Helen there in the setting-room pretty soon come and say, "Mary, it's time."

It is like that, Time: a little pain and you get a result.

Mary sits where sun slants in as if out of the old time. She remembers littlegirl's self: back forty years, back to the sea-island of Edisto: sun slanting in on the whitelimed cabin through Spanishmoss, big black Cousin Willum taking his stiffness yonder to the yard and wetting on the chickens until it went down and the time come again to rise off that mattress where she sleep with Cousin Dubya Junior and Cousin Ruby and start another day in the sun and cotton. Back a bit further in time the sun slants in upon a cobbled street in Charleston, upon the Wesley Jackson family, upon the one she calls Mommer and the one she calls Pap. Mommer is black as her cousins Willum and Sariah (she knows that she is not of their flesh), and Pap (she knows she is not of his flesh) is brown Indian and has a small tight mouth and beaky nose like a hawk's. Mary herself is her funnylooking light color. One day churchbells wake her and Pap lifts her up to see sailboats and she says, "The sea has teeth." Pap sets her stride the cannon on the Battery and a lady on horseback stops and glares at her with shaller-blue eyes, like she some kinda Jonah ain't worth a whale's time to swaller. She starts to cry wondering why Pap is studying up on that lady with pain in his face. The lady spurs and it is another day in that time forty years ago: Cousin Willum totes the mattress, boxes and sacks, loads them on his wagon by the mimosa tree. Mommer wears her hat. So they are going. They climb on the corncob mattress. Willum hums up the mule. Mommer cries. The sun dries shiny skin where the cry is. They ride. Riding: the road to the sea-island of Edisto is like a long tunnel under stars that you go in, never a way back, just tunnel on like to an ittybitty light you of seen but wore out fetching: she remembers: they stop to pick blackberries to go with the cornbread. The birds at daybreak give her sea-feelings from their *caw caw* above the lonesome of wheelcreak and harnessjingle. Some time later she sees the chil'ren peering at her over the slat, behind her the sandtrack arrowing, shadders of palmetto fronds like teeth, the forest looming, folding away a whole lot of swamp has queer smell like hardboil egg. She sees chickens clucking in and out of saltgrass by the whitelime cabin, sees, too, a clearing that will be the share for cotton. Something skitters in the wagon, the chil'ren giggling when she screams at the single bleached claw. She has never seen a sandcrab before. She clings to Mommer. Then the bigeared snagtoothed stringy-necked woman in white headcloth, her eyes rapt in a sweet albino gaze, comes and scolds: this is Cousin Sariah, who, other times, whups tar out of Dubya Junior and Ruby. Mary will one day say, "She don't whup me becos I'm good," and Mommer says, rolling eyes like nobody -knows-my trouble, "She de Lawd's chile." That night in the sweaty dark of the cabin Lil Brother Boy spit blood. That night the hurricane lamp lights up Mommer sobbing her talk to Sariah, rain drums on thin shingled planks. Mary wonders where is Pap. One day boll weevils eat the cotton, one day Lil Brother Boy dies becos his throat done swole up from a crow flying by, and she goes sometimes to oceanside and gets her big sad sea-feelings. One day Willum hitches mule to wagon and they ride again, downroad over plank bridge thundering like *dum dum dum* on a hot afternoon, and she and Mommer are in a train and then in fault country, pines so dry they have needles only on the crests: in Pap's camp he and other blue-striped men walk in chains, the mean-looking man Mommer frowns on carries a shotgun on his shoulder like an ax, in Pap's camp crows are setting, waiting in the pinetrees for death. Mommer cuts her finger scaling mullet, dies. Then Mary is Willum's and Sariah's. They say to nevermind what Pap done. She is up to the inlet at high tide teasing fatback at big darkgreen crabs and Dubya Junior is snaring them in the net when they hear from afar in the swamp the *owroo owroo owroo* of hounds and a shot go *clap-gadap-dap* then birdthickened silence and she runs screaming *Pap* too late even before Willum holds her and the dust clouds over the po-lice Model-T whining spinning swaying into nothingness downroad until quiet against Willum's sweatsour overalls she asks *Did they shoot him?* and he says *Naw honeybabby naw he been out dat swormp three fo days tho.* Other times she and Ruby and Dubya Junior take the yaller bus to school. By and by she is sixteen. The man Lucas saves ten dollars from the C.C.C. job building beachhouses for whitefolks, and Lucas is black as Willum and she fixes to take Lucas as soon as picking is done but dust spins into the palmetto teeth from the mailman's brandnew thirty-six Plymouth coupe. Sariah calls across the clearing *Mayree you Mayree* and she thinks *Pap's dead* and Sariah calls *Ledderrr* the sound rolled out thin in the heat. When she comes, Sariah has that letter. *Man say hit yourn. Speak de wards chile.* Something loops out of the envelope, spooks a chicken, and Mary picks up twentydollar bill and reads the letter (only phrases remembered now, 'Dear Mary Jackson . . . recently returned to Poe's Hill from Mission to Persia . . . good Christian girl to be company for our daughter Kitty who is ten . . . to defray expenses . . . let us know your traintime in Raleigh . . . cordially Mrs. D. D. Pentecost') and says *You all keep the money Sariah* but Sariah blinks custardpink eyes and says *Take it. You de Lawd's chile.*

Manny has said to her, "Mama, why did Mrs. Pentecost put herself to so much trouble to find and hire from three hundred miles away a girl she could have found here in Vinegar Hill, during hard times too?" She has said to him, "On account Mrs. Pentecost, her daddy, Major Ball, come from Charleston, reckon the news got out of South Carolina and up to North Carolina." This is in March.

Manny scorns her for serving white people, caring for them too, and cannot know: she has her color for a reason, her gradually growing woman's guessing-knowledge of Mrs. Pentecost's secret.

In April then.

Morningglories climb the corrugated blue tin roof of her house on Watauga Street. The persimmon tree puts out sticky brown pods, limbs brushing roof making sucking sound like ocean at Edisto swishing into hot sand, going, coming again. One evening Manny comes home from Crabtree's Cannery, mows the front patch. Scent of grass lingers on air. Pap says, "Mighty nice smelling grass." Manny bust loose with, "What exactly did you do: lay one of their whiteass bitches?" It is time. It is five years since she waits at the barbedwire while Pap limps stoopnecked, sacked into Salvation Army clothes, not even knowing where the gate to parole freedom is until the warden tilts his straw and says, "Now you keep this old Injun away from white womenfolk, y' hear?" Sitting in the rear of the bus, Pap has the fear-stink on him that abandoned dogs get in kennels. His fingers scratch up and down his thighs like swollen caterpillars.

In May then. She tells Manny, "They were good people," Willum and Sariah and Ruby and Dubya Junior and the man Lucas, "and I pre-chated how they looked after me when Pap was in the camp, but I had this dream like one day going to marry me this telligent man like your daddy, Sergeant Justice Emmanuel Branch. He turned out a savior man. I going to have me a babby don't need to do no sharecrops and going to Jesus college and me going to have me my own home all paid up and ready for Pap and what's mine, like yawl here. The Lord was in it, too. Along come that invite from Mrs. D.D. Pentecost," telling Manny, not knowing Pap will stir in his rockingchair by the woodstove and bang his fist on the armrest and cry, “Pentecost!”

“Do you know her?” Mary asks. Pap never forgets a name. Say “Abraham Lincoln.” Pap knows him.

“Go on, Mama,” Manny says. “Knows her aw right.”

“You don’t know her,” Manny says.

“Who?”

“Go on, Mama.”

“Mrs. Pentecost,” Pap says. Manny turns in the bed and leans bearded chin on the palm of hand. Mary looks too. Pap works gums and nods to hisself, says, “Man said Miss Kate married man name Pentecost. It was in the papers, man said.”

Before she can stop him, Manny is begun shaking Pap by the shoulders. “She? What did they convict you for, anyway?”

“Now I’m ready for the results,” thinks Mary.

“I ain’t did nothing. That’s truth!” Pap says. He has pushed Manny’s hands from his shoulders and made a kind of crab gesture sideways with his hands when he says with his eyes down and his head shaking, “They say I . . . messed with some pore crazy white chile.” His voice is low, a whisper.

“I’ll get you a glass of water,” Manny says, finally treating Pap proper like he grandfather. When he is in the kitchen, Mary’s gaze lifts Pap’s level. “Manny is got to know. You never hurt nobody? ”

“Nome.”

“How come you know Mrs. Pentecost’s maiden name so good?” Manny comes and asks, holding back the glass of water. “Or did you know her kin in Charleston? Was she at your trial?”

“Mary says I never done nothing to nobodies.”

Mary shakes her head. “Don’t, son. Not now.”

“Was Kate Ball, later Mrs. Pentecost, a witness against you? That’s all I’m asking . . .”

“Answer the question, Pap.”

And Pap nods.

"Let him have the water, son." It is then she kneels and pulls out from under her bed Sgt. Justice E. Branch's battered footlocker that the Marines sent back from the Pacific Ocean, on account the Japanese hand grenade he threw himself on to save his men . . . opens and from underneath mothballed linens draws out the bundle of Miss Kitty's letters tied up with Mr. Max's.

"Listen," she begins when seated again. "Mrs. Pentecost say for me to th'ow these letters away. Say the girl's too young and we got to do right. Now, I ain't stupid. Stopping love letters ain't right . . . She was fixing, though, to send me back to the cotton and the man Lucas if I don't pre-chate the benefits of Shut Up."

LISTEN.

Reverend Pentecost eyes popped like cueballs in poolpockets on account he gassed in the First World Woe. He still had uniforms and Sam Browne, once he dressed in them, marched up and down with the radio on for Armistice Day. He drank sherry and wine just to pee on those mean Pro'bition folks. He sung hymns good like *Watchman Tell Us of the Night*. Sometimes he went out to soldier camp to give Special Request Service, preaching. A too nice man, he didn't marry Miss Kate Ball, he married the New Testament, be-kind-to-dumb-animals stuff. After supper he retired and Mrs. Pentecost went to her room next to the kitchen and took off her hearingaid and Miss Kitty retired to her bedroom and done did homework. She was sixteen all right.

One night I wash up dishes and locks doors good fixing to retire to my mattress on the floor of the pantry but see lightstreak from under Miss Kitty's door. I knock and go in and she and me set a spell having good old time talking like we used to. O Lord she could make me laugh! That night she pretends she's a fancy woman ain't no good to the human race. Dress herself in silks and heels and black lace pants and paints her face and smokes from this cigarette holder: Presdent Roosefelt did that. We airs the room and hides her fancy stuff where Mrs. Pentecost won't look.

But on another time I knock, no answer. Figure Miss Kitty sleep.

Couple nights on it come up Sunday, I'm off. Been to service at Pisgah and am downtown changing bus at the stop next the pictureshow. Soldiers everywhere full of sass. The pictureshow letted out. They come under the marky and sure: there is Miss Kitty all dress up fancy like she do for me. Only she has her this man, too. I couldn't see too good. He look like a sad sack older than she, got slit eyes and pencil moostash tells you blues in the trend. They sashay off.

Me, I go on home, wait up for her in the room. Long about one in the morning by the *ping* of the old clock hear this breathing noise, in she come by the front window. 'Hmph,' I said. Reckon I give her a start. 'Mary!' she said. 'What yawl doing here?' Her eyes is wild and her mouth is sassy. 'Studying your trouble.' I said, 'Your mama find out, you be skint alive and me, I pick cotton, *uh huh*.' By and by she tole me his name is this Bud. Wife trucking out, world down on him, joined Air Corps, going overseas any old time. 'He's so lonely,' Miss Kitty said. 'Naw, he ain't,' I said. 'You're down on him, too, on account he's Jewish,' she said. 'Lord,' I said, 'I don't care if he's a little green man with pink polka dots from the moon, I'm just down on trouble.' But her eyes was wild and her mouth sassy. She said this Bud wanted to marry her soon as he got di-vorce which he ain't got. She said she met him three weeks ago when she played guitar for Woe Relief at the soldier camp. She said, 'I want to make him happy even though he's leaving soon and we may never see each other again.' She begun to cry and wasn't sassy no mo. I set to thinking of Mommer's troubles when they took Pap away, and Sariah's when they buried Lil Brother Boy. I'm thinking why the Lord give out pain? I figured: sometimes better to roll your happiness into one big apple and eat it while the taste is sweet. Trouble was, while she fixing to make this Bud happy, she got blues. If you going to give happiness, you gotta start by getting and keeping some for yourself: I learned that. So, 'Honey,' I said, 'maybe he's O.K., maybe he'll get di-vorce and come back from the woe and marry you, but he still have to meet your folks so's he can pre-chate how you are sort of special deluxe.' Slow she smiled, give me big hug. Me, I pick cotton all night with my old friends, the boll weevils.

Only by the time next morning Mrs. Pentecost fixing her a yoghurt in the kitchen, 'Ma'am,' I said, grits and eggs and pancake stack ready. 'Ma'am,' I said, 'I believe the Lord would want us to share our blessings.' 'Amen to that, Mary,' she said. I told her how sad it were to see homesick soldierboys wandering around Poe's Hill, specially Sunday. Mrs. Pentecost face come up bright. She says why not ask a soldier for Sunday lunch. 'Ma'am,' I said, 'I don't know how come you think of all the good ideas. That reminds me,' I said, 'Miss Kitty been out to soldier camp for the Woe Relief show, says everbody there likes this officer called Captain Bud but they's afraid he going to die on account he so homesick for his wife's cooking on Sundays.' Stuff like that. Then it's breakfust time and I'm serving the stack and Mrs. Pentecost asks Miss Kitty does she know this poor soldier called Bud. Lord have mercy, Miss Kitty like to choke. I wink eye at her and say, 'You remember, honey, the one from the soldier camp everbody's sorry for on account he's pining away Sundays without no special deluxe fried chicken and his wife's homemade apple pie? That one.'

Pretty soon it's fixed. Sunday lunchtime come and we got old Bud.

Well, I felt sort of sorry for him, myself, he really *did* look like he mos dead like John the Baptist, head chopped off. And he really was homesick for his wife's cooking, tell by the way he stuffed hisself with my special deluxe fried chicken and homemade apple pie. What it was, was he really and truly wanted his mama. He told Mrs. Pentecost that his mama was just about the purest soul on earth and if he had one dream in life it were to make one million dollars so's give her ever penny of it. Stuff like that. 'That's beautiful,' says Miss Kitty, eyes shiny. Mrs. Pentecost, you know, she thought different. 'Young man,' she said, 'if your mother is as pure as you say, then I advise you not to give her no one million dollars on account it would be the *ruin-ta-tion* of her. We are born in sin, flesh is weak.' Pretty soon she had Bud's mama about roasted in the fiery pit and Bud gets this sick look on his de-capitated face. Miss Kitty has to scuse herself she's so embarrassed by him and everbody, including me. It were the last we saw of old Bud. Miss Kitty, she went out the window one more time and come home crying her heart out on account of Bud saying she was a really nice girl but he was just a low-down *schlemiel*, he knew it, whatever that was, and anything between them didn't mean nothing becos there was only one woman in his life and that was his mama. Boys love mothers, daddies love daughters, I guess, *proper* speaking.

Next morning Mrs. Pentecost said to me, the Reverend's holding a request service with airmen at Pre-Flight School, would maybe bring a soldier home next Sunday. I found Miss Kitty laying in bed studying that pink steamboat wallpaper she had with white folks strolling with the top hats and parrysols past slaves. Real cheerful, 'Honey,' I said, 'your daddy's going to bring home a nice man.' Her face got twisted looking, hot. 'Say lesbian to me, say it!' 'Honey,' I said, 'that ain't a word I use.' 'Say it!' she said. 'O.K., 'I said. 'Lesbian.' 'Fine,' she said, 'that'll remind me how I hate men.' Then she fell on my neck crying. I said, 'Stop, honey.' She stopped.

That next Sunday spring was just making a summer.In come this lieutenant for lunch: it was the Mr. Max.

Listen. There is Miss Kitty pining in the kitchen all morning. Do

I think she ought to be a nun? Uh-uh. Do she look all right? Uh-huh. Do I think people had to get married to have family? Pends on who people is. The doorbell ring and she look at me wild. 'What if he's goodlooking and warm and sincere, what can I say, Mary?' 'Go on,' I said, 'don't have to say nothing to no man, just wait your time. When his tongue hangs loose like a hounddog's on account he cain't stand no mo yearning, and he pours out his misery-heart, give him a little friendly en-couragement.'

Already I figure this Mr. Max may be O.K., for I can hear Reverend Pentecost laughing and then, suddenly, old Mrs. Pentecost laughing too, and she ain't exactly sunshine. 'Huh,' says Miss Kitty. 'If he makes *her* laugh, he must be a real drip. My hair all right?' She got this laughing-look in her eyes. We went into the setting room. That's when it happened. Miss Kitty saw this Mr. Max and I know him and she going to truck on down.

For lunch we start with crab in shell. Reverend serves some wine and says the grapes by the Cas-a-peen Sea was big as your thumb and quoted him some Song of Solomon and Mr. Max quoted him some poetry that was right pretty like 'where did the snow go day befo yesterday.' After crab we have the special deluxe fried chicken and marshmallowed yams and limas from my V-garden and hotbread and, for dessert, pecan pie with ice cream. Mr. Max come to the kitchen after lunch looking mighty unmarried and said it were the best meal he ever et and I said, 'Well, Miss Kitty cooked most half of it' and 'When are you coming again?' Trouble was, Miss Kitty done scrunched down to her eats and had her three helpings chicken and yams like she's whole lot mo int-erested in eats than in no man. Maybe lesbian? I'm dumbgasted. When Mr. Max he go home early, I said to myself, 'Mary Jackson, where was you at when brains was give out?'

Only, that evening he come back! I and Miss Kitty both at door. There he was holding old bunch of roses. He didn't have to say nothing. He just give them to her. She looked at them roses. She looked at him. She took them roses and ran into her room. Mr. Max looked pretty low and said, 'Trust me to hurt her feelings.' I said, 'Mister, you don't know but that's the nicest thing ever done did for her. Wait,' I said. I went to her room and said, 'Well, you ain't still pining for Captain Bud, is you?' 'No, Mary,' she allowed, 'it isn't that. It's he wouldn't respect me if he knew the kind of tramp I am.' 'Stuff,' I told her. 'Go on now. He's waiting. It's time for you, girl. You got a result.' So she went and spoke to him, and she must of said the right thing on account he started coming regular to the house, mos ever evening. The Pentecosts liked him. Of course they was old enough to be him and Kitty's grandparents, they couldn't stop talking a lot of stories when they should of done Shut Up and gone bye-bye. Mr. Max heard all about their travels to Persia, how they went by ox-cart, how the (how do you say it) Bolsheveeks tried excute them for giving comfort to some boys and girls got chopped by sabers, stuff like that. He was like a son to them, making like he Miss Kitty's big brother, and there was Mr. Max acting like it warnt right to joy a girl when he going to woe. And there was Miss Kitty herself—why, she could of grabbed holt that man and tole him she was having *his* babby even befo they done made one of their own for a fack becos she wants him real bad and right now.

MANNY LAUGHED. "Mama, I'm shocked at you."

HMPH. ANYWAY, ALONG ONE AFTERNOON we-alls on the porch, me and Mrs. Pentecost watching Miss Kitty and Mr. Max holding hands walking. You could just feel Mrs. Pentecost thinking. So, 'Ma'am,' I said, 'I'm worried.' 'What about, Mary?' 'Oh,' I told her, figuring to rile her up so much she'll want that marriage, 'I don't think she's good enough for him.' '*What?*' she uproars. 'Mary Jackson, how *dare* you make in-sinuation about our family!' She drew herself up like that horsewoman done when I was littlegirl and said, 'My father was Major Ball of the States of America Confederate Army. Kitty has been bred right. I will inform Lieutenant Stebbins we claim kin to Washington's grandfather!' Well, little bird tole me them Washingtons have mo slaves than Carter has liver pills, so look who's stuck up bragging?

"KNOWS MAJOR BALL GOOD," said Pap. "Meanest man I ever work fo. Washington, knows the name good, Booker T. Washington."

"Take it easy, Pap," said Manny.

LISTEN. I SAID TO HER, 'MAYBE YES, MAYBE NO. I bet they don't get married on account her being sort of low in his eyes.' About then Mrs. Pentecost got this real thoughtful look on her face. 'We'll see about that,' she said. I figured I done hep give them a little mo time to make the babby what's already made, though no bigger'n a bedbug.

Now, the Pentecosts had them a cottage at Nag's Head by the ocean. Come July we usta go there, and this time in nineteen forty-two Mr. Max was taking furlough to join us and arriving on that rattletrap bus you used to change on at Sligo. We went. The day befo he due, I and Miss Kitty go out crabbing in the tide inlet behind Kitty Hawk. I rowed and ship oars in some pussywillow as water glass over at turning of tide. We dropped fatback and waited. By and by the big crabs bit. We was quiet as sun. I drug in first. Little bit, little bit mo. Line was tight, heavy. Must of been three or fo little buggers all trying to get them a hunk of meat befo Miss Kitty sposed to dive net. Well. When I say so, she leans over the oarlock there and—*blam!*—she drops the net in the boat and the line went slack. She sets down looking like pain.

'You been to doctor, honey?'

She saw I thought. She shook. 'You missed time,' I said.

'Yes,' she said. We both thought a while. I might could of asked her was it old Captain Bud. But, far as I, if it ain't Mr. Max, oughta be. I'm shut. 'Tell him tomorra, honey,' I said, pretending. 'You-all have you a nice little babby when he has to go.'

That done it. She cried a bit. Pretty soon up she sets kind of stiff like that lady on horseback in the old days, a lot of bone in her and a lot of sass. 'No,' she said, 'I can't lie.'

Mercy. I guess the Pentecost family don't lie, all but one. 'He loves you, don't he?' She allows it. 'You love him, too, don't you?' She allows it. Maybe she'll write and tell him everthing 'soon's he gone,' she says.

'What you scared fo?' I said. 'I bet, first thing, you and him going to Norfolk, Virginia, to the preacher, and he go to woe and won't know a hill of beans he ain't a father.'

She just set there. She fixed me with them blue eyes and said I got to promise never tell him nothing. So I'm shut. Seemed like those days there were a right way and a wrong way and everbody taking the right way, and sometimes that's the wrong way. Even me. Had me a good line and ten cent of fatback. What I do? Cut bait. I cut bait and set watching crabs tear fatback to iddy bits. You got to wait your time. You got to get your bite on the line, bring in slow, not a sound or shadder to spook them. Ease up line till your crab is so close you can see them mean little eyes lit up in the sun like two bitty balls of tapioca, then *splush!* Dive yo net and scoop quick and dump the bugger into yo bushel basket befo he sidedaddles away . . . Maybe Miss Kitty wait too long already, though.

There's the Lord's Time, but if you want His Time to turn out to be *your* time, you got to give Him a little co-operation.

Mr. Max come on the bus. Soon's him and her set eyes on each other, you know it's finally hot time in the old town tonight! Only, we got a bad sign right off. Ho-rizon had this ex-plosion. Coast

Guard said a tanker blowed up by German submarine. Next day the beach was black with oil, slimy, and there was a poor sailor floating face down in little breakers. Could of been Mr. Max, done dead in airplane and no chile begot to carry on his seed.

One time Reverend Pentecost talking woe stories. Miss Kitty shushed him, said to Mr. Max, 'We all want you to enjoy your leave and not think about the woe. When I write I'll tell you all the home things.'

It reminded the Reverend how he used to write letters from the trenchmud even when they was bombing. 'You'll write us, won't you, son? I mean you write to Kitty here, don't bother with us old folks.'

'I'd be pleasured,' says Mr. Max. 'I'll write if you do.' He give Miss Kitty a close look.

And I recollect that, that *if*. On account it would make all the difference. Anyway, up pipes old Mrs. Pentecost all fluttery-buttery: 'I reckon you might find my chile's writing disappointing, I mean a chile of her delicacy and breeding to be raised in a mission home and surrounded by heathen and shut off from the world by great snowy mountains, a chile like Kitty is not yet ready to take on the duties of young womenshood.' Stuff like that. 'Hot dog!' I say to myself. 'Miss Kitty is got to tell him now, they going to run off get married quick as catch measles.' Becos Miss Kitty seems paying no nevermind to her mama, she looking deep in Mr. Max's eyes so long the Reverend chuckled, 'Mind the serpent, boy, mind the serpent.'

I went out and th'owed sand over my left shoulder. Air was queer. Sand didn't blow, though.

A strange week. Sposed be hurricane making our way. Coast Guard come along in the jeep, give warning. Everthing too quiet. Sun stayed hot, wind low. Tides swole, coming to the piling under the cottage, drawing long ways back and leaving all kind queer fish and skates layin' on the beach. Even a babby whale. Me and Mr. Max and a bunch others pushed and pulled that whale into the shallers and just about give it up when all on a sudden come a gret big old wave that ain't due on the tide for couple hours, set the whale float. Lord in it. Like I say, give the Lord a little co-operation, man. About that time Mrs. Pentecost acting up, too. Says to me real snappy, 'Mary, where they at? What they doing?' She made me promise not to let Miss Kitty out of sight, specially when they-all's walking, evenings, in the moon.

Reminds me. On account strange tides, part the beach a mile down where ain't nothing but dunes and saltgrass got changed. There was this big shaller pool all dug out by the tide in one night. End of week we three walked down there. It were warm and moony. We set and watched moon in that pool and they teased like, 'Mary, there's a real good pictureshow up the beach in Norfolk, Virginia, if you run you'll be just in time.' We did that a while. By and by Mr. Max took a notion he could use a swim in that pool, only he don't have no trunks. 'Come on,' Miss Kitty said sassy. 'Who alls fraid big bad wolf?' They undressed. You could see some, too, in that moon. 'You Miss Kitty, you stop that!' I'm saying, 'Oughta be shame on you.' Though back of mind, I know they's good as married. Well, they messed around in that pool that don't cover up more'n knees. By and by I notice it getting mighty quiet in that pool. I cleared throat good, let them know I'm still studying. I look around. They was kissing in that water. Mr. Max set up pretty good for a white man. Miss Kitty mos blind you. The Lord made us good, I believe that, natural good, no sin-strings.

It was a warm night, strange. Wind quit and tide was sucked way back from shore and stars was sad. The mo I set the mo I got my old sea-feelings like I used to when I was lonesome on the sea-island of Edisto. I looked way, way out yonder into the dark of the sea like there might could be something there if I could just get a light to it. It's hard to ex-plain. There were three of us, and two of us is dressed only in moonlight, and right there you got a little pain on the way and no morphine except Jesus. Thing was, this Coast Guard jeep must of crep up. Becos, first thing you know, they of got a lightbeam blinding our eyes. You ever wish you was a wall?

Somebody shouts, 'That them?' Whoevers it were was with the guardsman must of said, 'It's them.'

'You all there, come on,' shouts this guardsman. 'Hurricane coming. We're taking you folks to Manteo right smart.'

It were awful quiet in that pool. Just two lit-up head like cabbages. Finally Mr. Max called out in a sort of loud angry voice that he's officer in U.S. Army Air Corps and what in tarnation do that guardsman think he doing, sneaking up like that. The guardsman couldn't *sir* enough after that. 'Sorry, sir, we're looking for Miss Pentecost, sir.' Mr. Max said, 'Turn off that fool light,' and the guardsman yessired. It's moonlight and time again. Mr. Max and Miss Kitty dressed up out of their birthday suits. When they was fixed to climb into the jeep, we heard this powerful moan like gnashing of teeth pro-vided in Hell. Miss Kitty cries out, 'Mother!'

Sure's you born, Mrs. Pentecost was asetting in the back seat. I picked enough cotton *that* time to put boll weevils out of work and on strike. I be dog if I ain't done dead already.

Now, listen. We vacuated to this schoolhouse in Manteo, scrunched in there with whole lot people, dogs and chickens. Reverend Pentecost got everbody sing *Watchman Tell Us* and *Those in Pearl on the Sea*. Wasn't too bad a time. Miss Kitty and Mr. Max even get to cuddle up a bit. Mrs. Pentecost, though, just biding time, like she was crabbing, and fixing to work herself into her own kinda hurricane headed my way.

We went back to Nag's Head next afternoon after the other, little hurricane. Not much damage, just a couple old hotels blowed away. Everbody felt bad on account Mr. Max's furlough over. Looks of him and Miss Kitty, life about over, too. I been to that inside-place, myself, later.

It were Reverend and Miss Kitty drove him to Sligo to catch the bus. Me, I sort of stay away from the cottage. Went clumb a big dune. Set. Had my sea-feelings bad. Once things go wrong, you got to get your line out and wait for the buggers to co-operate. After a while I girded up my loins, like they say, went to the cottage to have me some slave-time, women's-time Mr. Lincoln forgot about. *She* was waiting for me, you bet.

'Mary,' she said, 'you have betrayed our family.'

I said, 'No, ma'am. *No,* ma'am. You don't know the truth.'

'Well?' she said like she was waiting for the truth nothing but the truth. Which is quite a record in the family.

'Well,' I said, 'I don't really know, you ask Miss Kitty.'

'I'm asking you,' she said. She looked at me hard like that lady on horseback did when I was knee-deep in chilehood and her th'owing me overboard for even existing.

I kep trying to keep shut and she kep saying how sad it were I had turned out bad, and I did feel pretty low when I got to reckning how many good things the Pentecosts done for me. By and by I tole her the truth about Miss Kitty having a love-chile.

She scared me. 'It's come out in her,' she said in a softer kind of moan than hurricane wind, mo like her soul running down outta gas. 'The curse of our Ball family come out again in her.'

I pretended don't understand what she's talking about, but little bird is telling me good, Major Ball a sho-nuff boogiemans. Finally, I said, 'All we got do is telphone U.S. Army and they'll fix up a nice wedding. Miss Kitty's much more growed up than her age. We got to let her go to that man loves her.'

Whew. What Mrs. Pentecost said next give me the creeptime big. "Spose a father begets a chile on his own daughter. That chile can't marry, can she? God is looking down upon our vileness and bomination. His intended bride is run away. Wherefore should I stay my hand if my Isaac ain't Abraham's? "

A little while after, she told me I got to hep her stop them letters. Anything from Mr. Max, I got to get it from the mailmans befo Miss Kitty knows, and I got to find a way grab any letter from her, maybe saying I'll take it to the post office on my way to Reverend T. Willie Dukes at Pisgah. I was tole to th'ow away all the letters and not to worry on account of Miss Kitty being just sixteen. When we got back to Poe's Hill, I did that, only I kep them letters. It made me sick killing love off. Maybe still going to be O.K., and then some time I can give Miss Kitty all the letters and say I found them in Mrs. Pentecost's room after she done dead. Maybe not, though. Love goes on and on, silent love, letters not re-quired, just cosy-time.

Chapter Ten **Mary**

"So this was the woman who testified at Pap's trial," says Manny when she has finished her story. His eyes are bright, without submission. "I'm going to call Judge Debnam Babbage. I might go to Charleston for an investigation."

Mary decides to telephone Dr. Hasbrouck about the letters before she gets scared again. *On account he legal heir to he wife's property.*

It is a cool night for May. Up the incline of Watauga Street to Vinegar Hill Boulevard, and then she shuts herself into the white glare of the telephone kiosk. While Dr. Hasbrouck's line is ringing, big white moths blunder against the glass, brandishing their wings like haunts.

And last night: Sunday, June the sixth.

At Pisgah the Reverend T. Willie Dukes says you have to go down in the dark to see the light.

After church she irons her black dress and puts it on a hanger above Manny's cot in the kitchen. Later, out in the backyard on the path to the privy, she peeps in the shed where Pap already snores in the fishfoul air, his chromium reel glittering by a silvered window.

She retires, blowing out the kerosene lamp and snuggling under quilt. Justice Branch's service star blacks a windowpane. He must have decided to die without having time to think about it, just as she has arrived at truth in a swift, unlooked-for motion of darkness. You go down, though. There is still light in darkness.

As if no time.

He will need a good breakfust. Probably caught the bus from Charleston. Planes drone freightcars shudder their clanks. *Mayree you Mayree* calls Sariah out of dreamtime and she runs from seateeth into the jive of U.S.O. dance (*the name is Justice Emmanuel Branch baby and you better dance because they are shipping this gun out in seventy-two hours*) and Miss Kitty says *I am ten years old. This is my room. I used to look at the mountains all day. Now I raise the sash and see the milkman coming. Clip clop clip clop. Isn't that funny? Mother says you are going to be my sister. You have lovely skin. Can I feel it?*

Mary wakes in the twilight of dawn. What light there is in the room is spare and gray, without motion or intensity or promise or loss. It is time revealed as Time. A crow caws, flaps, vanishes into silence as though whipped off the planet by a flaw in gravity. She half opens her eyes, heart pounding waves of deafening: someone is out there, someone is peering in her window, someone pale as pigeon. She sleeps. When next she wakes, she hears brakes squeaking on Watauga Street and a metal door slammed and voices spaced between gunnings of a motor:

"See ya, Sam."

"O.K., man."

The car whines, reversing up the rutted incline, a car too big to U-turn at the deadend, then footsteps *scuff click scuff,* and it is the light of six o'clock: today is Monday. Already she folds the quilt and hunches and swings muttering, "Pap, he's home" though in summertimes Pap moves his pallet to the shed, yet muttering again as bare feet feel gummy cool of linoleum and she shifts into the pink silk wrapper she inherited from among Miss Kitty's things, "Manny's back from Charleston."

Unlatches front door: street tilts, gold rims the gray house opposite. At the window a tall man is studying his father's star, blue suit limberly draped, white shirt and dark tie, black beard, sunglasses: Manny.

"What a matter yo eyes? You wear dark glasses at night?" There is something changed about Manny. If she can just get him to Jesus college he'll tell Ole Pharaoh to git. "Find out something?"

"Information, yes." A sweep of hand: he breathes on lenses, begins to polish them with sassy motions of a breastpocket handkerchief. "Satisfaction, no."

"You see that lawyerman Judge Babbage sent you to?"

"Mr. Buck McKay. I saw him all right."

"You should of asked that man in the car come in."

"Big Sam the Salesman," Manny sighs as they enter the house. "He offered me a job in New York. He has a good car. Olds."

"You don't need no car."

"Nome. But I gotta split from Taboo City."

"You got you a good job at the cannery. Until you go to the Jesus college."

"Yessum."

"You sassing me?"

"Oh, nome." He hooks his arm as if he is throwing her a basketball.

"What you mean a job in New York?"

"Thinking about it."

She tries to smooth out the rough grain of her feelings. "Go on, then. Go to New York. Get you a big flashy car, get you a big flashy woman, too. See if she do for you good's me."

He flops onto her bed. He wears white gym socks and black

pointed shoes. "If I got a high-yaller woman, then I got children. If I got children, there's Taboo City," he says, "on and on.".

"Hmph," she says, thinking *He know now.*

"I wouldn't mind a new car." He grins, stifling a yawn.

"You should of took the bus. Now you got to go work in couple hours." She hears Manny chuckle strangely to himself. "What's so funny? What's got into you?"

"That Big Sam."

"What he do?"

"He sells Books of Knowledge. I know things they don't put in Books of Knowledge."

She leaves him in order to fire the stove and put the coffee on. When she returns, he is lighting a cigarette, the match flaring against his coppery face and black beard, the subtle hand wringing out flame, slowly. "Just started," he replies, unasked.

"You don't smoke in no bed in no house, naw sirree!"

"She . . . *she* . . ," Manny jets smoke and presses full lips, "she and Major Ball sent an innocent man to prison for life. And knew he was innocent, and the jury and judge knew that too. Taboo City."

"Well," she says, "nothing we can do now. Sides, you can't run away. Run off, only thing changes is the weather."

"I'm going to do something."

"No, you ain't. What old Mrs. Pentecost and old Major Ball done, just forget. You got a friend in Time."

"I'm making it my business, Mama. Goddam!"

"That's fine," she says, plucking the cigarette from his lips, "cuss a while."

"Hey!"

"Breakfust in one hour." There is a hiss as she pours water on the cigarette, mushing it. "Now you know your grandfather was a good man, you can stop picking on him."

"He's not my grandfather," Manny says.

She bites her tongue, says nothing.

"Big Sam the Salesman wasn't jiving me. I could make money in New York."

"Time you went to the Jesus college. Don't tell me no more crooked salesman."

"I'll get a basketball scholarship. Up North."

"Well," says Mary, "do it, then." She is hurt by him, yet proud of him too. She has waited years for Manny to learn what's good for him, and he gets a result in one weekend: Time itself. Already, though, he resembles Mrs. Pentecost with his pride. It must be all in the family. In the depths, too, she has always known Mrs. Pentecost was her mother. Because Pap seats her stride the cannon on the Battery, and the Pain Lady on horseback crosses in front of the *honk hoogar hoogar* of motorcars and glares at her own unspeakable result: the teeth of things.

When she brings Manny his coffee, he is sitting up, aged by beard and high forehead, skull capped by thin black hair. He reminds her of stations of the Cross. Her heart has long dedicated him to goals worthy of the most exacting demands of the spirit. "Drink some coffee, Emmanuel," she says. She seldom calls him that. Time she did.

He grins. "I guess you're a good mama even though you are a crook. You broke the law when you interfered with the delivery of mail. Mr. Buck McKay kept saying the word *iniquity.* He said people will put their faith in iniquity if you give them enough time and lies . . . You make good coffee." He holds the cup of coffee in both hands, draws up his knees, huddles over the cup, says, "Don't Jesus me, Mama. Like you always say, though, to love others you got to love yourself first. I need time for that."

AN HOUR LATER MARY WETS FEET ON CRABGRASS in the backyard. Water lies in puddles: *it must of rained in the night.*

Perhaps lightning made the pigeonface at her window. In the shed Pap is still stretched on his pallet among tools and sacks, the gleam of his chromium reel like the splinter of a star. His long underwear needs patching at elbow and knee . . . It is true, what Manny says: we have to love ourselves properly. She goes, lifts the latch of the pineslat privy, and sits in semi-dark amongst flies and hornets and dank reeks of lime and unventilated clay. Justice Branch was so crippled by piles he could scarcely walk, he wrote in his last letter from the troopship before the battle in which he saved his men by falling on the Japanese hand grenade. Through a knothole she sees Pap outside strapping on dungarees, bending, splashing water on his face from faucet. By the time she emerges into light he is on hands and knees by the tomato vines, digging for nightcrawlers. He will fish today.

"Manny's home. Come get yawl's grits."

He turns. His skull is veined and frizzlehaired. In their deep-sunken orbits his eyes still have iron in them, the long silence. "Gonna get Ole Red-Eye today," he mumbles. "Done seen that bass down in the shallers." Fingers probe delicately. He drops a worm into tin can.

"Don't make him re-member if he don't want to," she tells Manny when she has her men seated at the kitchen table. When white sails fanged the sky and a lady on horseback stopped and stared and she was seated on a cannon and Pap studied Miss Kate Ball, pain in his face, two of them knew about Major Ball's lunatic desire for forbidden fruit. "Mighty nice grits, Mary. Joyed the eggs, too," says Pap, rising, wiping tight little mouth on coveralls. Again Manny's voice seems harsh:

"Wesley Jackson!"

And Pap must sit, head bowed. Again Manny holds up the drawing he has made of a golden fish with an egg in its mouth.

"Try to remember, Wesley Jackson. Did you make a necklace

token like this and give it to Miss Kate Ball of Charleston?"

Pap wets lips. "Knows the name good." He glances away.

"Not the name this time. The picture. Try to remember."

"You draws real good, Manny."

Manny spreads his hands flat on the table and says, "You were spared during an Indian massacre when you were a baby. Major Ball brought you to Charleston, you worked for him, you knew his daughter Kate—later Mrs. Pentecost. At your trial both Major Ball and Miss Kate Ball witnessed against you . . ."

Pap leans forward, rocking slightly, hands clasped between legs.

"You were convicted of rape. It was a white girl who lived near the Ball house. Major Ball testified that he found the girl one night wandering in a daze out back of his house, in the stables where you usually worked. He said she told him what had happened, and when he described you to her, she said it was you . . . When the police searched the stables, they found this ornament on a broken necklace, like it had been torn off in a struggle. The claim was, you were wearing this necklace. But you testified that you made the ornament as a present for Miss Kate and gave it to her years before the incident. When she testified, she denied it. You have that?"

Pa stops rocking, clasps and unclasps his hands.

"I'm on your side now," Manny says. "My lawyer, Mr. Buck McKay, is convinced that you were wrongfully charged, wrongfully tried, and wrongfully convicted. Assuming that the girl was raped by somebody—it was never proven—we still have the fact that her so-called testimony was prompted by Major Ball to identify you as her assailant. Yet this hearsay was accepted by the court and left unchallenged by your so-called defense. The only concrete piece of evidence linking you to the crime was the ornament. We'll come back to that . . . Everything about this trial makes clear that you were made the scapegoat for the whole community: the illegal manner in which you were examined, the all-white jury, the harshness of your sentence, the lack of appeal and the refusal to admit new evidence. McKay found out somehow that when Mrs. Pentecost returned from Kurdistan in thirty-six, she went to Charleston on business connected with the death of her father, Major Ball, and at this time she changed her testimony in the Wesley Jackson case, but she was ignored. As McKay says, you never hurt anybody in your life."

"What I tol' the man," Pap nods at last. "Man at the camp say look in the papers. I say what do it say. Sho Miss Kate married the man Pentecost."

"Wesley Jackson," Manny says.

"Don't," says Mary.

"Wesley Jackson." The veins stand out on Manny's high lustrous forehead. "Did you or did you not give an ornament like this golden fish to Miss Kate?"

"Don't," Mary says.

"*He knows!* Now," Manny says as he takes a sheet of notepaper from his jacket, unfolds and reads from it. "'Do you recognize this ornament, Wesley?' they said.'

"You said, 'Yes, sir, made it myself.' Then you told what seemed a jive story about meeting Kate Ball in Chicago where she was studying at the Bible Institute. Q. 'Did you meet Miss Ball in Chicago?'

"A. 'Yes, sir.'

"Q. 'Why did you go to Chicago?'

"A. She sent me money and told me where she's at.'

"Q. 'Were you used to being employed by her?'

"A. 'No, sir. I work for Major Ball and quit to go to Chicago.'

"Q. 'How much money did she send you?'

"A. 'Train ticket and some for eats.'

"Q. 'Why did she send for you?' I have a note here where McKay said this question was improper. Defense made no objection. 'Why did she send for you?'

"A. 'She was sick, real sick.'

"Q. 'If she was sick, why should she send all the way to Charleston for you?'

"A. 'She took sick is all. I had to go do something for her.'

"Q. 'I see. What did you do for her, Wesley?'

"A. 'I don't recollect good. Give her the present, though.'

"Q. 'You mean to say you traveled a thousand and more miles in order to give Miss Ball your little ornament? That was mighty thoughtful of you, Wesley.'

"A. 'Thank you, sir.'

"Q. 'Tell us what else you did in Chicago besides giving presents.'

"A. 'Worked for the depot saving up to get married.'

"Q. 'You were fixing to get married, were you?'

"A. 'I decided to.'

"Q. 'How long did you work for the depot?'

"A. 'Oh, six, seven months.'

"Q. 'Which depot was it?'

"A. 'I don't remember good.'

"Q. 'Were you seeing Miss Ball during this time?'

"A. 'Time to time seen her. She was most sick.'

"Q. 'What did you do when you saw her?'

"A. 'Tried to ease her mind. Went for the doctor couple times.'

"Q. 'I see. Tell us more about your wanting to get married. Was there someone in Chicago you wanted to marry?'

"A. 'There was this lady. But she didn't want me to marry her just to hep her out, so I come home and married me another lady.'

"Q. 'Handsome fellow like you doesn't have much trouble with the ladies, does he? We'll rephrase. Do you have sexual intercourse much as you please?'

"A. 'No, sir. Do you?'

"Q. 'Will the court please request the defendant to confine his answers to the questions? Isn't it true, Wesley, that you have no control over yourself when you see a white woman?' An objection was overruled on that question.'

"A. 'No, sir.'

"Q. 'Now, Wesley. We have Major Ball's sworn testimony that you left his employment without giving notice—an act of rank discourtesy to the gentleman who saved you from the slaughter of your people, and, at his own expense and out of the goodness of his heart, brought you to our city to be raised among god-fearing folks. Now, Major Ball has dutifully informed us that at no time during that year was Miss Kate sick, as you said she was. Had she been sick, who but her father would have been first to be notified by the authorities of the Bible Institute? Gentlemen of the jury, Miss Ball testified that she never saw Wesley Jackson in her life in any city other than this one. And we have the word of this gracious Christian lady that the first time she saw your golden fish was not five years ago in Chicago but here in this courtroom. Isn't it true, Wesley, that you yourself have worn this ornament until one night, besotted with drink and governed only by your insensate and bestial lust, you happened upon, in an ill-starred moment, a pure undefiled defenseless white angel of the South and in the course of your struggle to violate the temple of her chastity and to force your will upon the unravished whiteness of her body'. . ."

"Thanking you for the mighty nice breakfust, Mary." Pap rises. She can see his fists tightening in a kind of palpitating hysteria, like small cornered rabbits. She has not looked him full in the face.

"Pap, you go on now and get ready. I'll make you some sammitches."

He does not look at her either. He does not even turn in the kitchen doorway where a steamy light wavers behind the bug-whiny morning-glories. She can feel him looking at her out of the corner of his eye, at her back already busy clearing the table, feel him stilling his heart with sea-feelings that make him seem akin to her. It is for her sake that he has kept inside his silences-- and his chains.

"He *knows!*" Manny cries.

"You should of took the bus," she says, thinking *He took me from Chicago and married Mommer to give me a home.*

In a distant part of Poe's Hill mill whistles are shrieking like Lil Brother Boy did when he swallowed carbolic acid.

THE LETTERS ARE GONE.

Manny is the Man now. All things in Time. His father had already used eight of his seventy-two hours of leave and used another two at the U.S.O. dance before making up his mind to do what she had already decided, leaving them two hours to find the Reverend T. Willie Dukes to marry them, leaving them sixty hours of married life together, all the happiness rolled into one sweet apple and then taken away forever, the strong brown body taken but never the spirit of a savior abiding. She goes to the window and touches the satin pennant with its faded star. The spirit is working in Manny, saviour spirit, not sin visited from Time.

Shuffling feet behind her, her heart filling to the brim: it is Pap so long alone with Time. Wearing his shapeless felt hat weathered now to burlap-yaller and pierced by fishhooks, he grasps rod and reel and tin pail in which are packed a jar of worms, sandwiches wrapped in greaseproof paper, and a thermos of coffee.

"Going to the river now?"

"Sho.

"Pap?"

"Huh?"

"Manny had to find out about me, sometime."

"Sho. Lemme have fifty cent buy some plug."

Finding her purse, she gives him a dollar. "Take the bus home.

You getting too old to walk ten mile ever day."

"Beholden."

SHE TAKES THE BUS DOWNTOWN, alights across the street from the Bright Leaf Hotel, and enters Mrs. Zabriski's airconditioned diner. Some black boys in T-shirts are standing around the glittering globe of a jukebox. The music throbs

love me love me
O O O bay bee . . .

"Cuppa coffee, dear, or what?" Plump, peroxided, rabbiteyed Mrs. Zabriski fingers the crucifix on her starched white blouse.

"The usual," replies Mary with a studied pause. There is something historically amusing about the way, for the first time, she neglects to say' please'. Mrs. Zabriski chuckles while pouring coffee from a pyrex globe. Mary's white cup has rings in it like her bathtub.

did you come
did you fee eel

"They grow up fast." Mrs. Zabriski leans over the counter in a confiding manner. "Mr. Zabriski is teaching me to shoot a pistol. So what's new, dear?" When Mary tells her that Manny has won a basketball scholarship to a big school Up North, Mrs. Zabriski blinks weak watery eyes and says, "It's a free country, dear . . . Jeez, I might have known," she exclaims with a sigh of disgust.

They are both glancing toward the glare of the street, both seeing the policeman rest one hand on the butt of his pistol and raise the other, cars stopping and, coming across the street from the hotel, walking with pigeon-like bob, the old lady in a white robe.

"Old Mother Pentecost," says Mrs. Zabriski. "They ought to lock her up. She found out I'm Catholic, see. She'll come in here, to tell me I'm going to hell, see. I said, 'Look, lady. Come here again and you gotta eat something in the joint, or what.' Know what she did? She orders a cuppa hot water. I think it's a gag, see. I bring the hot water in a cup. So she takes out this used teabag—used, I am telling you—drops it in the cup, helps herself to my cream and sugar, has a cuppa tea and don't pay me a nickel. She squeezed the teabag and took it with her. So what am I in business for—Communism?"

The rock music has stopped, the T-shirted boys are leaving. Mary watches them in the big mirror behind Mrs. Zabriski. She is reaching up to adjust her hair when one of the boys holds the glass door open for Mrs. Pentecost. Bending over her coffee cup, Mary can hear the pneumatic door closing like a long suck of breath.

"So what's yours, Mother Pentecost?" Mrs. Zabriski demands in rude voice. "Cuppa hot water, or what?" She begins to wipe the counter, crucifix dangling and jiggling about, eyes not flicked up but burrowed inside themselves.

Two small black boys shade their eyes and peer through the plate glass. The sun has drained their faces of color.

"The Lord will provide," Mrs. Pentecost says, softly.

"Well," says Mrs. Zabriski, "He's not providing today. So tell me it's unfair," she concludes with a dumb satisfied look that sweeps the diner's ceiling from end to end. Then Mary turns, lifts gaze.

"Hullo," she says as if out of breath. How ill and decrepit looks her mother. The blue-veined hands seem to make an involuntary motion, like a pair of loose claws. At this moment Mary is not aware that she has learned to make herself akin to people, with love toward them and sympathy. She would not have dwelled upon the idea that her rising and her stepping forward to grip Mrs. Pentecost lightly by the shoulders would express a new consciousness. "Don't you know your Mary?"

Mrs. Pentecost studies her with charmed eyes. "Mary, I declare!

Goody goody . . . I was going to pay you a call but I've had no peace in my heart."

"So they know each other. So I'm an idiot," Mrs. Zabriski is muttering.

"How about something t'eat?" Mary guides Mrs. Pentecost to a counter stool. "How about ham and eggs and french fries and a glass of yoghurt? Sit down."

Mrs. Pentecost sits, smiling, upright but bulgy like a badly stuffed bird. "Are you cooking here now, Mary?"

"If you don't mind," interrupts Mrs. Zabriski, "I hate to mention."

"I'm paying," says Mary with a frown. She picks up the menu and suggests, after a pause, "Why not Number Three, two eggs sunny side, two rashers of bacon, and a side stack buckwheat pancakes?"

Mrs. Zabriski licks her pencil. "That a good job you're doing, or what?"

"Number Three and a side order french fries and a glass of strawberry yoghurt."

"Oh," says Mrs. Pentecost, "goody goody."

"Number Three and a side french and yoghurt. Old dear must be starving, huh?"

"Mary," Mrs. Pentecost is saying with a wistful smile, "I would have invited you to visit at the Home but the ladies there, I never dreamed they'd be so *old* . . ."

Mary feels inspired. "Tell you what," she is suddenly saying, without thinking, "come on down have supper with us tonight. We'll have special deluxe fried chicken just like always. You know my house on Watauga?"

Mrs. Pentecost nods. "It didn't seem fitting to pay my respects."

"Well," says Mary, "don't worry about it. Take a taxi. After six. I'll pay."

A hand comes to rest on the back of Mary's hand. It is like a cold kitten.

"I'd be delighted to come. Dear Mary."

With eggs and bacon sizzling on the griddle, Mrs. Zabriski says in a loud voice, "Nothing personal, Mother Pentecost, but why do you walk around in a white robe and tell people they're going to hell? Are you nutty as a fruitcake, or what?"

Claw-like, Mrs. Pentecost's hand squeezes down on Mary's. Her eyes are shining like light on a blue tin roof.

TIME WAS FLOWING.

The afternoon sun dropped its yellow panels first on Miss Kitty's steamboat wallpaper, then on the chair where Mary sat, and then imperceptibly slid them across the carpet and onto the bed where Miss Kitty's Tom still slept. His face was aflame until inch by inch sunlight spread across his features: the slightly flattened nose basked shadowless and inert as a lizard, the lips curled as if in his sleep he has been graced with light and can look back in sorrow-laughter at all the begetting and begatting stories since Eden.

Mary rose and went into the living room.

"It's down to six minutes," said Miss Helen, looking up from where she sat on the sofa with her hands folded over the bulge of maternity dress. What with the small white suitcase at her feet and look of serene expectation on her face, she resembled a passenger whose mind has already arrived home before the departure of the train. As if no time. "I've called the ambulance."

"Want me to fetch—him?" Mary asked with a toss of head.

The other's face seemed to alight from its dream. "Oh," Miss Helen said with a fond snort, "I'm going to give him some cold tongue! . . What is it like, Mary?"

Mary thought. After a while she said, "Not too bad. Cousin Sariah, whose eyes sometimes turned right back up into her head like a dead dog's on account of tapeworms, and who couldn't read nor write but knew how to come in from the field, into the cabin and lay down and have her a nice little babby—she said to me, you is full of the miseries and just saying in a kind of slow rockingchair voice, 'Oh, Lordy,' when all of a sudden you say, 'Oh, *Jesus!*' That's it: a little pain and you get a result."

The ambulance came. When Miss Helen had been taken to hospital, Mary returned to the living room, thinking *This is the time we waited for. Not that time of womanblood alone with itself but this time when your soul is in the sun on a sea-island bright and breezy.* Sunpanels spread. Outside on the street chil'ren were playing, and motorcars began to park along the street, signifying the arrival of fathers, on and on. Just as the grandfather clock, deciding it wasn't ready for dying, *pinged* five o'clock five times, Miss Kitty's Tom groped his way through the doorway, stalled there glassyeyed, ashen and dishevelled from too much happiness celebrating fatherhood.

A sudden perspective opened in her mind: she saw a lady trying to shrink behind an iron post on the Raleigh railroad station platform, saw her biting her nails and staring at the Jim Crow car as the train halted one summer day in thirty-six: saw herself, Mary, then already stepping down and past the black porter who, acting as assistant ticket collector, had, ever since she had boarded the train at Beaufort (he had pronounced it *Beyoufoot* so she had pronounced it *Beyoufoot*), been practicing upon Miss Mary Jackson the gentle patronage of his art as if the lightness of her color, her age of sixteen, and the fact that she traveled alone (in a new pink dress purchased with the remainder of Mrs. D.D. Pentecost's twenty dollars) had inspired in him a tender regard for her welfare and a curious compulsion to wink at the other passengers: saw herself then trying to identify the Pentecosts among the crowd strung out along the platform and then in fact identifying the roundcollared old gentleman with the protuberant eyes as the Reverend Pentecost and the pretty little girl in pigtails as Miss Kitty: and she heard him say *Where in heaven's name is Kate got to?* and Miss Kitty say, pointing, *Look! Mummy's playing hide and go seek* and then saw the pigeon-white-faced lady with the gray hair tied into an iron fist of a knot step from behind the post and wait with an expression of wideeyed terror: and then heard Mrs. Pentecost, when she came forward, say almost inaudibly: *Welcome to the family.*

Miss Kitty's Tom saw her now as he rubbed his head and groaned, "Where's Helen? Getting drunk is the dumbest thing I ever did."

"Well," said Mary, sunshine in her voice, "welcome to the family."

Chapter Eleven **Mrs. Pentecost**

White sea unfolding, its torah thundering.

A wee *ticka ticka* as of swifts swallowing bugs in an English garden.

Mother Pentecost tuned her hearingaid and looked up. In the sky above Poe's Hill were the strange airplanes with propellers that reminded her of flails at harvesttime in the Caucasus.

If the sky fall.

Tall buildings sway in dooms of noon.

It was at the little hotel near the Dead Sea that she and Mr. Pentecost met Lady Mandeville-Gordon who said, *If the sky fall, we shall catch larks.*

The light was red, then green. Crowds swept her across the intersection of Depot and Main.

She raised her arms and cried with a joyful intonation: "MY LORD . . . TELLS ME . . . TO TELL YOU . . . THAT HE IS COMING AGAIN!"

The angels on their harps said come, And through the pearly gates came Mum.

Lady Mandeville-Gordon had quoted that delicious memorial.

Mother Pentecost was laughing to herself. She was feeling strangely, peacefully happy. A feeling of warmth, meridional and voluptuous, stirred in her like a current from the Holy Land.

When she reached the courthouse park, she sat upon a stone bench in the shadow of the Confederate Soldier. From a pocket inside her white robe, she fetched an apple that Mrs. Zabriski had sold to Mary and Mary had given to her. Half closing her eyes, she munched.

The helicopters went on threshing the sky
gathering up the laughter of village girls.

Chapter Twelve **Manny**

It was Sunday night on the road before it was Monday in Poe's Hill, Big Sam the Salesman's Oldsmobile towing the land from under them on springs so smooth Manny felt the land's hunger for his love. Tangs of the swampwater forests, pungencies of wet soil carried on the close night air: the in-fragrance of the land was in the air and touched him, intoxicating.

Then he was home. Lying on his mother's bed, he interpreted sounds that he had listened to all his life without realizing how he was juxtaposed against them. Already on Vinegar Hill the first morning buses were stopping, clearing their power nostrils. From the marshaling yards came the *clinka clinka clank* of boxcars. He was juxtaposed against these mechanical sounds, enemies of silence, devotion, and control. Something there was that was flowing from immemorial love, something ineffable growing. Weary but receptive, he lay and listened to his heart and heard again the voice that had helped to baptize him into the great spiritual brotherhood of the puny planet.

The voice of Buck McKay was communicative in a reserved way. "Extending sympathy with the mind is easy, and it's not enough. Besides, it can be dangerous to liberty. But, as for the other, extending sympathy with the heart, the glacier-slow movement of man toward some frail kinship with his kind—kinship of his own desiring and making from love and hope and sacrifice—it also may well not be enough. Nevertheless it is now the only movement in which his liberty has meaning. What is needed is a change in the human weather, atonement, compassion. But what we are likely to have instead is a spiritual Stone Age in which whatever fire first stirred in whatever brutish cave our nearer ancestors to cherish and to fear the new god of themselves will be gradually extinguished and finally forgotten, and then our cold, lonely, unsupported souls shall be set adrift, like the planet itself, among myriads of unknown stars."

Mysteriously drawn to McKay, Manny felt compelled to go and stand beside the lawyer at the window. As if this gesture served to permit a continuance of the philosophical discourse, McKay continued it in soft intonation. "The word 'brotherhood', Mr. Branch, wouldn't you agree it has become a bit shopworn and dreary?"

McKay looked at him sharply but did not wait for a reply. "Philosophers of science, though fundamentally concerned with aspects of human brotherhood and solidarity, tend to avoid the political implications of such words and concentrate, instead, on the language of evolution. Emergence is one such word, as in the emergence of the human species or the emergence of consciousness in our minds. The word *convergence*, though similar to emergence in the sense of movement, even, perhaps, of a directed movement, carries with it a particular vision: convergence refers to an accelerating process whereby the whole human species is united into a single interthinking group. We come together inwardly and in entire freedom. The enlargement of individual consciousness enlarges humanity. Our individual selves open up to the construction of a new world of the spirit."

McKay paused, opened the palms of his hands on a shrug, and said, "Hifalutin? Perhaps. And yet I am sure there are already millions of people who feel as if a supreme law were inherent in them or, if not inherent, at least a 'something' clearing away the old shrubbery and opening the possibility of a way, a new path, a sanctuary of hope. People of different races and cultures perceive their convergence in a new world. When we see, for example, a photograph of our planet as taken from outer space, are we not conscious as never before in history of our puny home in the cosmos and of our responsibility for it? When we become aware of the dramatic increase in human numbers, are we not conscious of the need to integrate our individual selves with other selves and with nature? This is a spiritual phenomenon, convergence, although, I suppose, the word 'spiritual' has also become off-putting. Coercive government, anyway, is not spiritual, and it is the enemy of convergence, which remains open to self-fulfillment.'

"Now, I come to the point." McKay again looked sharply at Manny. "We have been investigating your family tree. Some of its branches, so to say, leafed out in spite of violent and oppressive circumstances. And here you are, Mr. Branch. You, yourself, have emerged to a consciousness higher than that of your forebears, and you would not be on a mission to discover your roots if you were not already in full bloom as a convergence tree. I said, 'accelerating' and believe you will find, perhaps to your surprise, an enormous number of persons who are leafing out as you are, in different ways but with the same spirit. You are all on the same mysterious voyage to discover the tree of life—the convergence tree of trees."

That spareframed, dapper, gentle man with the astonishing head of stark-gray hair was gazing out of the window of his high-rise Charleston office. Beneath were rooftops of the old city, St. Michael's spire and domes of an Athens that never was Athens and a Rome that never was a Rome, yet a city in a way as old as these, brooding, visited and revisited by the sins of the fathers, in the remarkable period of only two and a half centuries now become, in Manny's eyes, the monumental Past and emblem of the building of a new world in The New World. "You were an only child, Mr. Branch?" McKay inquired with hawkeyed attention.

Manny nodded.

"You're not married?"

"No."

"You have—please forgive me—no children?"

"No."

"Mind you, Mr. Branch, incest is not the taboo it once was. I do not propose to horrify you, even less to advise you about personal conduct. From the beginning I have sought for an approximate answer to the question Why."

The propeller fan overhead went *shoo shoo shoo.*

McKay relaxed his attention. Clearing throat behind his hand and easing himself into a swivel chair, he returned to summation. He would write Judge Debman Babbage. Exoneration, due restitution . . . Babbage would advise and listen to instructions. "However, I must warn you," said McKay. "Both Mrs. Pentecost and the man you have believed to be your grandfather have exerted themselves for almost half a century that their secret may be buried with them. Of course, the secret is already guessed. People of our city have known it for years . . . Secrets are the very air we breathe, and when they slip from the tongues of charming gossips and veteran bores, we are thrilled. We are reminded of our inescapable past. We are accursed. Perhaps . . . perhaps in five hundred . . . perhaps in only a few decades . . . if we have time and haven't perished . . ."

His voice had dropped to a barely audible whisper. The propeller fan was heard—*shoo shoo shoo*—and the room felt crowded with a world of the damned whose souls, ubiquitous as dandelion blossoms, floated upon a stillness in the air.

Manny was on the road now. Big Sam the Salesman's Olds was towing the land from under them and just ahead loomed a buck, spectral, immobilized by the glare of two bloodless globes. Big Sam's horn was an agony of inhuman sound, yet it seemed a long time before the buck sprang with a curious delicacy of mottled limbs toward the sheltering gloom of a cypress swamp. *Not to add to the sumtotal since Cain*, Manny was thinking. *To live in silence, devotion and control.* He could feel himself breaking loose from himself, looking before and after.

And now home.

He called Mary's name and she came and listened. "Do you remember what I said when I was little, and the Reverend Dukes was sprinkling baptizing water on my neck there as I bowed?"

"Yes. I remember."

"I said the drops were the tears of Prince Jesus."

"Yes, you said that."

"It was a nice feeling."

"I remember," Mary said. "The tears of Prince Jesus."

"Funny I said that," Manny said.

"I wonder why you said that," Mary said.

Into the wilderness sprang the buck, and the voices of the damned, soundless as dandelion blossoms, raged against oblivion.

HE TOOK THE LETTERS WITHOUT HESITATION THIS TIME. It was already decided, weeks ago, what he must do, although he had not believed that, when the moment came to juxtapose himself against the wishes of his mother, he would pocket the letters in his workclothes, not breaking stride. He had deliberated and decided what he must do, this in the aftermath of a realization that his mother with the best of intentions was implicating him in crime. He had even taken the precaution of telephoning Dr. Max

Stebbins, to warn him to expect an important visitor at the farm by noon on Monday the seventh. He had disguised his voice. It was true, Dr. Stebbins had sounded annoyed and suspicious. That was why Manny had specified time and place, to gain credibility. But Manny, himself, felt unsure that his plan would work, so unsure that he had lapsed into a diffident mood and saved the theft of the letters until the last possible day before they were to be given to Dr. Hasbrouck instead of securing them at his leisure, well in advance. Now that he had the letters in his pocket, he felt as if Mary had almost been wishing for them to disappear, so openly had she left them on display. He was a little angry with her for tempting him to take seriously his sense of family honor and his hopes for the family tree. For now that he had the letters, now that he was in full stride and not directing his footsteps toward the cannery on Mill Mile—he had already lied to the foreman, explaining that a legal matter would detain him in Charleston until Tuesday—now that he was actually committed to his plan, he began to doubt its prudence. He had in Pap an example close to home of the good man who tried to put right the crimes of others and who, for his pains, had been punished for half his life. Clearly, it was a mistake to believe that other people would be grateful for help. Therefore—thus ran the logic of his new reflections—he was unable to say whether his delivering the letters to their rightful owner, Dr. Stebbins, was really a good thing to do. All he could say in defense of his plan was that originally it had been spontaneous. And now spontaneity, or what was left of it, would have to be enough. He was going to Bermuda Farm for better or worse.

The sun was high by the time he had traversed the city from east to west. He had passed the site of the Katherine Hasbrouck Memorial Hospital. He could still hear the sporadic ferocity of jackhammers a mile further on in a new suburban development where identical ranchhouses deployed spiky aerials against the sky. Later, crossing the six lanes of Interstate Highway, he had to dash to avoid the onrush of cars and trucks cruising at seventy and more miles an hour. Then he bore northwest along an unpaved county road and found and followed an old timber track that Pap had once shown him. At last the woods folded him in to natural sounds. In and out of sunstreams, butterflies floated in winking jinking glitter. The far-off *caw caw* of a buzzard seemed to come from the very soul of things.

It was mid-morning when he reached the ruins of the old sawmill. Flinging himself face-down upon a house-high mound of sawdust, he scooped out the crust and inhaled aromas of warm damp pinewine. It was good. He sprawled. Bugwhines and grasshoppery murmurations as well as the angry birdcries occasioned by his presence grew gradually fainter.

Memory streamed in with the morning . . .

Illuminated again was a man with shock-gray hair. Above him a propeller fan went *shoo shoo shoo* while Buck McKay was speaking in his quiet way: "It was friendship. Call it simplicity, call it innocence, but it began as friendship when Wesley Jackson and Kate Ball were still children, growing up together in the same house until certain manifestations of nature joined with the prejudices of society to cripple whatever that early relationship might have become. But a relationship nonetheless had existed. It was foolish of the prosecution to brush the fact aside, how she was in Chicago in the year nineteen and sent for him, her friend, who quit a lifetime's work for Major Ball and went. Let us merely accept his testimony about that. She was ill, and like a friend he gave her a little ornament he had made, no doubt to cheer her up. And let us interpret his testimony about saving up to get married and being turned down. Let us say that the woman was Kate Ball, herself. Why would he have proposed to go through a marriage which, shall we say, would have qualified him, certain places, as a candidate for the lynch mob? I can think of but one answer: devotion. Devoted friendship. Loyalty, constancy. To what? To what Kate Ball wanted at that time, and we know that must have been . . . Were you thinking respectability, Mr. Branch?"

Manny shrugged and said, "Wesley Jackson couldn't have conferred that, even if she had wanted it."

"Precisely." McKay's voice had not varied. "She wanted self-love. That, perhaps, a Wesley Jackson, a devoted friend, might have improved upon. In the end his coming to Chicago was sufficient to keep her from destroying herself. And the child she carried in her womb. She suffered more than morning sickness. She was sick unto death. She turned to the one person whom she knew she could trust, and he fulfilled that trust. Of course, Mr. Branch, I must ask you to accept, without argument at this juncture, that the man whom your mother, for good reasons, has been brought up to think of as her father—as your grandfather—is no such thing. He's something else, a kind of saint. But leave that."

"For the present, consider how preposterous his testimony appeared to the court. Because thirty-nine-year-old spinsters of that time didn't calculate on males to be at their beck and call every time they traveled from home and caught, as it appeared she had caught, a bad cold. For some in the courtroom, Wesley's story might have rung true. I find it difficult to believe that everyone in that courtroom was without exception hoteyed, sneering, and imbecile. Maybe a majority existed and was too afraid to speak out. Fear, a Gothic psychosis deeply rooted, has usually been the negative side of the American character, as anyone can tell you who is not an ostrich with his head buried in the specious quicksands of sentimentality. But I digress . . . The fact is that Wesley's story was left unexamined, and the relationship between a woman presumed to be white and respectable and a man presumed to be her racial, social and moral inferior went, if not unnoticed, unexplained.

Add to this that neither Wesley, who could not tell the whole truth without total risk, nor Kate Ball, who in five years had become so accustomed to the Chicago deception that she was willing to join her perjury to Major Ball's, were helping matters. That they succeeded in hiding the fact of friendship attests to a continuance of the original trust. One must imagine the aging spinster in that courtroom as rigid with fear that the defendant was going to tell all. But he did not. Instead, she betrayed him—and herself—and from that day she was accursed. But let us return to Wesley's story of Chicago in the year nineteen: the story has an inner pattern, one, moreover, that agrees in tenor with certain hints and shreds of gossip that are part of the fetid atmosphere one breathes. I anticipated the conclusion, a moment ago."

Manny nodded. "She bore a child."

"She bore a child. And the child was very slightly, but perhaps unmistakably, of mixed racial descent, shall we say."

"Black," Manny said.

An ironic smile creased the corners of McKay's mouth. "Is your mother indeed, as you put it, black?"

"No," Manny said.

"To me," McKay continued, "the whole business of pigmentation is a colossal bore. However, it arouses passions and causes great tragedies. Shall I proceed?"

Manny nodded. McKay was hawkeyed amid the *shoo shoo shoo.* "As soon as the child was born, Wesley with that capacity of his for taking up impossible burdens knew that he could acknowledge her as his own. Perhaps he went too far, was too persuasive, was too eager to commit himself. At all events, he took the infant with him back to Charleston and there found his common-law wife who was willing to raise the child as her own.'

"Now, if we go back, we are puzzled as to why Kate Ball refused to live with, let alone marry, her one devoted friend. You see, if this man and this woman were the parents, then it is too difficult to account for the conspiracy behind Wesley's trial. And so: I had not studied the records very long before I knew that I was sooner or later going to encounter the kind of taboo that might be violated when there is no anchor, when all seems permitted. I encountered it even sooner than expected . . . no need to drag out the circumstances. I happened to be dining at the yacht club when I heard someone mention a name that had spookily just risen into my own consciousness in connection with his testimony about finding the victim of Wesley's alleged rape wandering about in his stable. Major Ball. Major Ball was the name I heard.'

"This Major Ball died of jaundice. That was half a century ago — yet suddenly there are two people in this city of secrets who have his name ghosting upon their lips! Quite extraordinary . . . Well, sir, I turned to see who it was who had seemed to divine my thought. All I saw were two well-dressed elderly ladies sipping cocktails at a patio table. At once I recognized one of them as Captain St. George's widow. Curiosity getting the better of me, I rose and approached her, apologized for the intrusion, and explained that I couldn't help but hear the name of a man in whose affairs I was in a small professional way concerned.'

"Well, the ladies seemed to think this was hilarious. Since it would have been ill-bred of them to leave me with the impression that I was myself the object of their derision, Mrs. St. George said, 'Buck,' she said, 'Buck, I declare, we were just saying how we ought to change the name of my bloodhound, Lord Byron.' 'Oh?' I said. 'Yes,' she said. 'You see, my bitch, which is Lord Byron's offspring, has given her daddy a litter of pups. So I said I was fixing to change his name to Major Ball. Because the original Lord Byron only had a child by his half-sister. It's not exact enough, is it, Buck?'

"That afternoon I would have been found, Mr. Branch, a hundred miles from the city. There is a small eighteenth-century parish church among ruins of certain Low Country plantations. I went there, phoning the vicar, an old schoolfriend, beforehand. When I arrived, he already, being a gentleman of meticulous scholarly habits, awaited me with registers of births, deaths, and marriages, these marked at the appropriate places. He also awaited me with a number of semi-legendary stories to tell, and one story—circumstantially, of course—may throw light upon the question of your mother's progenitors."

Buck McKay rose, went to the office window and gazed beyond the huddled rooftops of Old Charleston toward the bright sky. The sun glistened on his brow and astonishing fleece of hair.

"I see," Manny said. "You mean that Major Ball and his daughter were not entirely white. There was a slave ancestor."

"Precisely," said McKay, turning from the window his ironic gaze. "They were white negroes. Like me."

WHIRROO OF A STARTLED BIRD, CRACKLING OF A TWIG: Manny sat up, shook his head, and experienced the sensation that he was being watched. A moment later he saw Pap not twenty feet away from the sawdust mound. Pap's toothless gawk and cocked head gave him a look of petrified surprise.

These two men seldom spoke to one another. That morning at breakfast had been exceptional. Then, tired from his trip, Manny had given in to the old feeling of grievance at having to share his home with an ex-convict. Now, more rested, he was in sympathetic mood. He rose without a word, and, spotting Pap's fishing equipment and lunchbox aglint by the side of the timbertrack, he picked them up and began to walk. He heard Pap shuffling along behind.

"You and me friends, ain't we, Manny?"

"All right with me," Manny said, striding on. "But don't bother to show me that damned leg of yours."

"All right," said Pap. "They put chains on my legs and brings me that tin pannikin full of shit to eat. I say to Mr. Burgess, prisonmans, what you doin' that fo, why can't you do right?"

"Just shut up about it, will you, Pap?"

Pap shut up. For about ten minutes he kept shut, just grinning toothlessly whenever Manny looked at him. Then Pap said, "Want to go fishing?"

"Maybe later."

"Want some watermelon? I know a place ain't far."

"You're an old crook, Pap. Stealing watermelon at your age. Besides, it's a racial stereotype."

"Mighty nice watermelons, Manny."

"Well," Manny said, "you rip one off when I'm not looking."

They emerged from the woods at River Road, crossed it, and started down the twisted rutted roadway that sloped to Bermuda Farm. Manny felt the old man tugging at his elbow. "You want to see something? You come on this way."

The next he knew, Pap had slipped into the dense underbrush by the side of the roadway. Leaving the fishing equipment, Manny followed as best he could. The air was hot, humid. Branches and briars slashed at his face and hands. Pap, like Br'er Rabbit, seemed to thrive on briar patches and was a hundred paces ahead, crouched at the edge of a small sunny field when Manny was about to quit in exasperation. Several times as he approached, he lost sight of Pap. Each time he identified him by his hat; the rest of him blended into shadows. Finally Manny, too, was crouching, wary of twigs and leaves where he would tread.

It was a field of goldenrod, part of a narrow timber cut, down the center of which marched telephone poles a-sag with a single line. Evident from the direction of the line was that it would eventually go to the farm.

Everything was very quiet but for startled birds sounding their cries.

Pap's face was beady with perspiration. He looked grave now, concentrating his gaze upon a spot in the field where what seemed to be a large pile of freshly-cut Christmas trees had been stacked.

"They ain't there now," Pap said finally, a trace of relief in his tone.

"Who?"

"Oh," said Pap, "couple men with sidearms."

"Is that right?"

"That's right."

"You wouldn't jive me?"

"They been coming in the early evening about sunset."

"How long?"

"About a week."

"What are they doing here?"

"Come on. I'll show you."

Part of the mystery was explained on their nearer approach to the stack of trees. Crudely camouflaged beneath them was a small pickup truck. Manny could hardly refrain from laughing. There was something incongruous, silly, about armed men hiding in a truck in this field. He checked his impulse to laugh until curiosity was satisfied.

It was soon satisfied. Setting to work at once, he and Pap stripped off the camouflage until a brand-new '65 Dodge was exposed to the sun. It was a government truck, according to the license plates. From a side window drooped a wire which, as Pap silently pointed out, led to and up a telephone pole; there, it was evidently spliced into the main line.

A redbird streaked across the golden-yellow field. The air was laden with odors of warm, burgeoning vegetation. The woods toward the river looked as if a milky polyethylene wrapper enclosed them and held in a humid swill.

When Manny found and picked up the first heavy stone, he had not yet decided what he must do. When he lifted it above his head, he turned and grinned at Pap. Pap's face lit, slowly, with childish glee.

"There are some machines I don't like," Manny said. He shattered the windscreen with the first stone. After that he was so busy demolishing the car that only in intervals did he hear Pap's high giddy laughter and whoops of delight.

IT WAS NOON.

At the barn a dog's excited barking was quieted as Pap lifted the latch; then a quivering, frolicsome Golden Retriever greeted them and darted toward the river, finally stopping to see what the delay was all about. "Pharaoh knows it's fishing time," Pap grinned. And went.

Stebbins was not yet home. Manny was not surprised. He had reckoned upon the possibility that the professor would be involved in graduation ceremonies. Vinegar Hill and South Atlantic University had always seemed worlds apart. Even the fact that some agency of the government had been keeping this professor under surveillance did not, upon reflection, seem surprising. College professors were the kind to get in trouble with the authorities. Manny decided to say nothing about the wiretap. Besides, the truck was a write-off now. There was no need to tell a man he didn't know and possibly couldn't trust about it.

From the look of the farmhouse, Stebbins was already in trouble, abandoned by wife and child with more trouble to come, letters identifying him as father to Tom Driver. The place was run-down, the paint blistering and shutters with broken slats festooned with morningglories. The grass grew a foot high, gone to seed. Fields were a tangle of tall weeds and broken cornstalks.

Manny waited in the shade of an oak tree. And waited and grew discouraged. Was it so important to deliver the letters? What had possessed him to think he could end his mother's involvement with the Pentecosts when, as he now knew, that involvement was in the blood?

He had almost decided to go fishing when rattles and jounces told him of an approaching car.

PART III

Chapter Thirteen **Manny**

He was still waiting inside the house an hour later, waiting for Stebbins to finish reading the letters. Everything had been remarkably cordial so far. He had been greeted as a friend and introduced as such to the pretty redhead, Fanny, who with a suitcase had also arrived in Stebbins's ruststreaked Chevrolet. He had been asked to help himself to sandwiches and milk from the refrigerator—he had done this—and he had even been asked to stick around for a swim in the river.

He was not quite sure what to make of Fanny. She had seemed open and friendly, and he liked her smile. She had something sweet about the sauntering gait of the mature young woman aware of her powers. She looked nearer thirty than twenty-five. From a certain softening in her eyes when she glanced at Stebbins, it was obvious she loved him. These were the first impressions. She had mentioned a headache and Stebbins had shown her to what he called the guest room, upstairs.

Seated on a sofa, Manny glanced from time to time toward the desk where Stebbins sat reading. The broad, slightly sloping shoulders and big hands scarcely moved. The head with its longish graying hair was also stationary. Only the facial muscles moved: the sunburned brow was furrowed, the eyes crinkled. Stebbins had the intense appearance of a man accustomed to slim odds.

Finally Stebbins straightened up from the desk, slid back his chair, and lit his pipe. "Thanks for the mail," he said with quiet mockery. "From what you have told me, Manny, the child born to Kitty Pentecost turns out to be Tom Driver. My wife guessed as much three years ago. Quite incredible."

Stebbins puffed on his pipe a while, then resumed. "Kitty had a love of life and a vision of its grandeur. She also had the bad habit of trying to force fantasy into reality by sheer will-power. She meant well, of course. Americans tend to prefer illusions to reality. Old Mother Pentecost spun the plot—if you'll forgive my alluding a little brusquely to your kith and kin?"

Manny had to smile.

"She," Stebbins went on. "She became, like Virgil's Sybil, a little mad, prodigiously struggling to shake from the brain the God that rides her. Then there's dear old Major Ball."

"Yes," said Manny. "It began with him."

"If it's of any help, Manny, one of Kitty's letters, written during a visit to Charleston in late summer of forty-two, mentions a deathbed confession alleged to have been made by Major Ball. Kitty was just appalled. She thought her relatives were being deliberately horrid to her. The letter, in substance, bears out what you've told me. I shall destroy the letter, have no fear," Stebbins said in anticipation of an angle Manny had not considered. "That should help bury the secret of your mother's origins. But, tell me, this brute, this Major Ball, was also, was he not, the one who assaulted a mentally defective girl and contrived to link the crime to our friend, Mr. Jackson?"

"I'll need to go back," Manny explained.

"Go back then."

When telling the story, Manny rose and stood by a window even as Buck McKay had done. And told the story as he had heard it—as McKay had heard it, too, from the vicar of a parish church in the Low Country, and as the vicar himself had heard it told in Gullah dialect by an old black crone who had been a slave, and perhaps as she had heard it, too: sepulchral voices sounding the unrequited history of their woe. And when he had finished the story, he felt as he had in Buck McKay's office while the *shoo shoo shoo* of the propeller fan riddled every silence, that the past was immense, dark, and burdensome, that iniquity was its burden.

"Actually," Manny concluded, shaking his head for having neglected to get to the heart of the matter: not the burden of history but the future convergence of man. When he explained McKay's concept of "convergence," Stebbins seemed to listen with a special intensity, though he remained silent.

"Let me see if I have it," Stebbins finally declared. "A so-called 'white negro' arrives from the West Indies a century and a half ago. He, as they say, 'passes'. He marries into the planter class and begets a child who grows up, begets children, who in turn beget children, one of whom is Major Ball, cavalry officer in the Confederate Army who, years after the Civil War, goes West, is present at an Indian massacre, and saves, or kidnaps, a child who has a black mother and an Indian father. Possibly Cheyenne, don't know. He names the child Wesley Jackson. In due course, Major Ball marries a Charleston lady of singular pedigree, a daughter, Katherine, is born, the lady dies. At some time or other an incestuous relationship begins between Major Ball and daughter. The girl, already half-crazed, grows to womanhood. Finally breaking away to become a student in Chicago, she realizes to her horror that she is pregnant. She sends for Jackson, her friend, privy to her terror and grief, and he takes the child to rear as his own. Five years pass. Major Ball commits rape. This time, with the assistance of his daughter whom he has presumably intimidated, he sees a chance to get rid of the person who knows the family secret, Jackson. But tell me," Stebbins said quietly as he tapped his pipe against the fireplace, "do you really believe Buck McKay's version of Mr. Jackson's motives? Was he really a saint, martyring himself, as you put it, 'in silence, devotion, and control'?"

"Not entirely," Manny agreed. "I think at first he was just ignorant of what he had let himself in for. Later, when he was sentenced, he seems to have remembered that he was entitled to live, too. So he escaped. But he was captured and, after that, remained silent. He was no longer devoted except to the child he loved as his own."

"Certainly no longer devoted to Katherine Ball. Soon after his imprisonment," said the other, "he was to learn of her marriage to Pentecost. She was full of remorse, but rather than try to free this innocent man she went seeking martyrdom for herself. With one rule for other people and another for herself, she gladly became a mother but, as it now appears, she didn't want Kitty to bear children. What does Kitty do but have a bastard! So Mother Pentecost, who has experience in that line, tries to tidy that business up, too. Always her race-fear compelling."

There was a silence. Stebbins filled the bowl of his pipe, struck a match against the fireplace, and held the flame over the bowl. "Manny, you mentioned a necklace with an ornamental golden fish." He blew out the match, puffed on the pipe. "You said, as I remember, that this necklace was discovered in Major Ball's stables, and that the prosecution exhibited it as evidence that Jackson was the girl's assailant. Jackson testified that he had given it to Kate Ball five years earlier, in Chicago, and *that* brought her to the witness stand where she denied the Chicago story and disclaimed any knowledge of the necklace. Who put the necklace in the stables?"

Manny puzzled over this. Finally he said, "I don't suppose Major Ball even knew she owned a necklace that Jackson had given her. That means that she put the necklace on the scene. That means that *she* was not only active in the cover-up from the start but also instrumental in linking my grandfather—excuse me, Jackson—to the crime. That's interesting. I hadn't thought of that clearly before. Of course, I can't get Pap to remember the necklace. It's as if it never existed."

"It exists," Stebbins said. "I have it. It's upstairs among things my wife left me when she . . . split for the main chance. I'll give it to you if you think it would be useful. To stir up Mr. Jackson's memories or, better still, to prompt Mrs. Pentecost to make a confession statement."

"Then it's useful," Manny said. "I'm pessimistic, though, about getting people to change. Evils persist."

"*Some* evils persist, Manny. There is progress. As McKay was saying to you, we are part of something evolving, something almost inconceivable to us because human history itself only spans a minute. Keep your faith in life. Be optimistic. The poet Melville, looking at the tragedy of his time, concluded that Nature, indifferent, would go on: 'Leaves must be green in spring.' It's a lift-off from the muck-heap. The neocortex has no room to expand, but consciousness is expanding, and that fact promises the 'convergence tree' he spoke of."

Stebbins spoke from his heart but was obviously troubled. His pipe had gone out; he sat, twisting it in his hands, contemplating something that passed behind his eyes. To Manny now he seemed a generous man. Reticent about himself, he had cooperated in an imaginative recreation of other lives. And yet—Stebbins, too, was involved.

"May I ask you something, Professor Stebbins?"

The other shook himself, half smiled. "Your turn," he said.

"Is Tom Driver your son?"

"He sure as hell isn't!" Stebbins burst into laughter. "I was a virgin until I was twenty-five. Kitty *imagined* me as having the honor. That's in the letters, all that effort of hers to tell a story, to believe in a delusion, to build a dream over the world, to create an artificial reality that would be a nice retreat—and that she could manipulate. Mind you, the imagination is our most precious power. But she used her power to distort the truth. The result, I find, is that I have picked up a reputation as a lecher and a libertine, a feckless American Don Juan."

"So it seems," Manny said. "Mama thought maybe this other soldier named Bud was responsible for the baby, but she went along with this jive about you. Partly because Dr. Hasbrouck had been told it was you."

"That's right, Manny. That explains a lot. Kitty must have told her husband an outright lie. In fact, she resembled her mother more and more. They were careless people, feckless fixers, lonely isolatos, to use Melville's word. But Dr. Hasbrouck cares, *he* cares. I understand why, now, he seduced my wife into running off with him."

"The story I heard was, you were his wife's lover."

"When we were young," Stebbins said with an intense expression in his eyes. "People change, Manny. People grow. That is, they grow into their real identities. If they want to know themselves. If they do not tell lies to themselves. I hope I'm a changed person. I hope I've grown. I hope I have an in-the-same-boat spirit. Leaves must be green in spring."

IN TIME, IN THE AFTERNOON, Manny would go with Stebbins and Fanny to the river, first to the bluffs, above, where a cool sound as of faraway percussions rose and where westward through a long green sea patchy with islands of farmland could be seen, snaking a-glitter like a suddenly flung necklace, the Tuscarora River, then down the path where slender saplings trembled, their leaves in slants of light.

It had rained in the night. The river was swollen, the current swift. He undressed behind bushes and put on the borrowed swimming trunks. Then, ahead of the others, he dove in. A few strong strokes and he stood in the middle of the stream where it was almost over his head. His toes dug in cold ooze; knee-high was warm current. Submerging, he rolled on his back and looked up. Wavering golden lights diffused themselves through the tug of murk. Surfacing, he breathed deeply. The air, the water, the green earth were good. He felt this as completely as at any time in his life. And there was light—light everywhere!

Chapter Fourteen **Max**

For a year or so after Kitty's death, Max had continued to feel as if he were living under a stone. The old apathy, the old sense of personal insignificance, persisted. He resented this condition. In the prime of life, he was quite able to recognize and accept certain limitations of his vital powers. That he was, without really knowing why, good at his job, that he turned out good students—which was his proper function—he could not, and therefore did not, deny. Although he would probably achieve little else for the rest of his life, he had at least achieved something. He knew in all justice it had been worth the undertaking, and thus he was spared boredom. Nevertheless, he was not happy. Something in his own mind was blocking his way to fulfillment and self-possession. Unless he could bring it into the light and identify it, he would not grow. And yet, disastrous as might be a prolonged failure to grow, he was not unaware of spiritual dangers that might lie in wait for him both during and after a journey to recovery. Deep down, he suspected, he had untapped reserves of energy and power; to tap and assert them could possibly, it seemed to him, subvert and destroy much of the materialistic, excessively rationalistic value-system in which he had been educated and by which, with a curious lack of success, he had tried to conduct his life. If there had not been thrust upon him events that fairly screamed out that there was a discrepancy between the idealism by which he thought he lived and the reality by which he was actually living, he would very likely have done nothing to restore himself to himself: he had grown so used to living under a stone that he was more than half persuaded that this was what life was all about, slow suffocation in solitude and terror.

But, first, his father died. It was Christmastime, sixty-three. Ginny complained of feeling too tired to make the trip to East Tennessee; she would enjoy a week's rest with the men gone. Max and Chris went without her—without her belittling and nagging. They were, man and ten-year-old boy, in a festive mood. A son who had lost a beloved father, Max began in those days, in his turn, the life of significant fatherhood. As they drove westward, especially when they climbed the snow-laden peaks of the Great Smoky Mountains as these opened to their mutual wonderment, Max felt as if he were giving from the essence of himself. In no time at all, Chris, too, was looking with enchanted eyes upon America. Max believed Chris would never forget. Whatever the teeming cities his son was destined to know, there would always be, now ineradicable, some image of magnificence, some measure intangible of ageless aspirations, some future for in-the-same-boat visions. For Max there flowered a fierce pride in his people of the mountains and of the open sky, the people of frontiers. Now his son shared the pride and the love. The flow of sympathy between man and boy was natural and unconstrained. He who in a few years would be a possible grandfather began to contemplate the future without fear and the past without guilt or regret.

It was only a beginning. Nevertheless from that conscious experiencing of himself Max caught a glimpse of meanings that might yet be more fully revealed. The funeral in Clayton, Tennessee, also woke him up: he had not known that Dr. Stebbins had been loved by so many people, and yet he had been, and he, Max, native son, was remembered and loved by many whose names he had forgotten. It was a humbling experience and also a gratifying one: he had roots.

During that same time in Tenneessee, Max also began to focus thoughts on his marriage. He attributed Ginny's restlessness, aggression, cruelty to a single cause, himself, mostly an undeserved perception but he could grant it. The marriage was crippling them both. He would continue the discussion with her about his leaving the university in Poe's Hill and finding a new job in a city, probably in or near New York, where Ginny would feel at home. He would listen to her. He would do whatever she wanted—if he could.

Inspired by this resolve, he set out for Poe's Hill a day earlier than had been expected of him. It was past midnight when he neared the farm. Chris lay cocooned in sleep. The night was clear and frosty, the moon bright. As he turned into the driveway, he had an open view of the farmhouse and of the car parked beneath the liveoak. In that moment he felt himself go cold all over. He switched off his lights and engine, quietly opened the car door and slipped out. Finding the gravel road frozen hard, he was able to tread upon it lightly and avoid stirring Pharaoh, in the barn, to the usual paroxysm of barking. When he was halfway to the house, he recognized the car as Dr. Hasbrouck's Jaguar.

He returned to the car zombie-cold, started the engine, reversed into River Road, and in low gear communicated fury to the accelerator.

That night he retraced fifty miles of the route he had just taken. In the morning, when Chris woke in a motel room, Max told him that he had pulled off the road too tired to complete the trip to the farm. Chris could tell the same story to his mother and be convincing because Max looked haggard. He did not sleep that night. He lay awake, tried to think calmly. He must not, he reasoned, become that stupid animal, a jealous husband. He must not judge hastily or without shouldering some of the blame.

Luckily, Hasbrouck was gone next day. Ginny, though surprised by their early return, seemed particularly effusive and eager to please.

"Did you rest up?" Max asked.

She gave him a loving look and sighed, "Gloriously, thank you. Just sleeping late, not a care in the world. I haven't seen a blessed soul since you left."

It was at this time that Max fully understood the expression, *to lie in one's teeth.*

That evening as they sat by the fireplace Ginny casually mentioned a Christmas card. An old school chum would just *adore* a chance to see her again in a *fabulous* Park Avenue apartment the day after Christmas. "Take a week," Max said, undeceived. "Chris and I will manage. The trip will do you good. What school was it where you met your friend?"

"A convent," Ginny said. With a blank expression.

Ginny's trip to New York was but the first in a series of trips that extended through the spring and summer of sixty-four and culminated in her walking out, with Chris, that fall. To check the little conspiracy out, Max would call or drop by Hasbrouck's office in the new administration's wing of Henry Memorial Building. Dr. Hasbrouck was invariably out of town when Ginny was. Usually Max let the whole thing go. Since Ginny had taken the initiative, there really wasn't much he could do except bide his time and to give her all the rope she needed. He was not surprised by her decision to leave him. He was a little amused to think of how she had manipulated Hasbrouck into getting her connected with the theatrical crowd, but it saddened him to think that Hasbrouck would dump her as soon as he was through with her.

At a price, however. For he had left himself without express cause for preventing Ginny from taking Chris away from him. In the fall semester his job became the most important thing in his life. He concentrated his energies upon it. He was determined to do the best work he had ever done, to explore ideas as never before, to participate in college life as never before.

Strangely, there was new hope in his heart. He had the will to live. He was going to come through. He would find his lost joy.

Max suddenly chuckled to himself. What was all this nonsense about new hope and joy? Of course he had come through! Why did he who accepted others not accept himself? He was a lucky man, a successful one, too. His book on the origins of the modern novel had, after all and only six months ago, been published by a university press in California. He hadn't truly anticipated that stroke of luck. Not only that, he had received from out of the blue, unsolicited and without any "pull" of which he was aware, a telephoned offer, followed by a contract, to join, as a tenured professor, the faculty of a new university in Santa Cruz, California. The Dean there had, almost apologetically, almost deferentially, explained that it would be another year before classes could start, the so-called "university" presently consisting of an administration building in a cow pasture, but a campus—nay, campuses—must be imagined as rising overnight. Max had not imagined this stroke of luck. Within three to four years there would be at least 10,000 students in brick and stucco dormitories nestled among the oaks and redwoods, with views of the ocean and free bus rides to the libraries at Berkeley and access to Monterrey where Robert Lewis Stevenson had once had a romantic fling. All that. Although the Dean had neglected to mention earthquakes, Professor Max Stebbins, unknown to the family or anyone at South Atlantic, would soon be on his way to Paradise, temblors and all.

. . .

LATE ONE AFTERNOON DURING EASTER RECESS, Max came home from the library in a richly reflective frame of mind. At sunset he was rocking peacefully in a chair on the screened porch. There was a scent of wild honeysuckle in the air. Pharaoh stretched contentedly at his feet. Crickets began their chromatic roar. Shadows swiftly lengthened from the wilderness. Then it was night. Still he rocked. He began to lose consciousness of time. Dry thunder rumbled, heat lightning flashed.

For a moment of hallucination he was hearing the drumming of shells, feeling the shudder of big airplanes . . . He thought of Sculley, his co-pilot, Sculley in snapshots in whimsical poses, mountaineer pivoting on piton, skier with arm about the waist of a giggling sunburned girl, philosopher smoking his pipe sitting in front of his stone cabin in the High Colorado Rockies . . . Sculley, killed in action, dead these twenty years . . .

Max wept, closed eyes. He saw Kitty as clearly as if she were alive in whirls of radiance. He was peering into some innermost self . . .

MAX DROVE SCULLEY'S CONVERTIBLE COUPE to the Pentecost house. He and Kitty had a date to go to a dinner dance at the officer's club. She was on the porch, waiting, dressed in long-length gown that exposed arms and shoulders and made her look older than a girl not yet seventeen.

When they had been driving for awhile, Kitty said, "Let's not go to the dance. Will you be angry with me?" He drove over to the curb, idled the motor. "I'm not exactly Fred Astaire. You're too pretty to keep all to myself."

She had lowered her gaze. She was fighting tears. He drew her into his arms and breathed her hair. "I'll be on orders before the end of the summer," he said, stroking her hair. "You and I will change. I don't want you to get hurt."

She tossed back her hair. "I love you," she said. She made it sound true, unlike the girls he had known in college.

"None of that, young lady."

"I don't want to think about the war," she said. "Promise you won't think about the war."

"No war it is."

"Max?"

"Yes?"

"I wanted to go to the dance with you more than anything."

"That's O.K."

"I'm really not a good girl for you."

"You're the *only* girl for me."

"You don't know me, Max."

"Is your mother worrying you again?"

"Why do you ask that?"

"Because that's the trouble, isn't it?"

Kitty smiled sadly and met his gaze. She brushed her cheek against his shoulder. "Let's drive in the country."

"Drive in the country?"

"I know just the place," she said. Some while later, as he was absorbed in his dilemma over making love to her, she asked, "Will you promise to always forgive me?"

Max made some asinine remark to the effect that *he*, for his part, was not going to ask *her* forgiveness.

"Look who's superior today."

"Today, the lady says." Max changed the subject. "Is there someone at the dance?"

"Am I that obvious?"

It was only a shot in the dark. "Kitty, I want you too much not to want something for your sake."

"You were right about the dance," she said presently. "Shall I tell you about him?"

"No."

"Good."

"Usual pains?"

"I had them coming to me."

"I'll try not to hurt you," he said.

"You'll hurt me most of all," she said.

"Will you please explain that?"

She laughed. "Ha ha. I know more than you—and you're twenty-two! I'm just a little shrimp . . . Drive on, boy! We're going to a river and we'll swim and watch the sunset! Did you know I'm showing you the place where you are to live one day when you come back? You must have a place to come back to—like your friend Sculley with his cabin in the Rockies. Hurry, hurry!"

Bermuda Farm, that day, was derelict. The fields were receding into a wilderness of scrub pine and waist-high weeds. Several large trees had blown down in the hurricane of thirty-eight and had narrowly missed the house. The house, itself, with its blistered paint and boarded-up doors and windows, had evidently not been inhabited for years. "Well," said Kitty, reading the expression on Max's face, "you have to use your imagination."

"I'll take it," he said. "What happens next?"

Print of her thigh against her dress, curve of her waist, the rounded buttocks, the small firm breasts: he desired her and yet at the same time he felt a pity for her, not love for her. She seemed to know more about him than he knew about himself. She was trying to tie him down. She was complicating his plans by stirring up emotions that had nothing to do with the waging of a war. He could make love to her and promise everything—or nothing—according to a general custom, but he would feel sorry afterwards. He always seemed to feel sorry for other people if he let them get too close.

"That's up to you," Kitty said, answering his question. "Do you want to go back or see the river?"

"You'll tear your dress."

"Good," she said. "I hate it."

They found a narrow beaten path to the bluffs above the river. No embarrassing explanations would be needed when he met Mrs. Pentecost. It would be a good idea, he was thinking, if he could prevent Kitty from sitting or lying down.

So he kissed her, standing up.

She searched his eyes. She seemed to see something in them that distressed her. "Hold me close," she said. She pressed herself against him. "You're very strange," she murmured."Do you know what I think it is? You've lived alone too much. You must have lived alone for about a hundred years. A lot of people are like that. I'll bet there are millions like that. But you mustn't be like that! Fight for what you want."

What she said was true and as expressive of her own needs as of his own. But then he was usually quick to acquiesce in judgments of his human lack. It was as if there were in him, removed from his perception but obvious to that of others, some principle of rejection that must condemn him to be the prisoner of himself, intact, unsupported, and alone. At the same time, in complete contradiction of that sense of himself, he believed that he had the power to love. He was beginning to find this out.

"I'm giving you a rotten time," Max said finally. "You realize how aloof I am. I think I'm in love with you. I don't want to pretend I know what that means. We're too young to know what anything means . . . I'm going back to the car. Will you hold my hand?"

This speech was embarrassing. Max could be sensitive to his own tone. He preferred not to talk about sentiments. He had heard some smooth operators in college, heard the sad songs and the lies of the men and women who were trying to prove something with their bodies. He had picked up a vicarious education in heartbreak. He had shied away from involvements with girls if he discovered, as he usually did, that he was being deceived or used. Several times he had, he believed, fallen in love only to find, just as he was about to reveal his feelings, that the girl was already engaged to someone else or was merely encouraging him until someone more exciting came along. He always felt sorry for such girls afterwards.

They were nearing the house when Kitty drew breath sharply. She had almost stepped on a diamondback rattlesnake drowsily slithering across the path. It did not coil, and it quickly disappeared.

Kitty looked pale and unstrung. In the car she sat quite still. Her eyes flashed at him. "Why didn't you kill it?" Her tone was so harsh and petulant she succeeded in making him feel guilty. The only rattler he had ever killed in the mountains had been one he intended to eat.

DURING THE FIRST WEEK OF THE BATTLE OF NORMANDY, Max and Sculley flew their Dakota almost round-the-clock, no sooner touching down at their base in East Anglia than seemingly it was time to take off again into the gray cotton-wool of English skies. Between missions, sleep was an instant blackout and dreamless abyss out of which one scrambled back to a wooden state of existence where life was something lived by other people somewhere else.

It was at this time that Max's image of Kitty first took on an obsessional quality. With one part of his mind he performed routine tasks; with another, he lived in the grip of an ideal love.

One bright June day, Max's squadron was placed on twenty-four-hour R&R. "Know what I'd like to do?" Sculley said as they were about to board a bus for London together with a group of airmen who were already half drunk. "Get away from uniforms, go some place quiet and civilized where people read books. Do you remember what a book looks like?"

Max shook his head with a grin. "Sculley, I don't even remember what a girl looks like. Where is your sense of priorities?"

Sculley looked serious. He was the broad-shouldered, sunny-faced Western type—cultivated, a thinker. His robust, honest nature somehow harmonized with a view of life that was decidedly skeptical. "Captain," Sculley said with his customary drollery, "we barbarians of the air forget that human beings still live down here on this god-forsaken planet. I want a peep at the golden age of humanism before the new Dark Ages arrive."

They decided to requisition a jeep and drive to Oxford. Down its streets they were rambling by noon. They toured colleges and libraries, idled in bookshops, went punting on the Thames in the languid afternoon, slap and murmur of easy waters making war assume its correct significance as universal madness. Toward sunset they had walked out of the city to the hilly plains to the southwest. From there they viewed beyond the quicksilver gleam of the river spires and towers that glowed in a melting golden light.

"Perhaps you're right,"Max declared after a long look at this scene. "It's golden, all right. It will serve as a symbol of humanist civilization. Do we want it? I recollect that Doctor Faustus gained knowledge and power—and lost his humanity."

"That's crucial," Sculley agreed. "but there have been other Fausts since Marlowe made his. Goethe's, for instance. Goethe's Faust beats the Devil by devoting himself to human well-being instead of surrendering to egomania. Modern man, insofar as he is a kind of Faust, may yet prevail against dehumanization. I admit, somewhere over the Channel right now is a 'darkling plain where ignorant armies clash by night.'"

Max thought then of that line from Matthew Arnold's *Dover Beach* and of a girl in that poem who was asked to be true. And said, "It's almost two years since she promised to write me."

"Forget her," Sculley said with an elaborate shrug. "She was just a kid playing the field. She's probably married by now and having babies and playing aggressive tennis."

"Do you think I know when I'm licked, Sculley?"

Sculley made a long face. "Do I think," he repeated with mock solemnity, "*you* know when you're licked? A fine question. Suppose I say 'yes': I imply that you are responsible but not tenacious, and you conclude that I am an ass. But if I say 'no', I imply that you are a hopeless romantic in love with love, not with a real, live, menstruating female. You likewise conclude that I am an ass. Therefore, all I have to say is that your ardor in this affair touches me deeply."

"Thanks."

"Don't mench." Sculley cocked his blonde head at him. "Item. You see enough of the girl to believe that she's the one the God of Chance picked out for you when He screwed up the world. But you don't clinch matters. Instead, you leave Poe's Hill under the sublime delusion that she is going to write to you . . . Mind you, the dears like to write letters, and they write them to a regiment of trousered imbeciles from the time they reach puberty or learn how to spell, whichever comes first . . . Item. You and the girl are alone in the woods, slobbering over one another."

"To put it crudely," said Max.

"To put it crudely," Sculley grinned. "It took you guys a couple of months to get your clothes off, and that's at the beach where somebody is watching you, and besides, fornication in sand is extremely painful to a wet penis. Still, I'll give you marks for kindness and tell you what I think: the girl was of two minds. She said she loved you—God knows why—and therefore, since she didn't write, you believe she didn't mean it. *That* hurts your pride. On the other hand, if we work from the hypothesis that she meant what she said—for I must admit the savages can be generous—we conclude that she has given you up *because* she loved you."

Max remembered Kitty's saying she was not good for him. When he told Sculley this, the other rolled over on his back and gazed at the sky. "I'm due for home leave soon, Max. Why don't I stop off in Poe's Hill and case the Pentecost scene?"

"Sculley, you're a genius. You'll marry her, yourself."

"That's the idea. And do something for me, will you, chum?"

"Sure," Max said.

"If I don't make it back—et cetera—go see my folks in Denver, get the key to my cabin, go there, altitude 9,000, say hello to my mountains."

Three days later Sculley was killed during a paradrop over Belgium at dusk. Shells were crumping; there were red bursts of anti-aircraft fire. Suddenly the fuselage rattled, the cockpit screen spiderwebbed. While the props continued their steady drone, Sculley's severed poll rolled under Max's feet. Blood jetted from the strapped torso.

Next day, as Max was sorting Sculley's personal effects to be sent to Denver, he came across a dogeared Greek anthology and in it some scribbled notes headed, "Four Recognitions of Humanism." Max read the notes and copied them. They focused certain thoughts of his own. They helped in a bad time.

THE SCREENED PORCH WAS DARK. Thunder growled in the vicinity of the farm. Trees were swaying violently. Even as Max rose and went indoors rain poured down and lightning glared at the windows like oxyacetylene torches.

Tucked away in his desk, his copy of Sculley's notes was finally found. He placed it open to the lamplight and read aloud to himself: " 'Four Recognitions of Humanism—'

" 'First, it recognizes the greatness of man—man the maker and controller who cultivates, builds, explores, sings, governs—

who has imagination and reason. Note that man also has emotion, which resists and rejects what reason makes and considers just. Through emotion we glimpse truths of the heart—we know that we have come as strangers and that our going is also strange—we know that indeed we make and control nothing—that we have no control over the forces of life and death such as the atmosphere of the earth or the explosion of stars.'

" 'Therefore a second recognition of humanism is that man is great in relation to the nothingness that surrounds and limits him. The most we can say for today's creation is that it was not here yesterday. Perhaps it is wise to think it will not be here tomorrow. It is here today, this magnificent creation. Let that suffice. Men who make tin gods of themselves—whose power is measured by pyramids of skulls—can neither control themselves nor order the lives of others. The same is true of nature: man's conquest of nature is a delusion of his pride. Nature, the all-creating, will continue.'

" 'A third recognition. The Greeks ascribed human limits to the gods and defined a condition of full humanity in a pious sort of way: man, they said, should know his place and keep it. Greek gods meant business. If you devalued persons, you wounded your own humanity. If you devalued nature, you brought the house down on your head—and the house could be a whole society. The Greeks taught us to recognize human wholeness. However, their limitation was, they really pictured existence as hopeless—until you got on the other side of it, up with the gods. Loving someone could be a disaster.'

" 'Where the Greeks praised, but feared, emotional ties, the Christians generalized kindness to a human condition and, contrary to popular belief, freed us from dependence upon an afterlife. Out of twenty Christian centuries has come to wide acceptance in the world, whether Christian or not, a third recognition of humanism: We are to know fully through brotherhood. We are, here on earth, that which we know. We can redeem life instead of lying helplessly enslaved to dark gods while vultures dine on our livers.'

" 'That proposition leads to a fourth recognition of humanism. We have the creative will and imagination to transform our world, within limits. We are responsible now—no support is forthcoming from gods—they have gone home. A man has the courage to resist powers, machines, or ideas that falsify and debase human dignity. A man has the sympathy and common sense and decency to realize on earth, not the false paradise of the collective state, but a justly individualized commonwealth based upon the mutuality of relationships in the human scale. We do not deny evil. Even those high laws of experience upon which aspirations must be founded can be smothered by man-made authorities—a rubbish heap of lies and idolatry. And we are easily trained to murder. But there is something in us allied with humanity against us. Tyranny will not prevail. The bow is drawn. The arrow of justice and freedom is aflame. It is being released, it is soaring . . .' "

Max put out the light and went upstairs to bed. Gusts of rain were soaking the floor but he kept the window open. In bed he did not close his eyes . . .

PARIS . . .

There were few cars in Paris after the war. He could see the M.P. patrol jeeps before they saw him. He wanted solitude. Sometimes he would linger for hours on the Pont Neuf staring into the chill chiaroscuro of barge-tormented, reflected light. He drank bad brandy at a small café owned by an Algerian black-marketeer with a pitted inflamed face.

He lived, himself, in internal exile. He had lost the wartime sense of purpose and direction. There was nothing in particular that he wanted. He liked to look at pretty girls but the fun was mostly in the looking. He didn't want consequences, responsibilities. He was sick to death of them. It seemed to him that he had become the victim of his own desire to do the right thing. His parents and teachers had taught him to do the right thing, and he had done the right thing; he hadn't made love because he hadn't married and when there was a war, he went. It seemed to him that he had done the right thing so long that his life was futile and barren. It seemed to him that the right thing, once in awhile, might be to do what *he* wanted.

One evening in October he drifted into a Montmartre café where a celebration was in progress. Laughter, handclapping, singing, an accordion playing, clouds of Turkish tobacco: and there was , standing on a table, wriggling her hips, cupping her breasts and singing, a blowsy young woman in a tight-fitting black dress.

Allons dans le bois,
ma mignonette,
Allons dans le bois,
du roi . . .

She sang and, suddenly, when the song was over, shouted, "Allo, Yank." She had lost some teeth.

She oogled Max, indicating his height to the crowd. "*C'est un grand enfant, eh?*" Max recognized a friendly insult in this and grinned back. "*Merci, petit maman.*" And heard the hoots and cheers as she rolled her eyes, fell upon his neck and smeared his lips with kisses.

"*Allons*, Yank. Okay?"

"Okay."

She led him outside to a park decorated with Chinese lanterns. She seemed to appraise him before she said, "You sleep with me tonight. Okay?"

"Okay. But money in hotel."

"*Ça ne fait rien, monsieur.* You like me?"

Certainly. She was content, then?

Naturally. Why not?

Perhaps she would like an American cigarette?

With pleasure.

Take two packs.

No, no.

They would sell dear on the *marche-noir.*

Monsieur the captain was very kind.

Not at all. It was a present for singing when he was *triste.*

Then she hoped he was not *triste* now. She herself had a brown baby to keep her happy. The Liberation.

She was not afraid?

Of course. But there was really no need to be afraid. She was afraid when she was pregnant that she would be too small, but an old man told her that she would be big enough in time and the old man had spoken the truth.

Max called her Mignonette. Since she lived near the café, it did not take long to climb the five flights of stairs to her room. They could hear the baby crying. Mignonette's pace quickened and she made a frantic gesture with her hands. "*Il a faim, pauvre petit.* O la."

In that moment he became fond of her.

It was a small room with a stove, dresser, crib and brass-knobbed bed. A clothesline strung with diapers gave off a faintly ammoniac odor. Max lay on the bed and watched while Mignonette suckled her baby which had an old brown man's wizened face.

It was like this, what he wanted now: someone brave and good who needed support.

Would he like a cup of coffee? Unfortunately it was chicory.

He recalled words from her song and said he would prefer nurse's milk.

La. Men were all alike.

Chicory would be good.

Bon. Was he married to a girl with long American legs?

No. In fact he might as well confess he was a virgin.

Mon Dieu. And what a beautiful man.

That was nice. Just for that he would ask permission to look after her and the baby.

Monsieur the captain was *tout grand serieux.* It was necessary to be always gay. This was proved by the old songs.

Mignonette smiled sadly at him with her bad teeth. She lowered the baby into the crib and slipped her dress over her head. In removing her undergarments, she turned away from him. He undressed quickly.

Perhaps they should drink the artificial coffee in the morning? Mingonette did not wait for reply but drew down his head. He kissed her unlucky mouth.

They lived together for two weeks before his orders came to take passage home on a troopship from Cherbourg. Whenever Max tried to persuade Mignonette to let him support her in some way, she became angry with him. He was to go away, not look back. She was content. One day he took the train to Cherbourg. Bells tolled in diapason from villages passed by. Late rusted wheat, caressed by the wind, were sleepy rhythms of a woman's body. Poppies were everywhere. There were gutted buildings, calcined walls with gaping holes where tanks had blundered through. Swollen-bellied children played in the rubble of fountains. The world was coming alive again. Peasant women wearing sabots and kerchiefs waved to the passing train. Hovering above the corn, thrusting against the wind were little stoic birds—skylarks.

Chapter Fifteen **Max**

Lying in bed listening to the rain dripping and splattering at the open window, Max was at last able to admit to full consciousness certain images and events of his buried life. He could monitor intuitions about himself and estimate, without morbid self-chastisement, their survival value.

His recollections of himself as a young man had already assumed a perceptible pattern. He was seeing that young man who had been himself from the vantage point of what he had become in middle age. He had survived by holding fast to a faith in his eventual emergence to a plane of increased awareness, the very consciousness with which he now perceived reality. If people lacked openness or leaned on him emotionally, he backed away. He, himself, had become more open, more conciliatory, more vulnerable as he grew older. Once, he had worked off on himself emotions he really did not have or that did not engage him at a deep level. He had been fond of exaggerating the goodness in people, and he wanted others to hold him in some exaggerated regard as a good, righteous, innocent man who would inflict no pain. It was for this reason, perhaps, that he had become so critical of his human failings. His *real* experience as a participant in a total war machine had been horror and revulsion. Perhaps he need not have sickened himself with worry about a lost humanity. Consciousness having become enlarged for him, he had found his way back to humanity.

Once more Max's eyes opened on an inner world . . .

Snowpatches on Tennessee hills. Melissa, his sister, was driving him to Chattanooga for a train to New York.

He scarcely knew his sister. They had not seen each other for eight years, since the time he had left home for college. She had married and settled down in Clayton. Her husband was a traveling salesman, easy-going, a little boorish. There was an emptiness about Melissa's life, but she would not discuss it because she was like her brother, proud.

She set her chin at a defiant angle."You haven't stayed a week. You've upset Mother and Daddy. They were going to bring the whole town out to welcome home the hero. Why do you have to go to New York all of a sudden?"

Max was feeling uncomfortable in his outgrown tweed jacket and gray flannels. " I really have no idea."

"Mother wanted you to speak to Daddy about going to medical school. They say doctors will make over fifty thousand a year."

"Good luck to them."

"Do you have a girl in New York?" Melissa asked after a pause.

"No."

"What happened to the girl in Poe's Hill you once wrote us about? Kitty—?"

"Pentecost. Probably married now."

"Don't you know?"

"Who cares?"

"You do." Melissa half smiled. He was glad she said that. But he spoke as if he were sore at her. "She never answered my letters.

To *hell* with it!"

"Don't shout at me."

"Jesus," he said. His mind registered a shock. He had idealized Kitty for so long that he no longer thought of her as a living person. Suddenly to think of her as such was to be zapped like an intruder in a rose garden who touches a live wire . . .

In New York he found employment as a junior executive in an organization that consisted of fifteen-thousand employees and one hundred and twenty-five vice-presidents. It was pleasant, undemanding work and paid well. He had regular casual sex with one of the secretaries who had been married young and divorced and didn't want complications. He rented a charming Greenwich Village apartment and gave racy parties in it. He became a connoisseur of the city, knew the theaters and restaurants, the hideaway bars and chopsuey joints. He carried about in his head, like a demented laboratory rat, a plan for scuttling through mazes of streets and subways. He bought a new Chevrolet, drove weekends to New England to ski or attend football games. That this way of life made him miserable did not, for several years, seem to matter.

Then one summer day he remembered his promise to Sculley to go to the High Colorado Rockies and "say hello" to the mountains. Suddenly city life fell flat. It was as remote to his real spiritual needs as a suit of armor. Simultaneously, the vastness of the American continent opened to his imagination like a pungent and secret bud. He decided to quit his job and go West.

When he had telephoned the Sculley family in Denver, he was struck by their warmth, their friendliness. Attracted more than ever to the West, he settled his affairs in a week and, on the evening of the day of departure, returned to his apartment for final packing.

Propped against his apartment door were a package and a letter from Kitty. After reading the letter, he ran to his car and sped in it uptown toward Pennsylvania Station.

"Dear Max," he had read. "Your sister has written me a sweet letter telling me where you are and what you're doing. The years are a single night, as they were to Rip Van Winkle. Although we have probably changed horribly, we could still be friends. Since a New York man would scarcely waste time in Poe's Hill, and since you may be too busy to write, I figured I could take the overnight train from Raleigh to Penn Station and drop by your place. I did. I told Mother I was going on a theater binge. Mr. Mason drove me to the station last night and I got in this morning early. I walked to Greenwich Village figuring I might invite you to share my breakfast. Mother packed more sardine and cucumber sandwiches than I can eat. Darnit, you were out. I inquired of this lady, I guess the superintendent's wife, what time you are expected home. She looked me up and down, you know. Finally she said you were moving to Denver and had probably already left.'

"Well, just in case you receive this, I want to wish you lots of luck. I've been traipsing around today wondering what present I could buy for you with the money Mother gave me to go on the theater binge with. I brought you an earthenware plate. I hope it's all right. Well, here I am back at your place and, sure enough, you're gone. The superintendent's wife said to leave things by the door; if you don't collect them, she'll give them to the mailman to be forwarded. It's six o'clock. I have a long walk to Penn Station and I have to stay awake tonight on the train, inventing the plot of the play I didn't see. I guess I'll have to make up something pretty deplorable about two people who have bad luck."

"Love, Kitty."

She cared for him after all! He felt transformed, thrilled with desire! This time he would hold Kitty in his arms forever! On and on he drove. There had been a terrible misunderstanding. On and on!

At Penn Station he left his car illegally at a taxi stand and on the run entered the great echoing concourse. Pigeons dive-bombed from vaults above. Hundreds of footsteps clacked hollow tongues. Steam issued from stairwells and a *tchug chug chug* underground was followed by a gush of acrid smoke.

Quick, quick. He couldn't find her. Quick, quick.

Nowhere. Gone.

Then there she was.

Pigeons were swooping down a cone of light to an uncrowded corner of the concourse, crusts were being strewn like handfuls of dice by a hand—the hand of a girl in a summer dress who wore a ribbon in her raven-glossy hair. Her face was sweet as she coaxed the pigeons.

Weal and woe of her stirred his heart. He stopped out of breath and gazed upon her in gratitude and amazement. Shafts of light broke soundlessly bright at her feet like blossoms of a pear tree, bridal. Her beauty was as strange as a maiden's in a myth and had entered his soul. She was life, she was joy!

Slowly she seemed to become aware of his gaze. Then, in one moment, her eyes participated in his and her lips parted. With a cry, he ran to her and folded her in his arms. The world around them seemed to drift away on a sea of meaningless murmurations.

Now words of endearment, breathings of desire, and one plea to be his in marriage tumbled together in a landslide of joyful energies.

She held him gently at arm's length and beseeched him with her eyes. "You don't know me," she said. "We ought to get to know each other first."

He had not expected her to back off. He had repeated the old mistake of thinking that she cared. He felt awkward and foolish.

"I thought we could be friends," she said.

"Oh, I see."

"Perhaps we could arrange to meet sometime.'

"We've just met."

"My train is leaving soon."

"It can go without you."

She considered this statement as if the idea were new. "I guess I could telegraph Mother that I'm staying a few days at a hotel. She didn't give me enough money to stay at a hotel."

"Kitty," he said quietly. "To hell with your mother. You're coming with me to the Rockies. We can get married on the way."

Her eyes laughed at him. "I'll be your mistress," she said.

"Wife," he said.

"It will be a dream over the world," she said in sudden rapture. She had closed her eyes. She opened them again and cried, "O I love you. And I forbid you to speak of the past!"

Max laughed on a somewhat cool note."You sound like a wife already."

Some while later, having liberated the Chevy from the angry gestures of cabbies, Max returned with Kitty to his apartment. She was obviously exhausted and overwrought. When he had cooked her supper, he packed his car with supplies and camping equipment while she, dressed in his pajamas, went to bed. She seemed to fall asleep at once.

It was after midnight when he finished packing and was preparing to sleep on the couch. A subway train rumbled and whined faraway and deep. She woke up, called his name in an anxious whisper, "Max?"

"Over here."

"Did you hear something?"

"Nothing unusual. Have you ever been away from home?"

"I've been to Charleston."

"Gee, Kitty, they don't make 'em like you anymore. Why stay at home?"

"Mother needs someone to look after her."

"How's your dad? You know, I like your old man."

"He died shortly after you left. I thought you knew."

"No-o." Since he was forbidden to speak of the past, he was hesitant. "I didn't know. I'm sorry."

There was a long silence in the dark of the room. Kitty broke it. "Darling, did you receive my letters?"

"When?"

"After you left us at the beach."

He stared at the ceiling. He suspected a trick. "So you wrote—?"

"Didn't you? But that's terrible! I wrote many times, but--"

"But what?"

"I was so ashamed. I thought you had not forgiven me."

"What were you ashamed of?"

"Of not being open with you."

"You were not open?"

"I'm not very brave."

"You've found the courage to lie to your mother and come and find me."

"Oh, I don't want to spoil everything!" she moaned.

After another silence Max said, "I wrote you, too. I thought you never forgave me for the way I behaved that day at the river."

She made a groaning sound in her throat. "Now I see. It's very sad . . . Oh," she went on, "I was such a silly girl! I wanted you . . ."

"Do you want me now?"

"O yes, my darling, I want you to come to me."

He went to the bed. She was soft and warm to his touch, her dark hair loosely falling, her breast gently rising, falling. There was a vague quality in her tone when she asked, "Do you have one of those . . . balloons?"

"Balloons?"

"You know."

"No, but don't worry," he said. "I want our children."

"Please, Max?"

"I'll have to find a drug store that's open."

"Hurry, then."

He had to drive uptown to find an all-night drug store. He ordered a month's supply of Trojans.

Upon his return the first thing that Kitty said was that they should leave New York at once.

"At once?"

She laughed."In a little while, I mean."

"What's the hurry?"

"Mother," she said.

"She doesn't know you're here."

"But I left your sister's letter in my desk. It has your address. Mother will soon be snooping around."

"She can't hurt us," Max said. Kitty was not easily to be reassured. Pressing fists against her cheeks and sucking in breath, then holding it only to let it go with a snort, she was worked into a passion. "I hate her!" she declared."She treats me like an idiot." She turned her glance slowly until it fell upon him. "Don't you despise me? Don't you see how destructive I am?"

"Don't," he said.

Their love-making was not a withholding. He did not think of her as someone apart. They moved as one.

"You reached me!" she cried. "O you reached me!" . . .

QUITE EARLY IN THE MORNING THEY LEFT, unrolling streets behind them like a dirty flag. They stopped in Pennsylvania to refuel and buy Kitty some clothing, and that night, in Ohio, Max pitched a tent in the woods. Already it seemed as if they led enchanted lives. In the big night the satin-rip of automobiles sounded far away. In the hazy morning the sizzling-up of bacon and eggs on an open fire seemed better than any truffles at the Ritz. Then another day, another night, and another and another: the beauty and vastness of the land mingled with his passion for Kitty.

They came to Western Kansas and camped on the prairie. Gigantic webs of heat lightning silently spun from horizon to horizon. It was harvest time. The sight, next day, of red combines easing, like toy submarines, through oceans of golden wheat, made the notion of stopping for a few days to work quite irresistible. Thus it came about that they drove to Oberlin, a small town, to the little stone courthouse where Max approached a farmer in a straw hat.

"Know where we can get some work, mister? I can drive a tractor, my wife can cook."

The farmer studied them expressionlessly. He spat and said, "Reckon."

A few minutes later a certain Mr. and Mrs. Smith had been hired for ten dollars a day and board by the farmer whose name was Steen, who took off hat and shifted feet in dust when he had been introduced to Kitty. "How do, ma'am. We got a bunch of roughnecks out yonder, but I reckon Mrs. Steen can show you how to handle them . . . Get yourself a straw, Mr. Smith. It's a hundert and ten. I seen bigger city-types than you get sun-cramps so bad they dasn't move their little finger without screaming."

Steen's farm—several thousand acres of wheat on the perimeter of which were houses, barns, a silo and a pinwheel windmill—increased Max's sense of abundance. Still, Max worried about Kitty: her new Levis and khaki shirt could not disguise her delicate beauty. She might cause trouble among the men; besides, she was too easily noticed. But, to Kitty, who was being paid to work for the first time in her life, the farm was but the scene of glorious adventure. He decided to keep his worries to himself.

After a week, his worries had almost vanished. He was sunburned, his muscles hardened, he had the beginnings of a dark beard. He came to resemble the men he worked with, most of them itinerants like himself, high school boys, ex-GI's, and a few who were said to be ex-cons. Twice each day they sailed in together from the fields and were called to a long common table where a rich steamy feast of meats and vegetables and pies was devoured as soon as Steen had read from the Bible. The women, and there were half a dozen, stayed in the kitchen except when there was a call to replenish the pitchers of iced water. In consequence Kitty was not unnoticed. When she appeared from the kitchen, her eyes sparkling and the color high in her cheeks, there was a definite quieting in the room. A number of men would follow her movements with their eyes and chew their food in a ruminating manner, like bulls.

Max had pitched camp in the prairie several miles from the shed where the men retired after supper. In spite of fatigue he was kept awake by mosquitoes, half-resting, half-listening to the night. His father had taught him to do that on hunting trips in the wilderness.

It was at the end of the first week that, as he lay beside Kitty, he heard the distant approach of a semi-trailer. He slipped out of the tent into the moon-blanched prairie. Several hundred yards away the trailer's headlamps dipped and swerved, coming his way. He woke Kitty. They dressed quickly. When the trailer stopped near the tent, they were in the Chevy; the brake was released and Max's hand was on the ignition switch. His heart was pounding. The driver of the trailer switched off his engine and lights, stepped out and called softly, "Mr. Smith?"

It was Steen. Max turned on his own lights. There was no one else but Steen.

"Over here," Max said.

"I ain't coming no closer," said the other. "You wouldn't be a man named Stebbins by any chance?"

"What about it?"

"Oh," said Steen, rubbing his chin in a mechanical motion, "one of the men heard a police call on the radio. You better move on. Here's your pay."

Max watched while Steen placed some bills under a stone and backed away.

"O.K.," Max said. "Thanks."

"Thank you, Mr. Steen," Kitty called out.

Steen half bowed. "Evenin', ma'am." He spat and said, "He don't look like no kidnapper to me." He climbed into the cab of the trailer and was soon gone out of sight.

They sat in the car without speaking, their feelings cheapened by Mrs. Pentecost. Max hit upon a solution: "Let's go to town and get married and report to the police afterwards when the law is on our side."

"You're very sweet," she said, caressing his hand. "It all sounds so lovely and nice."

"It would make me very happy," he said.

"I hope so," she said. After a pause, she told him that there was "something" he should know.

He dreaded that opener. He had heard it from too many girls. The old bitterness, the old sense of betrayal, swelled in his heart. "I don't want to hear it. I want to hear yes or no."

"Then it's no," she said with a toss of her hair.

"Why?"

"Because."

"That's not an answer, Kitty. That's child talk."

"I'm not a child."

"I didn't say . . . Kitty, I *love* you."

"You don't sound like it."

"Don't," he retorted hotly, "put the blame on me!"

She turned, faced him. "It's all my fault. I'm sorry."

"I'm not interested in fault-finding . . . I want you!"

“I know,” she said. “And I want you.”

“Then what the hell is going on?”

“I can’t.”

“Can’t what?”

“Can’t marry you.”

“Give me a reason. Please.”

“I’m afraid.”

“Afraid of what?”

Kitty lowered her gaze. Her hands were folded in her lap. “Mother,” she said.

“Jesus,” he said. “You’re letting her destroy—”

“I know,” she interrupted with a sob. “I can’t help it.” The anger went out of him. He moved to comfort her in his arms. “Talk to me. Don’t go away from me.” He spoke gently.

“All right,” she nodded. She ceased to cry.

Talking, they sat in the car, in the open moonlit prairie, in the approximate middle of the continent, and sought together to understand Kitty’s terror. It became clearer than ever that her mother had long exercised a morbid influence over her mind. That this had something to do with Mrs. Pentecost’s religious fanaticism, particularly with the belief in human depravity, Kitty and Max easily agreed upon. But there was something else, some motive, some warped energy in Mrs. Pentecost that they were unable to articulate even though they discerned its presence in an episode in Kitty’s childhood.

It came about that Kitty mentioned having a strong dislike of wedding gowns, so strong that she could seldom look upon a bride dressed in white without experiencing dizziness and nausea. Even the innocuous photographs of brides in the fashion pages of newspapers, she could not bear to look at.

“It’s the dress itself, not the bride, that triggers your reaction?” Max asked.

"I'm not sure," Kitty said. "You see, I remember Mother forcing me to wear a little wedding dress she had made for me."

Little by little that memory came back, how her mother had caught her taking down her panties and showing off for a little Muslim boy of her own age, nine. She was taken into the mission house and scrubbed with lye-soap until her skin bled. She was told that what she had done was extremely sinful and that she must never, ever, show herself like that to man or boy. Then, a week or so later, her mother had marched her several miles into the desert, out of sight of the Kurdish village where they lived and to a place where a bitter cold wind blew down from the Caucasus. Her mother was carrying a spade and, under her arm, a small parcel. When they reached the place, her mother proceeded to dig a shallow trench, the wind whipping away each spadeful of gray dirt as it was thrown. At first Kitty was curious. As time wore on she began to shiver with cold. Finally her mother put down the spade.

"What is it?" Kitty had asked.

"A grave," her mother replied.

Her mother unwrapped the parcel, shook out a small white dress, and ordered Kitty to put it on. Kitty protested: it was cold, she wanted to go home. Her mother came and took off her clothes and forced her to put on the white dress. When this was done and before Kitty realized what was happening, her mother bound her ankles with a belt and, after a struggle, her wrists behind her back.

Screaming, struggling helplessly, Kitty was carried and placed in the grave.

Her mother towered over her and said incomprehensible things, repeating. "You are the bride of God, you are the bride of God."

And began to rain shovelfuls of dirt upon Kitty's body until she was half buried and could no longer struggle against the weight.

Kitty swooned.

When she opened her eyes again, her mother was kneeling, praying. Kitty whimpered, "Let me go. I don't want to play anymore." Her mother rose and stood over her and said they were doing what God had commanded and that she would be set free if she promised never to marry a man but to be the bride of God.

As soon as Kitty realized she could be set free, she decided to trick her mother. She promised everything, just as her mother demanded, but she managed to cross fingers behind her back.

"So," Max commented when they had talked for an hour. "You'll have to choose between your mother and me."

She begged him to give her more time. He consented but explained that they would now have to worry about the police, traveling only by night until they were safe in Sculley's cabin . . .

The cabin was situated high among the mountain ranges of southwestern Colorado. A winding, precipitous road took Max and Kitty to a pass at nine-thousand feet. Here he found the half-concealed gateway that the Sculleys in Denver had described for him, a rocky, snow-patchy trail that ended half a mile further up. From the end of the road they made their way on foot, carrying supplies for about a mile before the trail descended to a green mountain meadow.

A blue lake was another sky. Mule deer grazed among the putty-colored aspens. A sliver of a brook jinked past wind-rippled grasses. On the farther side of the lake stood Sculley's redstone cabin. Behind it rose a majestic range of snow-patchy mountains glistening in the sun beneath the sky of cobalt-blue.

They found the cabin as Sculley had described it, in good repair, clean, sparsely but comfortably furnished, well-stocked with firewood both for the wide stone fireplace and for the potbellied stove.

They seemed to have everything for their comfort and well-being.

They had money, youth, no responsibilities. They had health. They had companionship, physical and intellectual.

Max knew something was wrong.

Perhaps it was the mountains. He loved the mountains. He had grown up in the mountains of the East. The presence of mountains satisfied him spiritually. But these mountains of the West, these gleaming white peaks, disturbed him. Their whiteness. Their austerity. Their sublimity. Their indifference! That was it. They cast cold eyes upon antsy mortals crawling on their flanks.

This was a chastening experience. It put him on guard. It toughened his mind to a certain degree. It made him query his style of feeling and thinking. All that intensity, all that sensuous excitation: was it, after all, but a style? Certain of his recent feelings, as they had expressed themselves, took on a burdensome quality. It was tentative, he didn't want it, but it was there. It placed Kitty at a slight distance. Perhaps his mind had played tricks on him. Perhaps he had not really seen her at Penn Station illuminated by shafts of light. Should he say that he had only seen a girl at Penn Station? And was his pleasant intercourse with her really so spectacular? Or should he say only that love was made? He wondered about Kitty's exclamation about being physically reached. Granting that he felt flattered, could he really accept that he had done anything to qualify for the sexual Olympics? As to their stint at Steen's farm, could he really say that all that backbreaking work in the hot sun followed by anxious, mosquito-infested nights had been exhilarating?

There was something wrong.

He seemed to allow Kitty to cast him into roles. He was passionate: accepted. But passion was cloying, if that was all there was to be.

He didn't want to escape. He didn't much like Kitty's dream over the world.

He decided that he must press matters with her . . .

. . .

YET HE DELAYED. HE WAS FOND OF HER. She needed support, protection. It seemed cruel to shatter her dream world.

One cloudless afternoon when they were dressing after a cold nude dip in the lake, he affected an offhand tone. "Well, honey, what say we get married? Think of all the happiness that can be ours." He accompanied this declaration with a clowning gesture, a shrug of the shoulders.

She studied him, frowned, and said in an even tone,"Our happiness doesn't matter. The world needs vision, not happiness, imagination, not your respectable little laws and conventions. You do understand, don't you?"

His anger was swift. He checked it, spoke evenly. "I understand that you are incapable of love."

"That's not true," she retorted. "I love you. I've always loved you."

"Why can't you commit yourself? Why this eternal separation between us?"

"What do you mean, separation?" Kitty asked with a look that seemed genuinely puzzled.

It took him a while to stumble through an explanation of what he meant. He instanced her insistence on the use of contraceptives. He expected her to bristle. Instead, she fell so silent that he wished he could unsay everything. "All right, dear," she said at last. "We won't use them anymore."

"Well," he said, "we'll think about it. I'm sure we can't afford an unwanted child."

"But you're right," she said. "We mustn't be separated." She came and leaned against his chest, looked up half-smiling and stroked his face. "I rather like you with a beard. I think you ought to get married."

He noted her *you* and said nothing more that day. Thereafter when they made love, they no longer took precautions. For the next few weeks it seemed to Max that their lives were melting together in a prodigality of natural feeling.

But there came one day when Kitty became feverishly ill. Her face felt hot. There was a delirious quality to her speech. Max was worried. He did what he could, bathing her face and hands with cold water from the lake, but her eyes remained glazed and by evening she was so weak he had to improvise a bedpan and lift her upon it. "I'm sorry you're seeing me like this," she said in a fading voice.

"I'm a doctor's son," he reminded her.

When her fever had abated after many hours, he built a fire and, stretching out on the stone floor, dropped off into fitful sleep. In the chill of dawn, Kitty was shaking him. "I've had a miscarriage. Best we go to a hospital in Denver."

When she was warmly dressed, she stood for a while and gazed about the room. "Goodbye, happiness," she said to the room. He started to say something about their returning next day but did not have the heart. Even her womb had rejected him.

He half carried her down the trail that morning. During the six-hour drive to Denver, their conversation was strained, touching only upon trivialities. By noon Kitty was being admitted to a hospital under her maiden name.

"Thank you, Max," she said when a nurse had come for her.

"Sure thing," he said, ruefully noting her formal tone. He wondered if he should kiss her goodbye. She was going, and, as she was going, said, "I've left a message for you in the cabin. You'll find it under the pillow. Take care of yourself."

And she was gone.

He was glad that he thought to give her several hundred dollars. He didn't know what she would do with them or where she would be going. He only knew she wished to remain free, never to get in the same boat with anyone.

He returned to Sculley's cabin after sunset. Scent of grass sprang at him and gnawed his heart.

He found Kitty's message scrawled on a piece of notepaper under her pillow together with the earthenware pieplate which she had given him. "Goodbye, my love," he read. "Don't worry about me and don't try to stop me. I am going home. I can never marry anyone. Will you listen to me? Will you try to understand? *I am nothing but a prostitute.* Will you leave me alone? Please. Kitty."

"All I wanted was to hope," Max said aloud to the cabin. For a few moments his self-pity blotted out every tenderness. To be deserted like this without explanation! Ridiculous, the crap about being a prostitute! He threw the pieplate violently against the fireplace and shouted at the top of his lungs, "Coward! Liar!" . . .

Drainpipes were awash, leaves pitterpattered. With the rainstorm almost over, the moonlight had returned, and through his bedroom window Max could see the silvery, tree-filtered mists already thinning, ephemeral as a dream. The thunder was marching distantly, slowly, still lingering as though waiting to be released.

Something was lifting from Max's heart.

His dream over the world of his youth had been a partial submersion. He had, partially, gotten back into the old feelings, into the old attitudes of passion, but , in truth, he was no longer to be identified as the person whom he had been focusing in wakeful contemplation. Not that he could altogether repudiate his former self: to do so was the gut-activity of saints and revolutionaries who were horrified by youthful sins and privileges and tried to root these out. He could nevertheless observe that certain aspects of himself had withered, certain others were preparing to unfold like new leaves. It was as if the spirit were a tree gradually absorbing and engulfing the barbed wire from which it has bled to live.

He thought, now, of trees. He thought of the old myths in which there were two trees, one of knowledge and one of life, and how to taste of the fruit of the tree of knowledge was to lose all paradise. And it seemed to him that he could interpret this to mean what Sculley had written in the notes on humanism, in effect, that the Promethean flame of freedom was for all mankind but was not intended to give men power over Creation. And it seemed to him that potentates and authorities on the earth were tempted to become as gods and that this temptation bore the sign of doom. And it seemed to him, also, that ordinary persons like himself were tempted to possess and control or, by a curious reversal, tempted to be possessed and controlled. And finally it seemed to him that the other tree, the tree of life, had not been forbidden but grew in Creation and through it was the branching into self-fulfillment and converging with others.

There was hope, now, and faith—faith in life. He was an infinitesimal but nonetheless significant part of a struggle for survival on a universal scale. There was already enough death, enough violence in the heart, already enough to urge him to resist it now that he was making live contact with himself and with the others who had shared the earth with him and were even at that moment sharing it, suffering and touching, if but in a dream, the heart of life.

He thought of mountains now. He reviewed and accepted his conception of them seventeen or so years ago. Anarchy, never quite absent from the American heart, drew men to solitude: a dead end.

His thought came back to Kitty. His will to illusion had after many years released its grip on his mind.

He felt prepared to face facts.

The first fact that he discovered was that he had wanted to possess her completely and for himself, and she, eluding him, had left him feeling powerless, as if she had robbed him of his soul.

What he perceived now, secondly, was the exclusiveness of their love. Where previously he had resented Kitty's success in declaring and showing a love that was not to be lived out as a social reality, now he could distinguish between two kinds of love: one, the romantic one which made passion an exclusive privilege of those with the time, money, and cultivated intensity to indulge in it, and two, the pragmatic love which valued the actual experience of the heart as over and against established authorities. In the eyes of authority, any passion tended toward the heretical and criminal, not, as it actually did, toward the heart of aliveness. This love could not have been converted into ordinary happiness without being subjected to the rules of convenience and commodity. What Kitty had wanted, as her later life made clear, was *to live*. The trouble was, her dream of a free existence had moved ahead of her capacity—and his—to make it a substantial reality. She had been afraid and she had not been open. The anarchy in her had led to a dead end.

He seemed to see her in vision again. She seemed to rise from his heart, releasing him to renewed life. Far away the thunder rumbled over the hills—it was she, ghosting on invisible feet away, away!

PART IV

Chapter Sixteen **Adam**

There is a snapshot taken when Hasbrouck was at Oxford in the twenties. He is tall and has a goose neck and narrow sloping shoulders. He wears his hair lanky like Oscar Wilde's. The eyes behind the pince-nez seem frozen into a blink. His arm is flung about the shoulders of a pale young man who is dressed exactly as he: high white collar, white bow tie, black gown and mortarboard. The young man's expression is cheeky, debonair. In the background of the picture is the Merton College wall against which Puritans lined up their fellow countrymen and executed them.

His name was Gerald, this young man who had a weak chest. Hasbrouck could never look at the picture without nostalgia tinged by remorse. The picture was yellowed now, pitted by decay, hanging framed among other memorabilia in his office in Henry Memorial. Gerald had been a prig, a snob, a profligate butterfly, though he was hardly to blame for having been pampered in damp and lordly mansions and sent to exclusive schools. To Hasbrouck, who shared digs with Gerald, the Englishman seemed to need affection even more than he: he, too, recalled childhood as a bottomless pit into which he had been thrust by hardshelled creatures like those in *Alice in Wonderland.* There had been for Hasbrouck a bleak upstate New York mansionhouse with forty rooms, obsequious, uniformed servants gliding about and talking in foreign tongues. Sometimes he had nightmares in which he became lost in corridors and passageways to nowhere. As he fled down them, doors opened of their own accord, became rectangular voids swirling with snow, and strange voices sounded in his ears. As much as he cared for Gerald when they were having blowjobs, Hasbrouck's New England heritage prompted him to try to save Gerald from slipping down the soaped stairs to depravity. Gradually Hasbrouck persuaded him that swimming in the nude at Parsons' Pleasure—where other young men might remark that Gerald was "like an Adonis'—would bring his TB to a dreadful climax. Gerald must find character to outlast porcelain skin and well-proportioned limbs—in effect, find a conscience like Hasbrouck's own, one based upon solid facts and stern encounters. Gerald must renounce his family which might once have stood for old-fashioned English rectitude and decency but now represented imperialism and racism. About the time that the snapshot was taken, Gerald renounced his family and proclaimed himself a communist. However, the liberation lasted only a few weeks. Gerald grew thin and emaciated and began to cough up blood. He lay in bed and fixed luminous dark eyes upon Hasbrouck as if beseeching and accusing him simultaneously. Finally there was that terrible night when Gerald raised himself feebly in bed and said in his chirpy voice, "I say, you bloody colonial, you're like a child pulling a fly to pieces." He died before Hasbrouck could expostulate with him.

When Hasbrouck left Oxford, his conscience kept bothering him about Gerald. He decided that if Gerald had lacked physical and moral fitness to confront the facts of the age—Marx, Darwin, and Freud—he, Hasbrouck, must not be found wanting. He cabled the family to send fifty thousand dollars at once to a new account in Switzerland, and he sailed to India, to the packed and pestilential cities which Kipling had described. There for some twenty years he put his conscience to work where victims of cholera raised sickening stench, where emaciated children awaited death by wayside burials, where scavenger dogs licked corpses clean, and where, now and then, the Imperial Police required the presence of a physician at a hanging. There in India Hasbrouck familiarized himself with sexual behavior by studying ancient books and by paying native men and woman to perform according to the books while he took notes and photographs and generally observed the facts. Later, at his own expense he published in Paris his research. This pioneering work was, later still, the basis of his scholarly reputation in America. His purpose, as he defined it, was to extirpate Puritanism and to exhort his fellows to enjoy sex without guilt or fear—even though he, himself, still had no sexual experience with women.

ONE SUMMER MORNING IN THE FIFTIES a steamship arrived in Seattle. Among its passengers was a bald, middle-aged American.

That summer, wars flickered over the face of the earth, in Korea, in Indochina. A so-called Cold War of frozen relationships had begun between the United States and the Soviet Union.

But wars seemed far away from the sun-drenched hills and fertile valleys of the Sonoma region where Hasbrouck visited after a brief stopover in San Francisco to see lawyers and bankers concerned, at continent's length, with the Hasbrouck family's New York-based financial enterprises. He had come to Sonoma to visit a man who owed him everything: life, in fact.

Of all the facts, he had reflected, few could be more satisfying than to save a man's life. This man in California had been serving with a regiment of Highlanders in India. Hasbrouck had met him at a social gathering in the hill country at the home of an Oxford-educated homosexual Indian planter. The Scot, with ludicrously bushy eyebrows and hair like smoked salmon, would probably not have attracted his attention had it not been for something said: the Scot, it appeared, was itching to fight Fascism in Spain. Here was a man confronting the facts. So Hasbrouck and the Scot went to converse privately on a stroll about the plantation and chanced upon the *pukka sahib* sexually assaulting a little Indian boy. The Scot drew a pistol and put a bullet through the planter's head. The kaleidoscope of events which followed proved to Hasbrouck his capacity for philanthropy. The boy and his family were bundled off to a city a thousand miles away. The Scot was supplied with a new identity as Mr. Ritchie McPherson, was spirited away to Goa, thence to Portugal, thence to war in Spain. Some time later in thirty-six, he entered the United States illegally from British Columbia, made his way to California, married the descendant of a Spanish commandant of the period before the arrival of the *gringos*, inherited an adobe ranchhouse and small vineyard, and had a daughter whose name, as Hasbrouck had learned through correspondence transmitted through the New York enterprises, was Epifania Beneficia McPherson, Fanny for short.

Hasbrouck was her godfather.

McPherson's ranch was located about ten miles of dusty road back in the Napa Valley. Since Hasbrouck wanted to surprise McPherson, he ordered the cabdriver to stop where a tree-canopied road began at a gate. He walked. Something about the place, the vibrant air, the spacious sky, affected him sentimentally. Here was a private peace that he had never found for himself. Duties had weighed too heavily upon him. Even here, however, the Hasbrouck money had made a fellow man happy.

Scruboaks and fleshtinted eucalyptus trees printed their shadows on golden foxtail grasses. In a dappled corral a sorrel mare nudged her foal.

As he approached the brown adobe house whose balconied second story was decorated with gourds and flower baskets of brilliant hues, dogs barked ferociously. The next that Hasbrouck heard was a metallic *wick-gashick*: lever-action rifle being armed: and he saw in the doorway, pointing the rifle at him, a slender girl in blue jeans. The long red hair she shook back caught the sun and was like windruffled wheat.

"What do you want?" the girl demanded. "We don't like *gringos* here."

"I say, are you pointing that thing at me? You must be joking!" he began but stopped. Why, the girl was positively menacing! He tipped his straw hat. Oh, he would tell the story! He was already promising himself that pleasure. He imagined the scene, the only scene of consequence to him in the world: high table at an Oxford college, witty chaps modestly arrayed, ruthlessness tucked well inside their *savoir faire*, Milord-this and Sir Basil-that, snoozy, pissing in their trousers from too much Croft's port, '26 or '29, and from a good litre or so of vintage burgundy or hock produced from the domestic bursar's cellar.

In that very instant he had collected the facts and drawn his own conclusions. He had nothing to fear. He made a little bow and guffawed: "My dear young lady, unless I am very much mistaken, you are an epiphany, my goddaughter . . . Allow me to introduce myself. I am Dr. Adam Hasbrouck, just arrived from India expressly to be of service to the clan McPherson. Surely you are *señorita* Epifania Benificia McPherson, Fanny for short . . . ? And your good father, is his name not—?"

The girl lowered the rifle and smiled, "Hi."

"Aye, Ritchie McPherson," came a whiskey-voiced burr from the doorway. Approaching was a stocky sandyhaired man, squinteyed beneath eyebrows so bushy they looked, as Hasbrouck always remembered them, as if glued on for a pantomime.

'The verra name as gi'n by yon wee mon, I'll be bluddy creepin' Jesus! Hasbrouck!" McPherson lurched forward and vigorously shook hands. "You look greet, wee mon . . . Fanny, run and tell her ladyship we shall have hogmanay this summer's day and bring a wee stone for fairst-footing."

There was feasting and drinking for three days and three nights.

Something in Hasbrouck warmed to these people, even to "her ladyship," a blackhaired woman in black who positively glowered at him because, it was explained, she hated all *gringos* but McPherson. That old rascal was of a type which Hasbrouck had come across before in queer corners of the world: born to be lucky in love and war without having to lift a finger, bone-idle, helpless, companionable, and, of all things, incorruptible except, possibly, when it came to money. Hasbrouck liked and envied him. Had he not saved the man from arrest for murder, to the tune of tens of thousands of dollars?

Perhaps the beauty and intelligence of Fanny McPherson were turning his head. Fifteen, figure softly rounding out. Dark deepset eyes flecked with green. High-spirited flush of cheeks, rich flame of hair. To the fifty-year-old expert on sex she seemed a Nausicaa, a Cordelia! Now she knew him, she admired him as her father's legendary benefactor. Those were the facts. A plan for her, slowly through the whiskey-haze of several afternoons, bloomed in his mind until, at dinner on the eve of his departure for Poe's Hill, he had decided to extend his philanthropy by a gesture of extravagance that would set his Calvinist and Dutch Reformed forefathers gnashing teeth in their graves.

"McPherson," he began, lifting wineglass to candlelight, "your Cabernet Sauvignon must be pronounced excellent and yourself the happiest of mortals. You have married a lady of beauty and aristocratic breeding who can also—my word!—cook superb chile relleno." Hasbrouck paused, beamed upon the woman whose face was an unsmiling mask. "And," he resumed, "there is your daughter. Your daughter, sir, as the great Robbie Burns has sung, is like a red, red, rose . . . I propose a toast."

McPherson, all eyebrows and mirth, rose, stood swaying with his glass. "A toast," he rasped—and belched.

Hasbrouck was standing, head almost brushing the ceiling, consciousness largely elsewhere probing long memories of the Oxford scene to give him correct tones and a winning way. "Someone, my dear fellow—I believe the Sassenach Bard of Avon—said, 'think not because thou art bereft there shall be no more cakes and ale,' and as you and I have come so near to destruction so often, I must say I resent unhappiness with all of my heart. That is not to say I think unhappiness is easily disposed of, but it's so easy to forget to be happy when the opportunities present. Therefore, may it please present company all to rise and join me in a toast—to happiness!"

Hasbrouck drank bitterly before he resumed:

"What I now have to say particularly concerns the happiness of yon bonny lass . . . Consider, young lady, the trillions-upon-trillions-to-one chance that has brought your loveliness into being. Think of a half-starved lad fighting for a crumb of bread in the squalid slums of Glasgow, and think of the very lad gone for a soldier. What do the imperialists care for this man should he die of a bullet or disease? They care nought! Let him behave as a man should and stand up for justice . . . and he is good as hanged. He escaped. But not to run away! No. To fight for a principle, to fight, we regret, the lost cause, to confront the facts of totalitarianism in their most immediate and dangerous form. He did that, too, and lived and found his way to this blessed land, this happy valley . . . Now, if you'll bear in mind, my dear, that I am a physician, I'm sure you will not be offended as I refer to certain, how shall I say, elemental *facts*." Upon his last word he lavished emphasis. Smiling, nodding, measuring cadence, Hasbrouck said, "The sheer prodigality of Creation, my dear, think of *that!* Why, one man in his time wastes billions of sperms. Think of *that!* Think of the odds that you would end up on a bedsheet or in a paper handkerchief! But no! There came a time when just *one* of those sperms wriggled its way to the maternal womb. Think of *that!* And even then, you might have been aborted, wrapped in a paper bag and tossed into the garbage can . . . No offense intended, mind you . . . *because*, señorita, against all these odds you have *prevailed!* It is a miracle, the most wonderful miracle—*life!*"

Hasbrouck paused and drank. Then he spoke slowly in order that the girl would feel the weight of his magnanimity as if they were in Oxford together at the high table in his brain.

"What will you do with this gift of life? . . . As your godfather, I have decided to make you sole beneficiary of a Trust of one hundred thousand dollars, the income from which will enable you to pursue your education without distress and to live independently for the rest of your life. On one condition." Hasbrouck held up his little finger and said, "When you are prepared for university, you will come to Poe's Hill so that your godfather shall have, as his reward, the pleasure of observing the full unfolding flower . . . What do you say, girl?"

Catching a glimpse of the girl's expression, he wondered why anyone who had just been offered what he had offered should look so infuriated . . . Ingratitude! Curse the swine! Even their surname had been invented for them. . .

Shakily, McPherson rose and spoke. "We thank'ee, Doctor Hasbrouck, from the bottom of our hearts. For m'sel, ach no, I kenna be longer beholden, but as t'is for the wee bairn, I'll say godbless'ee and I'll say n'more. She shall attend your pretty little college."

Hasbrouck beamed, flushed with the perspective of his benevolence.

HASBROUCK DID NOT KNOW HIMSELF. He should have been in the guest room at the far end of the house; he was not. He was in pajamas. He must have wandered from the house which moonlight at last established for him in a dark grove some hundred yards away from this place stinking of horse manure: the barn of course. As he began to reason, he identified hoofthud and hayswish of animals in stalls, yet his mind had gone away. They swarmed about him, images of brownskinned bodies moving, moving until satiated. There was panic in his loins. He half-crawled, half-careened into the open air and stood with back propped up against a eucalyptus tree. He felt the flesh of his penis and was, though athrob with desire, impotent.

He had an image and connected to it: is professor in Switzerland was treating a madman who had chopped off his penis and presented it to his wife.

His mind went away.

When it came back, he saw the girl. She was unsaddling a horse by the barn, by the barn in the moonlight unsaddling a horse. What? Out for a midnight ride. Of course. Out riding. Opening her thighs for a horse.

He shrank into the shadow of the tree.

His mind went away and, when it came back, the girl was passing close to him. He could hear the sweet swish of her jodhpurs.

She passed by and went toward the house . . .

He would have shot me too if I hadn't offered him philanthropy, Hasbrouck thought some minutes later. He flopped into bed too drunken-tired to give the usual concentration to images of orifices slippery as warm wax.

. . .

SOON AFTER SETTLING DOWN IN POE'S HILL, Hasbrouck established an irrevocable living Trust for his goddaughter, securing to her a monthly income of several thousands for life. Since he lived to serve others and spent little upon himself, he kept a clear conscience about his wealth. His love of mankind ranged from purchasing arms for rebel forces seeking the overthrow of Asian, African, or South American governments to this sentimental endowing of Fanny McPherson.

When eighteen, Fanny, obedient to her father's wishes, matriculated at South Atlantic University, graduated four years later, *summa cum laude* in biochemistry, and entered the university's medical school the same year. Grateful to her benefactor, sweet and kind by nature, she would send cards on his birthdays and sometimes make a surprise visit to his office just to share with him a friendly word. Their relationship extended no further. After Habrouck married Kitty, he was particularly careful to keep it distant. He had discovered that Kitty, who admired but did not love him, was madly jealous of women who came near him.

A time arrived when Fanny herself needed his professional help.

It was sixty-two, less than a fortnight since Kitty's burial. Seated in his office was his twenty-four-year-old goddaughter, her hair awry, her face pale and drawn, her eyes lusterless. "I read in the papers of your bereavement," she said. "I'm truly sorry. Perhaps you read of mine." Hasbrouck had detected bitterness and waited. "Carlos Brodie," she said.

That name set his adrenaline flowing! So much were he and Willie Koontz and Archie Leary just then involved in making Brodie's suicide the cause for overthrowing the Scroggs-Blacklaw regime that for the moment he suspected Fanny of spying for the opposition. Brodie's nameless "girlfriend," who was supposed to be his student, had been the alleged "cause" for the firing. There was Koontz' belief that Brodie's girlfriend had been "hired to compromise him": the very words. Hasbrouck sucked in his breath. "So you were the one."

Fanny nodded gravely.

"I was the one Carlos was living with when he was fired." She paused. Her eyes flashed. "There were so many horrible lies! . . . After he was fired, he said he was under surveillance by government agencies. He had to go away, he had no hope. It was all my fault."

"Why do you think it was your fault?" Hasbrouck queried with more than professional concern.

Fanny made a helpless gesture. "Well, you can only fire a tenured professor for gross moral turpitude—whatever that's supposed to mean—and that's what they said about his living with me. We loved each other. He was getting a divorce. We planned to get married . . . He was going to resign anyway. He would have been welcomed anywhere in the world until these *gringo* pigs, at one stroke, destroyed his honor." She lifted her gaze to Hasbrouck's. "They wouldn't listen to him. They just kept saying he was living with one of his students and this was against professional ethics. Carlos pleaded with them to understand that I am a graduate student in medicine, not neuro-psychology—though we met because I was fascinated by his research on the nervous system of monkeys—but I wasn't his student, I wasn't taking his examinations. He called me his colleague . . . And they fired him . . . If I'd only known."

"Known what, my dear?"

"Known how the system works. Carlos and I could have been more discreet. We had nothing to be ashamed of. We were open, honest about everything. His marriage had ended. His soon-to-be ex-wife had been having affairs for years. I don't know why he thought he had to die."

"Was it political, do you think?" Hasbrouck leaned forward over his desk. "Did you believe that federal agents kept Professor Brodie under constant surveillance?"

"That was all so ridiculous!" Fanny cried and went on rapidly. "Carlos told me how he got blacklisted. His scientific work required him to travel abroad to the Soviet Union. He thought it amusing that our government could suspect him of selling secret documents about the nervous system of the monkey! You won't believe this, but the reason he was watched is that his wife swore he was a Soviet spy. She got so up-tight she telephoned Washington and lied her head off. Carlos found out about it. That's when he left her."

"She sounds psychopathic," Hasbrouck said, not having to think about a conclusion formed weeks ago.

"I'm sorry for her—now," Fanny said. Her eyes moistened. "He was such a fine man. He had everything to live for. He struggled all his life. As a child, he had cerebral palsy. One of his hands was shriveled up. He had to speak out of the side of his mouth . . ."

She fell silent.

Hasbrouck thought and said, "His ego-state was not strong. There was nothing you could have done to save him." He proposed that Fanny take a rest, return to California, resume her studies in the fall. She shook her head again, vehemently."If I quit work now, I shall go to pieces. Work is my salvation. I'm going to finish my M.D. Why, I keep asking myself, do we not build bridges to one another instead of seeking domination? Is it all biological, or does consciousness free us to create a better world?"

"Oh," Hasbrouck replied,"some people, un-American blackguards, incompetents, have to be weeded out." He heard his own words too late. He realized his mistake. Too late. Envy and hatred were part of his secret repertoire. Without them he could not have arranged for agents to dispose of Carlos Brodie. Without them he was no match for Max Stebbins in a cold war caused by Kitty when she was still a Pentecost.

Fanny was regarding him in a curious way.

You blundering fool, he said silently to himself. He had just added his goddaughter to the enemies who surrounded him, who pressed in from every side, fangs glistening for a strike.

ONE MORNING JUST BEFORE EASTER OF SIXTY-FIVE Hasbrouck woke up feeling, well, old. He'd been working too hard for years, driving himself to copy-edit proofs of the book which was to be his crowning achievement, "Psychoeroticism of Culture." He was devoting his energies to making South Atlantic University a first-rate institution. Usually his kinder dream of himself as a master builder could lift his heart for an hour or two each day. He was convinced that universities were institutions of primary importance to the welfare and survival of mankind; that in them was the future shaped; and that without a fellow like himself around to insure that freedom of inquiry and thought were not crippled, that future would be no more inspiring to contemplate than a sewage system. On the other hand a university was no longer a loose conglomeration of teachers and pupils conducting a philosophical dialogue in some Athenian olive grove. It was a big business. The business of education was one of the biggest businesses in the world. Accordingly, as *eminence grise* of South Atlantic, he had to conduct business efficiently. One had not just to pursue knowledge but to produce it and be seen to be producing it. Teaching didn't count, though professors were required to go through the usual motions. Production counted. When the product had reached a world market, the image of the university would be first-rate. The devil of it was, one had to make hard decisions about the productivity of one's colleagues. In order to assure the growth of the business, one had to weed out the good-for-nothings, the liberals, the unreliables, the incorrigibles. One had to collect information about everyone. When all the available information was gathered—through the chain of command leading from the Department of Defense or through the ramifying network of subadministrators and student spies—one had to draw conclusions and painfully apply the guillotine. Indeed, in the first year or so of the new administration, quite a few heads had rolled. A few more heads and production would be booming, assault on the humanities finally launched.

He lay in bed and groaned. He had no friends, no one to comfort and advise him. How generously he had committed himself to others from Gerald at Oxford, now more than forty years ago, to, at present, Ginny Stebbins whose career as an actress in New York had been supported by the Hasbrouck connections. Yet no one had loved him. Kitty? Kitty would have loved him had it not been for Max. She had said so . . . or more or less. *I will marry you, Adam, if that's what you wish, but first there is something I must tell you.* Her words had shivered through him then and did so again and again until he seemed to suffocate in their avalanche. She had told him about the wartime romance and something about Colorado and something about Tom Driver—and left him to draw his own conclusions. Whenever he observed Max and Kitty together at parties, he suspected he had married Kitty in order to spite Max, who in turn had had the callous effrontery to appear in Poe's Hill with a wife and child. True, Stebbins was productive. He had now published a book, all the more reason his head must roll.

Hasbrouck shook himself and went into the bathroom. What he saw in the mirror was a hairless chest with flabby pectoral muscles. He was just old with a face like wrinkled chamois leather.

Sometime later that morning he was in his private airconditioned office suite awaiting the appearance, as appointed, of a hospital intern and recent Doctor of Medicine—Fanny McPherson. His nerves jumped, his hands felt clammy and left smears upon the glass-topped desk.

The whelp first, he thought. He flicked an intercom switch. "Send Mr. Widge in, will you?"

"Yes, sir. I'll have somebody find him." Sally was a wised-up secretary.

"What the hell do we have him on a work-study grant for if he's not here when I need him?"

"What can you expect from a creep like him?"

Presently Widge sauntered in smirking. Wearing sunglasses, a Brooks Brothers suit, and white canvas tennis shoes, he resembled a kind of tourist. "Greetings," he said.

"Have you made your arrangements?"

"You mean that asshole, Mason?"

Hasbrouck knew he didn't have to reply to the whelp. To Hasbrouck, Widge was the nadir of the new generation. Funny how things worked out. If Kitty had not been "hitting up," if Mason had not supplied the "snow." Hasbrouck relished his command of the jargon of the addicts. A week ago he had impressed Widge by indicating not only what he wanted but also where it was to be obtained: Mason's store.

Widge dangled his sunglasses. 'He said it would take at least a month to get that much stuff. He wants more money."

"How much?"

"Two thow."

Hasbrouck thought and said, "Tell him on delivery."

"He wants it now. Says it's too big a job for him."

"O.K." Hasbrouck decided. "Use Sally's cashbox."

The intercom buzzed.

"Hang on," said Hasbrouck without having to glance at Widge.

"Dr. McPherson to see you, sir. Shall I ask her to wait?"

"Send her in."

He hadn't seen Fanny for years, not since the Brodie affair.

Twenty-seven now, poised, still a strained look about her but still remarkably pretty with her golden hair tumbling over an internist's whitestarched jacket. She allowed him to peck her on the cheek and then stood, mocking him with dark eyes.

Making the introduction, Hasbrouck placed one big hand on Widge's shoulder, another on Fanny's. "I want you two to have a good look at each other. You may meet again."

Widge was licking his lips with the tip of his tongue.

Fanny rounded on Hasbrouck hotly but said nothing as he turned his back and spoke evenly, distinctly, "Get your rat's ass out of here, Widge," and waited until the door clicked shut.

"I'm going, too," said Fanny.

"Wait," he said.

"You seem to be playing a game, Dr. Hasbrouck."

"Wait," he said. He turned, folded arms, swept her with his eyes. "Do," he motioned with a flick of hand toward the upholstered chair that faced his own across the expanse of desk. "Do sit down."

"I'm due to make rounds at the hospital in half an hour. I only came—" she broke off and sat down. "All right. What is it you want?"

He also sat. He clasped his hands and rested his chin upon them.

"What is it I want?"

"You've changed," Fanny said, cocking her head at him.

He remembered too well a night about a dozen years ago when he cringed in terror and sex-fear behind a eucalyptus tree as she swung carelessly by. "You don't know me," he said. "I'm really quite a good chap in my way. But there's nothing ordinary about me. I'm quite an important man, you know. There are things I have to do." He was noting that his hands had separated. He leaned back in his chair so that he could wipe his hands on his trousers without being observed. "Things I have to do are not always pleasant. Do you follow me?"

"Perfectly." She didn't take her eyes off him while she pulled the hem of her skirt over crossed legs. "I might as well tell you, ever since Carlos died and . . . We had that little talk in which you implied that he was a Cold War spy . . . I've been giving half the income from the Trust to charity."

Hasbrouck studied her, impressed. "Might one inquire why?"

"Be my guest. As my father would say, I kenna be beholden to a man who betrays confidences."

"Go on."

"What I told you about myself and Carlos was confidential, professionally and every other way. Yet, as you know perfectly well, you used that information in order to disgrace the administration of General Scroggs."

Hasbrouck could feel a smile creeping thinly across his lips. "Pigs. *Gringo* pigs, I believe you once called them."

Fanny glared. "That's not the point. The point is--"

"—I see," Hasbrouck interrupted. "I have always regretted the fact that your name did get bandied about a bit in all that fuss, regretted it enormously, and particularly a few leaks into the press. But," he waved his hand limply to and fro,"that's all over and done with now. Let's move on, as they say."

"Someone remembers," she said.

"Who? . . . Oh, I see. You. Why didn't you tell me sooner? My door is always open. As to your conclusion that I am responsible for a breach of professional etiquette, why, girl, that's preposterous! . . . Everybody knew about you and Brodie. Everybody. The government knew, the police knew, Mrs. Brodie, and you, no doubt, had your own circle of friends . . . He was a victim of the Cold War. You didn't realize . . . ?"

Oh, he had blundered again. She was unconvinced. Her face was crimsoning, positively glowering at him as her mother's used to do. He considered a moment and decided it was time. "See here, my dear, there's something I want you to do for me that will not be unpleasant in the least. In fact, I rather think you'll take a fancy to the man."

She peered at him through dark eyes. And began to laugh in derision, then stopped. "My *dear* Dr. Hasbrouck, you were always too good to be true. And now you're a matchmaker. Excuse me, but I find that quite hilarious!" She laughed to stop again. "You seem to have totally misjudged my character!"

"We shall see," said Hasbrouck, feeling his thin, good-humored smiles still in place. His mouth was dry, his armpits wet. Why was it that a peasant could kill a man and desert his regiment and have all the luck whereas you could have a lifelong, principled devotion to humanity and end up a miserable wretch?

(extraordinary facts gentlemen)

One man escapes from a wilderness into a vineyard, whereas the toiler in the vineyard is surrounded by enemies: why? Hasbrouck felt his mind whirling in circles, spectator and victim of itself.

(to be quite honest with you
gentlemen
that is to say
which reminds one
of another story)

He felt an almost irresistible compulsion to wash his hands. He must hurry. Get the rite words in the rote order. Who the devil said that?

(was it Oscar
gentlemen
Willie Yeats
ahhh Joyce
as one was about to say)

He overheard himself resuming:

"On the contrary, my dear, it is your character upon which I am relying. As you, yourself, put it a moment ago, someone may remember things. For example, I remember that a certain Highlander, whose anonymity I have helped to protect behind the name of Ritchie McPherson, is wanted for murder and desertion. I have him, so to speak."

It was out now. Let it sink in. Glance away. That's it. Give the girl time.

Turn back now.

Aha!

Positively glowering. As her mother used to do. Looks as if she'd like to spit.

"*Gringo* is far too good a word for you," said Fanny with an awed inflection to her mockery.

"Thank you," said Hasbrouck quite scathingly, he judged. "Your father's secret is quite safe with me. I'm not asking you to do anything illegal or promiscuous. Don't become like Widge and put a bad construction on one's motives. Have a little confidence, girl! Would I betray your dear father?"

He paused an instant. This was much better. He was into stride.

"All I'm asking you to do is to get to know a man whose wife has left him—all alone. You'll like him. He has quite a winning way. Oh, I promise you. Now, is there anything wrong with that?"

"I wouldn't know," said the other. "I know that, if my father is arrested, you will be charged, yourself, as an accessory after the fact."

An instant later Hasbrouck concluded that he was standing up to this challenge very well. He had to give the girl credit: she was clever, a good player. He felt a smile creeping back upon his lips. "I'm aware of the risks," he said. "To be quite honest with you, no one is going to get hurt and we shall all be laughing . . . Blow me down, you hit the nail on the head: I'm a matchmaker!"

WHEN THE INTERVIEW WAS CONCLUDED about a quarter of an hour later, Hasbrouck flicked the intercom switch. "Sally?"

"Yes, sir?"

"Book me a flight to Washington for tonight, will you?"

"Any particular time?"

"Usual set-up," he said. "Sally?"

"Yes, sir?"

"I'm agitated."

There was a pause. Sally's voice scratched back."I'll be right in. You be good now and lie down."

He went to the small study adjacent to his office and stretched himself out on the Ottoman sofa. There were no windows. Light filtered under the closed door. He was able to reassure himself about his memorabilia, all where they should be. Next to where he lay his head was the snapshot of himself and Gerald at Oxford. He was going back there now, easing down.

He heard the door opened, closed, someone tiptoeing. He breathed the French perfume which he had bought for Sally: essences of the rose and odoriferous ambergris from the intestines of the sperm-whale: facts of life. He did not need to open his eyes. He knew what Sally looked like at forty-five, plump and blowsy with a loopy look on her face. She resembled a face on a pack of Egyptian cigarettes.

"Feeling a bit agitated, are we?" Her voice was purring now. Her fingers were caressing his brow.

He sighed. "They don't realize I work eighteen hours a day." He sighed again as she slipped the silk bandana over his eyes. He inhaled its aroma of old perspiration, his own, comforting somehow.

The frenchkissing now. The warm rubbery tongue.

When the frenchkissing stopped he was ready for all the predatory nonsense. He let Sally do the unzipping and fumbling and sucking. Slowly at first and then with urgency he swooned into a dream of scaffolds.

Chapter Seventeen **Max and Fanny**

Earth

by

Fanny McPherson

Eastwards toward dawn, Earth is like an old crone with sawnoff breasts. Across the eye of the heavens there pass, obscured by the advent of light, all the indecipherable glances of the stars. The desert valley is cold. Soldiers have waited in that valley that lies between ranges of mutilated mesa. When, up the valley, dynamiting started a fire, when the fire held out erotic promise like the spurt of a match behind a windowpane, the soldiers had briefly flickered into view, thousands of them seated on the sands.

The valley is flanked by high mesa and blocked to the north by recessed columns of basalt. Indeed there is a resemblance to a basilica: nave and apse the floor of a Genesis sea heaved a mile up, dome the undeceived sky, altar the zero-point of a mile-wide dustbowl. At zero-point the fire becomes a thin S-plume, like incense. Soldiers in combat fatigues, weapons slung, wait for the truth of the morning to march on.

And it is marching on. Already the sun bleaches the flame of snow on faroff mountain peaks. Blood of dark barrancas begins to flow like molten ore from crucibles. The lunar chill is gone.

Then a voice blats through throats of amplifiers: twennynine, twennyeight . . . The mesas bleed from rims like old crones with sawnoff breasts. Mountains lag shadows to eternity. The soldiers turn about, facing away from zero-point.

Three, two, one.

Dawn.

There is no dawn like this dawn. There has never been a dawn like this dawn. For a moment the light is infinitely, massively complete. Every valley is exalted. Mountains are baroque. Sky is magnesium white. In the next moment the land fulfills the promise of that early, simple fire: it achieves the voluptuous quality of inner thighs. Men are salt. The truth of the morning marches on. At an unspoken signal, soldiers turn and face zero-point. There is no sun like this sun cradled in the valley between rocking motherland. This sun is a prodigious serpent-writhing feather-gorgeous flame.

Casual groups of soldiers form, light cigarettes.

There is a sound rising and falling before it appears no sound at all but the beating of the heart of solitude and apathy as when snow swirls and whirls through cones of arclight along deserted streets, as when dead fireblackened trees, candelabra-limbed, reproach the wind like clumsy giants blinded by stars.

Time bends the cyclone stalk toward the surprised morning. Soon there will be coffee. The soldiers will be herded into trucks in order to tour the perimeter of zero-point and inspect the smouldering of uniformed straw effigies aflame, the vegetable kings. Across the eye of heaven a small tempest mushrooms.

On the soldiers descends a dust as fine and lascivious as cosmetic powder.

. . .

"**DEAR DR. MCPHERSON,**" Max scribbled on the manuscript he had just read. "Have you actually seen an atomic test? Certain details, such as the use of dynamite (to check whether instruments are properly registering?), would not ordinarily be known to persons like ourselves. Moreover, you describe an open tactical exercise of a kind conducted more or less secretly in Nevada in the early fifties when you were in your teens! Admitted, since you tell me you're Californian, you would be familiar with deserts—that mutilated motherland. Nevertheless, forgive me, but I'm worried about the authenticity of this piece which you say is a 'prologue' to 'peace studies' now being undertaken by you in time spared from a busy life at the hospital. Secondly, the Bomb is too incredible and insane an event to be fitted into the ordinary scale of language—i.e., you've been forced to compress much into myth and metaphor, and to resort to cosmic irony. However, on the bright side, your thinking seems clear and strong: that apathy—powerlessness—is a source of peril to life on earth strikes me as an idea worth further exploration in one form of rhetoric or another. Keep writing. Let me know how your study progresses, and, if there's anything further I can do to critique it candidly, don't hesitate to 'drop in' as you did this morning.

Good luck. Max Stebbins."

He did not immediately turn from his desk to study the woman who had, indeed, "dropped in." He slipped her manuscript into an envelope. It would be better if she read his criticism later. She would probably be boiling mad about his suspicions. Perhaps he'd stated them too bluntly. And why? She seemed an honest, cheerful person. She was a professional, a doctor. Even assuming that she had literary ambitions, even assuming that she had a friend who had recommended him for her reader, even assuming that she was naive enough to drop in on him, unannounced, at the farm, he did not think of her as the hustling type. Something didn't jibe. He felt sorry to have met her this way. He really liked this Fanny McPherson, had instinctively felt close to her from the first moment.

Outside, Sunday morning sparkling after the rain.

Sleeping late after his long meditative vigil with Kitty's ghost, he woke dreaming of piloting a silent aircraft, of floating, the earth lost in billowing seas of cloud, toward a massive mountain wall of pure undifferentiated snow-whiteness, incredibly sun-brilliant. Scarcely had he shaved, dressed, and cooked breakfast before Pharaoh started growling and there was the *pud pfft pfft* approaching the house. He had gone outside. She was straddling a Lambretta, the woman in white poloneck sweater and blue jeans who was removing helmet and goggles and shaking out long golden hair and, seeing him, greeting him in a naturally easy and friendly manner. She sang out some comical Spanish name preceded by "Doctor" and laughed: "My father was drunk when he named me." She said *dronk*, just a trace of accent, perhaps Hispanic.

"What can I do for you?"

She had her story cooked up. She served it rather breathlessly, sweeping hair from her eyes, fixing his eyes with her own.

"Are you sure I'm not bothering you, Professor Stebbins?"

"I'm prone to heart murmurs, doctor," Max said.

Why in the hell had he said that? Living alone too long, he supposed. *Going to fall in love again. You never learn.*

He turned to study this woman now. She was regarding him as if puzzled. An unmistakable current of emotion was passing between them. He was already thinking, *She might be a wonderful woman for me*. In the silence, he smiled, then she smiled. A soft smile, not mocking or flirtatious. In spite of any appearances to the contrary and in spite of her wonderfully intrepid character, she was a good woman.

"You're nice," he murmured aloud, not even trying to switch off the flow of feeling. That trace of grieving in her features: she was lonely, too, and touching his excited heart. "I apologize for the rotten joke about my heart, but I may have been looking for you all my life."

"I was looking for you, too," she said.

No, he thought. *She meant that*. She was not being seductive. Something was happening between strangers, swiftly, whatever pretence was masked. "I'm too old for you," he said. Fearful of infatuation, he wanted an obstacle erected immediately.

"Age is how you feel."

"I'm still married. I have a son almost eleven."

"You're unhappy," she said.

"It was a bad marriage."

"Why?"

Max met the twinkle in her gaze. "Ginny packed up and left last year. I don't blame her. I guess I had it coming. She wants domination, possession, money, success."

"Yuck," said Fanny.

"I held onto an illusion."

Fanny's look was sympathetic. "People can't stand much reality. T.S. Eliot. Pardon me." He pondered this and said, "As long as illusions don't become delusions."

"Is there no way out?" she asked.

"Yes," he said without pause. "Evolution of consciousness. Emergence of wholeness. One world. Equality. Should I go on?"

"I like what you say," said Fanny.

"Don't you think that pompous?"

"Why should I?"

"Ginny, by now, would have told me I'm bloody pompous."

"I like to hear you talk," said the other. "Tell me more. Tell me about your son."

He had wanted for a long time to talk to someone who could understand him. What about it, if his heart were bleeding? What about it, if separation from Chris burned like a boil on his heart? "Chris," he began, and love and bitterness mingled as he spoke. He and Chris had always adored each other. Ginny thought of her son as a possession needing to be groomed in a certain way in a New England boarding school. On the other hand, he thought it better that Chris be off to school than have to be exposed to two adults who were living a lie. So, in a way, he respected Ginny for packing up—and now, for wanting divorce. Yet he believed Chris would be happier living with him than without him altogether. When he visited Chris in New York at Christmastime, the bliss of a week's comradeship was dashed as the hour of Max's return to Poe's Hill came around, for then there was a gentle boy and his doting father, weeping the both of them unabashedly. It became time to leave. Doors had to be opened and shut, and at a streetcorner a shivering rheumyeyed Santa Claus tinkled a bell, and a haggard man, who could be an emblem for himself some future day, huddled in an army-surplus trenchcoat and gnawed, ravenously, on an eel. "I have hope for him," Max concluded. "He has good sense and a good heart."

"You're a loving man," said Fanny. There seemed to be nothing forced, nothing problematic in her tone. He made a clownish gesture, nodding after a shrug. "You're lovely," he said. She wrinkled her nose at him and scoffed, "My friends don't talk that way."

"You're some kind of nut."

"That's better. True, too," she half smiled. And glanced away, suddenly frowning, biting her lip. When she rose from the sofa, she seemed to appeal to him with her eyes. She drew her breath and said, "We seem to have gotten into a relationship more deeply than we bargained for. I don't want to get hurt, Max."

"I don't want to lose you," he said.

She half smiled again. "I don't want to lose you either, but—" She started toward the door.

"Don't go," Max said, rising. He felt an urgency he could not restrain. "Are you free? Are you spoken for?"

Turning to face him, her eyes softening. *Spoken for*: what an oldfashioned phrase he had just blurted out: what a fool he was just when, last night and early this morning, he had censured romantic longings. Yet he knew he was sincere! "I think we might be about perfect for each other," he declared, eyes cast downward before he stepped forward.

She waited for him, returned a long kiss. She was making a groaning sound in her throat as he caressed her body, breathed her hair. "Oh, Max."

"Stay."

"All right."

'We've got to talk. We've got to be completely honest."

'I know," she said.

"I'll start with one question,' he said, stroking her hair. "Who sent you here and why?"

She drew in breath sharply. But relaxed in his arms. "Dr. Hasbrouck, my godfather, is blackmailing me."

"I see," said Max after a pause. "And the sketch? Did you write it? Is that part of the ruse?"

"Part of the ruse, yes . . . It was the only thing I could think of for getting your attention. I did write it, though it's based upon notes taken by a scientist—friend of mine. He's dead now." Fanny's eyes were beseeching. "I'm sorry."

'Don't worry about it," Max said. "Hasbrouck has done us a favor. I think I love you."

"I think I love you, too."

"Let's talk in bed."

"All right," she said.

HE WAS IMPOTENT THE FIRST TIME.

As he and the lovely woman beside him in bed lay back, hot and unsatisfied, it was she who murmured softly, "Don't be unhappy. I'm happy. You just have a lot of images whirling around in your head saying *Don't*, and you think you have to prove something to me, and I'm willing to wait for as long as it takes . . . Your body is pleasing to me. I can stay till midnight. Then I do rounds on the maternity ward."

Max relaxed. It was true, images of Ginny, his parents, Kitty, Mrs. Pentecost, even Hasbrouck kept whirling in his head, but he knew he was free and he knew with an absolute clarity about destiny that the woman beside him was the one he *had* waited for all his life!

They lay and talked well into the afternoon and drank a bottle of red wine together.

Then his body became strong. Even then he was over-excited—too long, he thought, in prison—but his strength returned to him and he came into her even as she clung to him and cried,"I'm coming . . . Oh, I love you!"

ALL WAS WELL. THEY USUALLY MET IN HIS OFFICE about noon and had afternoons and evenings together until Fanny was due at the hospital. They made plans and set goals. He would sell Bermuda Farm—the state was already interested in developing the area as a historical site and recreational "facility"—and Fanny would complete internship in or near Santa Cruz where he would soon be making a new life. When he was divorced from Ginny and married to Fanny, he would do his utmost to have Chris come to live at home with them. They even had a plan for a mutual intellectual effort: they would take up "peace studies" together, he from the point of view of the Arts, she from that of the Sciences. No longer chained by the past, Max saw himself entering a future in which peace studies would be the primary study for humankind.

However, for the time being there was undeclared war, Hasbrouck's war. They decided that the best defense was to act as if Fanny were complying with his instructions and Max were going down the primrose path. When Hasbrouck's cards were on the table, Max and Fanny, acting in concert, would try to upset the game.

It happened that Fanny had been instructed to lure Max to a beach house at Nag's Head the weekend following her presumed seduction of him. On Saturday they set out in the Chevy and reached the Atlantic late in the afternoon. A short drive down the coastal highway of the Outer Banks and Max felt glad for having come. It was not only that the pioneering of the English-speaking peoples made, in this very place, its symbolic appeal to his spirit, but also that he had returned, after twenty-three years, to the place where he and Kitty had been young. He accepted this memory now as a dream that is green once only. And there was the sea. This was the sea with the ocean-river making warm and habitable a goodly portion of the civilized globe. He drove, breathed briny air and listened to the breakers.

But he had other things to think about. "Suppose Hasbrouck is at the house?" he wondered aloud.

Fanny commented, "Remember, I had two specific instructions: you were to be here this weekend at Nag's Head, and I must be with you at the farm on the afternoon of June the seventh. Now, I believe, he's just playing with you. Little conjuring tricks."

"For which he sells his immortal soul? We shall soon see, for here is the House of Usher, otherwise known as—" he slowed down, turned into a sandy driveway, and squinted at a sign—"

'NAG'S HEAD NOOK'—how original!—otherwise known as the House of the Horse's Ass."

"Do calm down," said Fanny.

The house was long, squat, and turquoise blue, no trees or shrubbery in sight. There was a motorboat attached to a trailer and a red sportscar beside it.

As he approached the house, Max could hear being played inside it a record with an ear-blasting, pelvic-thrusting beat. After he rang the doorbell, a young man in T-shirt and candystriped swim trunks opened the door.

Widge.

"**LOOK WHO'S HERE!" GUSHED WIDGE.** "Ole Cheesecake and—hiya, sir, c'mon in, I got my folks' place for the weekend . . . And don't you worry, sir, we got lotta booze and the chicks look good this time of year. Meet Kooks, my, uh, fiancée.' He pronounced it *fee-and-see.*

Max's glance had already taken in the obese young girl who was trying, it seemed, to imitate the sluttish drool of a nymphomaniac. She pressed right up to him, giggled, and spoke in a lewd nasal twang, "You're a trip, a whole trip."

"You said it, kid," said Max.

"C'mon, lover, let's dance." Kooks tugged him into a room with fitted lemon-yellow carpets. The hi-fi was sending forth a sound on the near side of hysteria:

I'm comin I'm comin O babybaby

Max just had time to see Fanny fluttering her eyelids before Kooks grabbed his buttocks and pushed herself against him with a rubbery motion. She said something inaudible.

"What's that, kid?"

"I said let's orgy."

"You said it, kid. How about a drink, kid?"

"Sure. Your bod is fantastic."

"Here's lookin' at you, kid."

"*Well*, Humphrey Bogart!"exclaimed Fanny half an hour later when they had managed to escape to a private bedroom and had locked the door. She closed her eyes, wriggled her hips, snapped her fingers. When she opened her eyes, he was silently laughing at her. "I think your bod is just fan-TAS-tic."

"Far out, kid," Max said. She snuggled into his arms. She was all he wanted.

"I really love you," she said.

"I'm glad," he murmured drowsily in her hair. His brain shook its cobwebs. "Because of Hasbrouck, we'll have to stay here in this house tonight. But let's take a long, long walk on the beach and not come back till the weirdos cool off. You know what Widge thinks he's getting out of this? He told me he expects me to pass him in English so he can graduate." Max shook his head in incredulity. "No way. No work, no way."

DRESSED WARMLY BUT BAREFOOTED, they walked along the strand for almost an hour before surroundings began to look familiar. Among a cluster of new cottages were some unpainted weatherbeaten ones which Max recalled having seen in the summer of forty-two. A little further down he recognized a sanddune from which he and Kitty and Mary Branch had meditatively looked out upon a war-torn sea.

The Pentecost cottage was gone without a trace. Where it should have been was a tarmac parking lot for a neon-lit motel.

Max whirled around, wounded. There in the breakers now glimmering in the sunset, he and Kitty had helped a stranded whale catch a neap tide. *My daughter is just a child . . . I'll write if you write me . . . Mind the serpent, boy, mind the serpent.*

He felt Fanny's hold on his arm tighten. "What is it, darling?"

"Voices."

"What kind of voices?"

"The dead."

They resumed their walk. After a while Max said. "Please forgive my mood. I am not estranged from you. We have come as close as I've ever been to anyone in my life . . . May I tell you a strange thing?"

They walked in the surf now. First one wave spent itself at their feet, cooling them, then another and another.

"I've been having a dream lately—since the day we met in fact. The dream keeps repeating itself . . . I am piloting a small plane. There are no sundazzled cumuli, only bright blue sky and something else: a snow-covered mountain, just a sheer brilliant mass of whiteness. In the dream I seem to be heading straight into it. I can't control the plane. The controls act of their own accord. The whiteness of the mountain looms larger and larger. It is a happy dream. The mountain, I seem to yearn for it. I seem to expect revelation. I am calm about this."

That woman who was all joy and comfort spoke to him then: "I do not dream as you, but I have thought of non-being many times without dread, absorbing, thinking rather of an impenetrable mystery—scientifically. Our bodies and brains are just so many atoms, yes . . . but our wisdom, our truth, our spirituality, are these not energies, energies *created* in us or by us? There is something in us, working through us, something non-material that, conceivably, exists in a timeless dimension. The Swiss psychiatrist, Dr. Jung, not too long ago was postulating a theory he called 'synchronicity,' an acausal but meaningful coincidence, like telepathic communication at the same time over distance. There is *something!*"

They walked and he held her close, as close as anyone had ever come to his soul.

There is a great joy, he reflected. A great joy. Streaming from the sun. Joy abiding in the grace of the deep, wave after wave whispering us the song of life, the song of earth. Even now earth-girdling seabirds sing in the grace of their glide. Even now, sweet woman companionable walking with me here, there is a great joy, for we are part of the whole. Wave after wave. And we shall not be lost but green in our grieving . . . All is one. Here, walking by this life-giving sea on this good earth where green grasses toil in the grace of the wind, we are free of the chains of flesh and mind. We are part of the whole and cannot be lost in the elements in which we are free. All, all is joy! Wave after wave after wave . . .

Chapter Eighteen **Fanny**

During the first week in June, Fanny received a telephone call at the hospital. A woman named Sally identified herself as Hasbrouck's secretary.

"He has a message for you. You're to hang in there and confirm whatever Widge says. Have you got that?"

"Yes," said Fanny. She could only vaguely surmise what that message meant but she knew that Max, like Carlos, was in danger.

"Have you a reply for Dr. Hasbrouck?"

"Tell him not to worry."

By the end of the week she understood the message completely. An official letter arrived from Dean Archibald Leary. Charges alleging gross moral misconduct had been made against Professor Stebbins, a faculty committee had been set up to investigate these charges on Monday night, and she was requested to be present as a material witness.

She loathed Hasbrouck now. She recognized the viciousness beneath the thin veneer of his benevolence. Hasbrouck had learned from her own lips how Carlos Brodie had been singled out and tormented. Now she was forced to participate in similar proceedings and expected to perjure herself. She had kept her nerve. Hasbrouck's little conjuring tricks seemed feeble and ludicrous; he could complicate simplicity itself. But she had underestimated a certain malignancy in his character. Accordingly, she now took very seriously the threat to expose her father to international authorities if she failed to do what Hasbrouck wanted.

She began to worry about how Max would be taking the news of his trial. She knew, because of what happened to Carlos, that a man's whole livelihood and honor were at stake and, more than that, his life.

Fortunately, Max knew he could depend on her. She had determined from the sudden beginning of their love that she would not shift the burden of her dilemma onto him. She would put her father's life at risk before Max's.

Unfortunately, she was on duty the entire weekend and would not be seeing Max until Monday morning. She did manage to reach him by telephone once, on Saturday, but the connection was so poor they rung off as soon as they had reassured one another that everything was going to be okay.

After an anxious, exhausting weekend, she pressed through the crowd assembling for Commencement and arrived at Max's office about mid-morning, Monday.

As she was about to knock, she heard Max shout angrily, "Get the hell out of here!" The door was jerked open. A young man dressed like a roué burst through, leaving a parting shot: "You blew it! They'll hang you by the shorts!" It was Widge. He brushed past Fanny, stopped, smirked. "Well, Ole Cheesecake. See ya tonight, baby . . . When you gonna give me a piece of the action?"

"Get the hell out, I said!" Max in the doorway, his eyes narrowed, his jaw jutting out: she had never seen him angry before.

She laughed as Widge sauntered out of sight. "You've frightened the little *gringo* bastard."

Max's good humor returned. "Come in, dear. Great news."

When they were seated side by side, he took her hand and began to explain. "First, that *student* has brewed a tempest in a teapot by lying to the authorities and the newspapers, charging that we were involved in a sex orgy that night at Nag's Head. The telephone has been ringing all weekend—incidentally, remind me to get it repaired—anyway, reporters, friends, and anonymous citizens who seem to have the our-girls-were-pure-till-you-came and the get-out-of-town-before-sundown approach to life—anyway, Widge has flunked my course and came here expecting me to change his grade in return for a withdrawal of his charges. Anyway . . ."

As he drew breath deeply, she squeezed his hand. "You're all nerves. Calm down. Tell me the great news."

"Coming to that," he resumed. "That day we met and you told me the story of your father, I had a hunch. I cabled an old friend of mine in London—retired R.A.F. squadron leader with influence in high places—and he has cabled me a confidential report. To wit, a sergeant-major disappeared from his regiment in India in thirty-six, but neither he nor any other Highlander of the period is wanted for a crime. What's more, our friend the squadron leader, in his droll humor, suggests that no Indian planter, homo or not, would have needed to resort to rape. Secondly, no Indian planters were executed in the time and place where your father has been convinced he so executed one. In other words, if Hasbrouck betrays the man known as Ritchie McPherson, it is unlikely that he, your father, will have much to answer for."

Fanny reflected ruefully, "Something convinced Ritchie he is an outlaw."

"Some*one* did—Hasbrouck. My theory is, Ritchie was blind *dronk* and Hasbrouck invented a story which both of them came to believe actually happened. Why? Hasbrouck wanted to send a sacrificial lamb to the slaughter in Spain to be a surrogate for his own fantasy about being a revolutionary. At any rate nothing ever happened to Hasbrouck, though *he's* in the records, you may be sure! He was reported as bribing natives to perform sex acts while he made scientific observations. The authorities evidently let him get away with this clinical voyeurism. If he'd been involved in the shooting of a planter, the story would have been different. That's the news."

THEY DROVE TO THE FARM WHERE MAX WAS EXPECTING a visitor in the early afternoon. Feeling groggy from fatigue and the heat of the day, Fanny excused herself from the visitor—Manny Branch—and went upstairs to the bedroom to take a nap. So much was happening she needed to pull her thoughts together and be clearheaded for the trial. In the meantime, something else might happen. Hasbrouck's instructions had been that she be present at the farm on this very afternoon.

After a while she was dozing off when Max entered, looking pleased with himself, rubbing his hands. 'How are you, dear?"

"Come here," she said.

She pulled his head to her breast. "I'm fine. You seem happy."

They kissed. He rose to go, his eyes glowing. "Manny has done a good deed in a naughty world. Tell you later." Max, after rummaging through a bureau, removed a necklace and went.

He returned after an interval. He and Manny were going for a swim. Would she like to come along? "I'll just rest," she said. "Take care."

"Oh," said Max from the doorway, "the telephone's busted. I was wondering why the lunatics haven't been threatening me this afternoon . . . I won't be long. You're beautiful."

Then he was gone, her laughing man.

From the window, she saw him running boyishly across fields. He disappeared in the woods which shimmered as though seen through a glass-bottomed boat.

Cafroom!

A car coming: Fanny peeped from behind a curtain and saw Hasbrouck's Jaguar stopping by the front door. Two people climbed out, Hasbrouck in a tropical suit and the other a woman about her own age.

Ginny, thought Fanny. *That's why I'm here.*

"He's home. That's Max's crummy car," said the woman.

"I told you before," said Hasbrouck with an irritable tone.

"He must have heard us by now. Call."

"I'll do nothing of the kind. I told you before, it's quite embarrassing knowing he keeps a woman . . ."

"Shut up, why don't you?" said the other. She smoked a cigarette and spoke without removing it from her lips.

Cupping his mouth, Hasbrouck called, "Anybody home?" He disappeared from Fanny's sight. Presently she heard him call from inside the house. "Anybody home?"

Fanny could feel her heart beating faster. If they were to both come in, she would go down and face them alone.

"No answer, Ginny."

"Probably at the river."

"That's a thought," said Hasbrouck. "You go ahead. I'll pop into the loo for a sec."

Ginny started walking. Fanny slipped out of the bedroom and crouched by the stairwell where she had a partial view of the front door and livingroom.

Hasbrouck entered.

She expected him to turn toward the kitchen, near which was a downstairs toilet. Instead, he scurried into the livingroom and quickly removed books from a recessed shelf by the fireplace. Presently he was replacing the books. Fanny ducked out of sight.

She had decided what to do before she heard the front door

slammed shut, even before, once again from the bedroom window, she saw that huge animal striding toward the woods, his hands clasped behind his back as if he were—as her father had discovered—strolling across a Fellows Garden in Oxford.

That was it: Hasbrouck was always pretending to be an English toff, puffing on imaginary cigars, listening to improbable royal fanfares, imitator in all things—even in performing the sort of fifth-rate cloak-and-dagger trick which she had just observed. Playing a role, he cast other people into roles. Ritchie, for instance. She seldom heard her father speak in heavy Scottish accent, but on the occasion of Hasbrouck's visit to California, Ritchie had laid it thickly on: the stereotyped Scotsman performing. No wonder Hasbrouck and, on that occasion, Ritchie, seemed too good to be true and larger than life.

But something else too. Fanny's thought raced as she waited for Hasbrouck to vanish into the woods. What she hadn't understood until Carlos was destroyed was apathy: there could be a condition without passion. That which seemed on the surface larger than life was in fact smaller and meaner and cheaper than life, a cold war of relationships.

In these terms she regarded Hasbrouck. She didn't hate him. On the other hand she couldn't pity him until he had been exposed.

The woods swallowed him. Fanny moved quickly.

Hidden in Max's bookshelf was what looked like a carton of cigarettes. She had already guessed that the carton would contain a substance far more lethal and incriminating than tobacco. In another moment she knew she was right.

"Stupid *gringo*," she muttered when she had opened the carton and found that it contained enough cocaine to overdose all the doctors at the hospital.

PART V

Chapter Nineteen **Max, Kitty**

The Tuscarora River springs from the Appalachians and meanders down some four hundred miles of wilderness and fertile farmland to the ocean. It is not a big river; little of it is navigable except by canoe. Early settlers avoided it in their push westward. Gradually, however, people came and left here a tumbledown watermill, there the gaunt granite teeth of a railway bridge blown up by retreating Confederate armies. The Indian, retreating long before these, left arrowheads, not least on high bluffs in the vicinity of Bermuda Farm. There is a legend of the Indian maiden so tormented by the Devil that she leapt from the bluffs—but was transformed, as she fell those several hundred feet, into the redbird, prolific in the region. Max knew that another kind of transformation was coming. Within a decade a hydroelectric dam would be constructed not far downstream from the farm. The river and thousands of acres of wilderness and farmland would be obliterated. The dam, the very prospect of which was sending property values soaring, would provide more than power for cities such as Poe's Hill. It would also give their inhabitants recreation. There would be speedboats whining where now the redbirds flew. There would be pleasure cruisers equipped with television, with refrigerators, and with toilets that flushed directly into dead water. Instead of catfish, future fishermen would catch beercans, excrement, condoms, and sanitary napkins.

Max stood on a blowing rock of the bluffs. Far below him, Manny Branch's head bobbed in the water.

Soon, Max was thinking, he would leave for California. He had no illusions about it: the story of Progress would be repeating itself wherever he went. Still, he had always been essentially of the West and wanted that larger sky.

The significance of Kitty's letters was just fully dawning upon him. If he had received them during the war, he would not have had rankling in his heart, all these years, the sense of failure and inadequacy. Perhaps she had not rejected him, after all; perhaps she had requited his love and then renounced it. But renunciation was a positive, earlier knowledge of which might well have cleared his path of its moral and psychological entanglements. Now in the summer of life he saw himself as a man radically opposed to every form of tyranny, a kind of Jeffersonian man, not an Emersonian subdue-the-wilderness-for-God man like his father and his father's father and generations before them.

He had had his dream again last night, the premonitory dream which he had disclosed to Fanny. The blank white mountain seemed nearer now.

Ah well, he would swim.

He turned and there, quite close, stood Ginny and Dr. Hasbrouck.

"Hello , Max."

"Hello, Irish."

"Old boy," said Hasbrouck,"you'd best come with us to the house. We have urgent matters to discuss."

"As you wish," said Max, silently worried whether he could

protect Fanny from the sort of outrage Ginny's and Hasbrouck's intrusion, in itself, threatened.

THE PRELIMINARY SKIRMISHING had taken about half an hour, Max and Fanny on one side of a coffee table, Ginny and Hasbrouck on the other. Hasbrouck had done most of the talking. Ginny smoked and sulked.

Since a game had to be played, Max waited until it came his turn to speak. "You want me to acknowledge Tom Driver as my son? If I do this, you, Ginny, may be willing to take me back. If I don't, you proceed with the divorce and Adam's lawyers launch a million-dollar paternity suit against me. Right?"

GINNY:

That's the way the cookie crumbles.

MAX:

Yet you ask this of a man whom you no longer love and who no longer loves you. You're so full of guilt you'd like to project it onto me and toss me overboard.

GINNY:

You're the one thinks he's so bloody superior. Next, you'll be comparing yourself to Our Lord Jesus Christ.

MAX:

Our Lord Jesus Christ?

GINNY:

Jesus has been a great comfort to me lately.

MAX:

Then confess to me, my child, what hast thou done with my son Christopher?

GINNY:

Chris needs discipline. I'm removing him from his present school and placing him under the charge of the Jesuits.

MAX:

We shall see . . . what the divorce court permits.

GINNY:

I shall have total custody, no fear. The university will fire you for moral turpitude, the police will convict you of sex with minors. I shall expose you for adultery. What is your name, darling?

FANNY:

Epifania Beneficia McPherson. I'll write it down for you on a prescription for sleeping pills. You'll need them.

GINNY:

You and your Chicano tart would hardly qualify as guardians.

MAX:

I thought you were a *nice* bitch.

HASBROUCK:

See here, you insolent whelp!

MAX:

My apologies. I'll take that back. Ginny, you're not a nice bitch . . . Tell me now. I thought we were having an amicable separation culminating, say, in a civilized divorce based upon the breakdown of the marriage. Do I understand you to mean you feel so aggrieved that you want blame fixed solely on me?

GINNY:

How dare you live here in sin while you neglect your own son!

MAX:

A school for cuckolds.

GINNY:

Of course, if you acknowledge Tom Driver as your son—come to terms with yourself for once—Chris and I will welcome you home after your years in prison. You're going to lose your job tonight. You're too old to succeed at something else. I shall soon be in the money. I'll see that you're looked after.

MAX:

I'm touched.

HASBROUCK:

What an indecent fellow!

MAX:

Just a minute. What am I supposed to do about your adultery with the old fart here?

GINNY:

What?

HASBROUCK:

How dare you!

MAX:

Your adultery. There's one for Jesus! Cast the first stone! I've been wearing horns for some time and being civil about it. If you're going to play games with the law, I shall be forced to sue Adam for alienating my wife's affections. It will cost you plenty.

HASBROUCK:

Seducer! Corrupter!

MAX:

Are you positive Kitty named me as father of her bastard?

HASBROUCK:

You smear Kitty. Bless her heart in heaven, she cannot be here to defend her honor.

MAX:

On the contrary.

HASBROUCK:

What do you mean?

MAX:

Shall I read to you her testimony in the matter? It's here.

HASBROUCK:

Ah, I see . . . The colored boy sold you the letters.

MAX:

You don't look so white yourself, old boy. Shall I read the letters, selectively of course? Ginny?

GINNY:

Well . . . all right.

MAX PICKED KITTY'S LETTERS UP FROM THE TABLE and began to read them: "The first letter is dated August 26th, 1942, from the Pentecost cottage at Nag's Head. I had spent my furlough with the family there and had just left them, being under orders to go overseas . . . 'Dear Max' . . ."

> I wonder where you are now, Max, what you are thinking. In ten days I'll be home in Poe's Hill, hoping to have a letter from you awaiting me there. I want to know everything you see and do. Write me your deepest impressions, as Mother would say . . . Mary is taking care of Mrs. Toogood's tabby's litter of kittens because the hurricane blew off the tin roof of the Toogood store so the cat took shelter under the tin roof where it lay, and the kits were born there. Life must go on! . . . Something terrible happened today. Another sailor's body was washed ashore from the torpedoed tanker. Father laid his jacket over the body. I've been crying all day. Nothing must happen to you, you *will* come back! . . . Mother has another view of religion from Father's, as you know. Sin, sin, sin, that's her view. Today she announces that the end of the world is nearer than she had thought. She's taking the bus back to Poe's Hill tomorrow in order to consult with her preacher there, an evangelist called Billy Raven. While she prepares for the wrath to come, Father and Mary and I have to visit her kinfolk in Old Charleston . . .

Charleston. August 30, 1942 . . . There are so many of Mother's kinfolk here that we could judge ourselves not only the Best Family but also the Only one, the family Ball like Old Man River, just rolling along. Modestly, we claim descent from people in history books—from Charlemagne and other Southern gentlemen—though we know damned well we were here before the Flood! . . . All day long I've been 'shown off' to a hencoopful of *charmin'* old ladies. Cousins Annie and Louise are my favorites. They speak of themselves as of a single organism. Says Annie with a look at Louise, '*Our* stomach is out of order today.' They dress as twins in long white pique skirts and white kid gloves fresh out of boxes from pre-war France. Before the war they used to throw away their soiled gloves because they could easily buy new, but now they are down to the last box. They're quite impatient for the liberation of France for reasons having little to do with a crusade for freedom. Did you know you are fighting to provide us ladies with white kid gloves? . . . Cousin Georgiana, however, is a vicious, frustrated old prune. She has set out to do what the others are too well-bred to do: to hurt my feelings. She said such horrible things about Mother that I knew they couldn't be true and even now I'm so mad I could wring Georgiana's stringy neck. She began in the most offensive way: 'I suppose, Miss Kitty, you are aware that your grandfather, Major Ball, was a debauched and blackhearted scoundrel? What? You're not? Well, surely you must have heard, et cetera.' On she went and, dear God, I was forced to listen . . .

"I'll skip here," said Max as his eyes identified the passage that confirmed the discoveries of Manny Branch. But he re-read the passage silently to himself: 'According to Cousin Georgiana, my grandfather, just before he died, confessed that he had lived with my mother *as man and wife* since she was about thirteen. How could such a vile story have been made up to make me feel horrid! What can I say to anyone if all these years they have been believing this revolting lie? How am I to see Mother again without thinking of the lie? Come back and take me away and help me to *live*, Max dearest. Major Ball raped his own daughter. Major Ball got her with child. Surely you must have heard, Miss Kitty, surely you must have heard . . . What if I am like my mother?'

Hasbrouck shifted restlessly, twiddled his thumbs. "This is getting us nowhere," he complained. "Do get on with it."

Max resumed his reading:

> Charleston, Aug. 31st. 6:00 A.M. . . . Mary told my father I wasn't well, and he came in and we had a long wonderful talk. I said nothing of Cousin Georgiana Prunehead's filth. Mary will mail this after breakfast . . . I don't think I ever realized before what a truly good man my father is. I know he has some weaknesses, and these used to infuriate me, especially his not standing up to Mother. But he's strong inside. And he's good company when he has sea air in his lungs and is away from her. He speaks of her with unfailing kindness. He told me of her courage when, during a snowstorm in the Caucasus, she delivered herself of a stillborn child and next day resumed the journey they had been making from Tiflis to Kurdistan via *ox-cart*. They saw Mount Ararat for three days, an experience that seemed to revive her at once. And Father, too, he was something of a rough diamond when he was young before the Great War. He traveled by camel up the Fraser River to Lake Caribou in British Columbia, panned for gold there,

and was a loggerman in Oregon, never a cowboy but he rode a horse into the Badlands of Dakota and studied fossil rocks, and his calling to the ministry came about through science, through understanding the miraculous Creation. If he hadn't been gassed in the war and made half-blind ever since, he might have had better luck as a scholar, but he gave up his studies and became a missionary. He says, with his big round eyes twinkling, the wild Kurdish tribesmen liked his horseback riding much better than his religion . . . I told him I wanted you to live in his family's homestead on the Tuscarora River. He is, as President Teddy Roosevelt used to say, 'dee-lighted.' He says you have the love of the land in you. He says the love of the land is indispensable to the sense of common responsibility that holds people together . . . He looks so ill and tired. I don't think Mother's kinfolk are any better for him than Mother. How a man as sincere as he is can put up with slanderous gossip and sly innuendo, not to mention snobbery and prejudice, I declare I don't know. Even Cousins Annie and Louise bob their heads together and screech like a pair of sick parrots. For instance, they told me that a poor Negro, who had worked for Major Ball in this very house where I am staying, was sentenced close to life imprisonment for assaulting a half-witted girl from the neighborhood. 'We know he was innocent,' said Cousin Annie, nodding enigmatically to Cousin Louise. 'We know things.' And Cousin Louise nodded enigmatically to Cousin Annie and said, 'We are silent.' Thank goodness we'll be leaving for home soon . . .

137 Cornwallis Street, Poe's Hill. September 10,1942 . . . The mail must be delayed. Maybe my letters haven't caught

up with you as yet. Gloom prevails here. Every day another classmate seems to be missing—'joined up.' An early fall does, however, brighten the scene.

Green day soon catches fire
Leaves the thorn of desire

I've been reading John Donne's poetry and I'm full of paradoxes. But now is the time to be straight with you because I love you. As you know, there was 'someone else' before we met ('And now good-morrow to our waking souls . . .'). He was a big baby twice my age. I guess I knew he was lying to me. We've made a pretty mess of things. I keep myself going by imagining that his child, the child I carry is *ours*. The world is so loveless, I despair of bringing into it a child not made of love. I want my child to grow up believing in something—dear God, in *something!* I want to preserve, if I can, the memory of what you and I have been to each other. This will be my child's inheritance: to have you as spiritual father . . . Both Mother and Mary already know about the child and assume that you are the father. I neither affirm nor deny their assumption because I shall be waiting to hear whether you agree to 'spiritual fatherhood'. . . I'm going to see life through, whatever happens. Even in misery, it is wonderful to be alive. I feel very humble and grateful. I shall gather falling leaves and dream of early daffodils.

It was Fanny who broke the silence. "Thank you for reading that," she said softly. "She must have been a beautiful person."

Max refrained from comment. He leveled his gaze first at Ginny, then Hasbrouck, and waited.

'What do you say, Adam?" This from Ginny.

Hasbrouck mopped his face and neck with a handkerchief and addressed himself to no one in particular. "Some trickery here. Max may have forged the letters and given them to Mary Branch to give to me."

'The envelopes are postmarked," Max said. "Your wife's handwriting would be impossible to imitate."

"You're a good player," said Hasbrouck. "I, for one, am not convinced."

"Suit yourself," said Max. "There is one more letter."

> 137 Cornwallis Street. Poe's Hill. December 7, 1942 . . . Dear Max: A year has passed since the declaration of war and almost five months without seeing you or hearing from you. Some day, perhaps, another woman's love will reveal what I feel about you . . . When born, the child is to be taken up for adoption. Mother made the arrangements, although, had you been willing to 'affiliate,' I might have resisted them—and her . . . Father died six weeks ago after a severe stroke. Mother has had masses of wonderful letters which have been a great help to us, but she finds answering them very exhausting, particularly to people whom she and Father knew best. I have been answering for her. That is one reason why I am late in letting you know.
>
> He was not well when we were in Charleston, but he was cheerful and making a huge effort. The stroke was on a Monday. Luckily he had a single room at the university hospital so we could be there day and night. He just kept going until the Friday morning, then died in the afternoon. It was horrid.
>
> The funeral was on the following Wednesday. It was a lovely crisp October day. There was a service at the university chapel. It was packed and people were standing

inside. Somehow I had never realized how well-known Father was. The coffin was covered with the Stars and Stripes. Father's medals were displayed alongside one beautiful red and white wreath. We sang his favorite psalms, 'Eternal Father Strong to Save' and 'Who Would True Valor See.' It was a fine funeral. We felt desperately proud of him. He himself would have thought the service okay. Mother was quite magnificent. We took the lead from her. I see now that Father would have been lost without her. It was in its way a good partnership.

The dean of the chapel took the service and said Father had such spirit and zest for life while at the same time standing for all that is right and proper. The dean asked Mother if she wanted anyone to 'say a few words' and her reply was, 'No, thank you very much, if people don't know by now that D.D. was a good man, then they wouldn't have come.' Judging by the number of people there, I think they did know that he was a good man. It was a good remark, Mother's.

I have left school now. Mother does not allow me to leave the house. I have no desire to go out. The House of Pentecost once felt, to me, as if it were suspended on air. Now it has been dashed to the ground. Those of us still living inside have been crushed and forgotten.

Love, Kitty

"When will Hasbouck's war end?" Max pondered aloud in dismay fifteen minutes later as the Jaguar sped out of sight.

"Ginny's not bad," said Fanny. "But she'll never change. She thinks she has Hasbrouck's money in the bag. They believe they're off to Hollywood. Actually they're off to prison. What a big deal."

Max chuckled to be companionable. "I think the old boy's

infatuated with her."

"Not with her, but because she was *your* woman. He wants to strip you of everything except your funky old car."

It was true. When Max had read the final letter, Hasbrouck had querried, "How much do you want for this farm, cash on the barrel?" When Max informed him that the property had recently been appraised as worth a quarter of a million dollars, Hasbrouck had not flinched. "Don't sell to anyone until you hear from me in two days. Ginny and I are flying to Los Angeles tonight to find the right chap to direct her in the film I'm producing. Which reminds me." Hasbrouck had risen, was already making for the door. "I've recused myself from chairing your committee tonight. Archie Leary will take over. You'll get a fair hearing. If I were you, old chap, I'd sell up and get out of this town." Max had to smile. He said nothing. As soon as he could, he did not restrain himself from pleading with Ginny, 'For God's sake, don't go with that man!"

Ginny had hesitated as she crushed one of her eternal cigarettes. "Is this dump really worth a quarter of a million?"

"If we settle our affairs amicably, you shall have your share. But don't go with that man."

"No," she said after a long pause. "A star is born. Goodbye, darlings."

MAX APPROACHED THE HOUR OF THE HEARING with confidence, aware, for a start, that charges of gross moral turpitude were rare and difficult to prove. However, such were the peculiarities of academic institutions that he knew an offense need not be criminal in nature to produce dismissal from office and virtual disbarment from one's chosen profession. Part of what was at stake was something rather medieval: his honor, that old quixotic abstraction vaguely related to the quality of a man's devotion to the common welfare. Although Max felt confident of acquittal, he knew that some people could, possibly, ignore the facts and greet him with hoots of derision and cries of execration. Funny, that had been the resolution of Kafka's novel, *The Trial*, the very book Ginny had been reading when he met her.

At eight o'clock in the marble corridor of Henry Memorial Building there had assembled, in fact, a small mob of people he didn't recognize. An armed campus policeman cleared the way for Max and Fanny. An eerie hush descended on the mob, and a few flashbulbs exploded in his eyes like incendiary bombs.

It was a relief to be shut inside the relative sanctuary of the Jasper Henry Room. Thick white carpets, oil-gleaming imitation Chippendale chairs, a limp American flag, a long conference table made of laminated wood, and, peering benignly down on all these furnishings, the painted countenance of the Founder, a bearded man in ministerial black who had made his fortune in the slave trade. Ginny had been right about tackiness and mediocrity.

The committee had already been seated at the one end of the conference table, Dean Archibald Leary at its head. To one side, evidently present as an observer, sat President Wee Willie Koontz; opposite him, looking fidgety, sat Widge and, looking demure at 250 pounds, Miss Kooks.

There was an atmosphere of strained formality. Members of the committee, whom Max knew by sight but had never had personal dealings with, fiddled pencils and glanced away from him. Leary did the talking. Fanny was motioned to a seat beside Kooks, Max to the isolated end of the conference table. He was asked if he objected to the presence of President Koontz. Max, quickly considering that that small man smoking his small pipe might be an ally, replied in the negative.

Leary, the ardent Yankee, cleared his throat and began. "Certain offenses alleged to have been committed by Professor Stebbins are to be investigated here. Their purport is gross moral turpitude involving the corruption of the young by a responsible member of our faculty. Late last week the following charges were made, to wit, one, that at Nag's Head on a weekend a month ago Professor Stebbins joined with three of his students—namely, Miss Fanny McPherson, Miss Lena May Kooks, and Mr. Bob No-Middle-Initial Widge—in sexual activity involving group sex, partner swapping, and two acts, on the part of Professor Stebbins with a minor, Miss Kooks, of deviate intercourse; and, two, that, prior to this weekend, Professor Stebbins threatened to block Mr. Widge's graduation unless he made arrangements for this, uh, party, which he subsequently did, procuring his family's summer home at Nag's Head for this purpose; and, three, after the alleged incident took place, Professor Stebbins threatened Mr. Widge with grievous bodily harm if the alleged incident were reported to proper authority. Mr. Widge has come forward. I shall begin by asking him if I have correctly summarized his allegations."

Widge, lolling head to one side, said, "Yes, sir."

"Does anyone else wish to comment on the allegations as written?"

"Yes," said Fanny.

"Miss McPherson?"

"*Doctor* McPherson. I'm a Doctor of Medicine interning at University Hospital. I am not Professor Stebbins's student. I'm his mistress."

Several committee members chuckled audibly. Wee Willie Koontz's face lit up in merriment.

Leary proceeded. "Any other comments?"

"Yes," said Max. "Miss Kooks is not now and never has been a student of mine. Mr. Widge introduced her to me at Nag's Head as his *fiancée*, though I imagined at the time that she might be associated with a kind of institution far more ancient than a university."

"Let me understand this correctly," said Leary, who may have been repressing a smile, Max couldn't be sure. "Of the three persons named in the allegations, only one, Mr. Widge, has been your student at all, and one, Dr. McPherson, is not a student but —ahem—your mistress . . . I will now ask Professor Stebbins how he will answer, substantively, the allegations that have been made. Take your time. This is not a kangaroo court. You are free to present facts as you see them and to interpret the facts with a view to placing them in any light you deem favorable to your, uh, case."

Eyes were now upon him. By a curious reversal Max, called to assert his innocence under conditions of solemn foolery, felt a strange resurfacing of his old despondency. Was there, obscured to his perception, some flaw in his character that exposed him to, and justified, the contumely of his fellows? Or was his exposure simply the common fate, each person contending among bewildering, warring passions? Whatever the answer, he was now to speak for himself. 'Gentlemen," he began, "if my life were a pilgrimage, I would have to judge it peculiarly bogged down in the slough of the non-event." Max then went on to explain that his so-called "trial" was based on a non-event, that Hasbrouck, blackmailing Fanny, had planned it, so that eventually three persons would give perjured testimony about something that had never happened. As for Miss Kooks, her sexual advances had been so obvious from the time of his arrival that he and Dr. McPherson left the Nag's Head cottage, returned late, locked the bedroom door against the others, and drove home early next morning. As for the allegation that he had threatened Mr. Widge, the truth was exactly the obverse: as recently as that very morning Widge had pulled out a knife and threatened him unless he agreed to change a failing mark to a pass. He, Max, had refused to be intimidated. "The truth, I fancy," Max concluded, "rests with Dr. Hasbrouck for reasons best known to himself. For the time being, please request Dr. McPherson to corroborate the facts as I have related them."

While speaking, Max noticed that Dean Leary and President Koontz exchanged meaningful glances. Turning then to Fanny, Leary queried, "Is this true that Dr. Hasbrouck has been blackmailing you?"

"That is true," said Fanny without hesitation. "Dr. Hasbrouck is my godfather and has tried to blackmail me by exposing a certain 'non-event' in my own father's past . . . At the present time Dr. Hasbrouck should be at the airport, along with Mrs. Stebbins. I would suggest that this hearing be suspended until Dr. Hasbrouck can be called before it, unless he's already in jail."

"I move to suspend the hearing," said a committee member.

"Seconded," said another.

"The motion is to suspend the hearing until Dr. Hasbrouck's testimony can be heard," declared Leary. "All in favor say Aye."

"Aye," was the committee's unanimous voice.

"The motion is carried. Will somebody please call the airport?" Leary and Koontz rose and approached Max and shook his hand warmly. "What a lot of crap," said Leary, the pawky humor of the Yankee in his tone. "Jesus H. Christ, we've been waiting donkey's years for someone to bust that old fakir, Hasbrouck. We are in with a chance."

President Wee Willie Koontz stopped puffing on his pipe. "Something fishy. Long time," he remarked and resumed smoking.

Leary was more expansive. "Stebbins, always liked the way you stuck up for Carlos Brodie. Of course Socrates was invited to commit suicide for trying to make people *think*. Here in this school for scandalmongers, ideas flourish but men are condemned either for a lack of production or for misconduct which might prove a non-event. Either way, Wee Willie and I have virtually had our hands tied because Hasbrouck has enough goddam money to buy the whole university."

A few minutes later one of the committee members came and whispered in Leary's ear. At first he nodded gravely. Then he shook his head and raised his arms in a gesture of incredulity, exclaiming, "Jesus H. Christ, gentlemen, Dr. Hasbrouck and Mrs. Stebbins have been arrested in possession of a large supply of cocaine! Can you beat that?. . Hey, *look out!*"

Everything happened so swiftly that Max had just felt the body hurtling past him, had just heard Fanny scream, and had just seen Widge sprawl motionless on the carpet, the switchblade that had been in his hand glinting on the carpet, before it was clear that Widge had lunged at Fanny and had collided with the fist of Wee Willie Koontz. Someone was already shouting for the campus police. Koontz was dusting his hands.

"Lucky punch. Coldcocked him. Olympic bantamweight. Let's have a drink," declared the president of South Atlantic University. His pipe, short as his stature and words, was tucked into a broad grin.

Chapter Twenty **Manny**

He saw her first through the window on Watauga Street, Mary, busy in the kitchen, silhouetted against window's blaze of dying sun. Cooking supper and dressedup, too, even in her crazy bonnet: he would tease her about that. You would go down many roads, you would pass through many a city, you would be wandering for many years among many nations and peoples, and always it would be slow—glacier-slow, Buck McKay had said—the tree of man's evolution to convergence. It would be slow, slow and burdensome, but the convergence tree was spreading its branches and, little by little, wherever the evening suns went down, wherever he would be, just then, appearing and being at one with his brothers black and white, the people of the planet would kindle their fires and strike off their chains and arise, in a new dawn, free. He thought he would always remember her as he saw her now, the good woman comforting, protecting, and prevailing, and he was glad she had not yet taken down the star and presence of his father. The war, after all, was not over. Indeed, it had just begun to enter the days when many a son, as he, would go forth to spread the word like a flame: love.

Goodbye, Mama. I must go now.

He entered the house. Things were sizzling on the stove. There was an aroma of frying chicken and baking bread.

"You always cook with your Sunday hat on, Mama?"

She swept him with one of her best looks. "Hmmph," she said.

"You know I did the right thing, Mama. The letters belonged to Dr. Stebbins and he 'sho pre-chated' them. Had me a swim, fished a spell with Pap, thought about everything, felt good. I got to go now, Mama, right away tonight. You know that."

"New York? That sales-man? Hmmph."

"Maybe that, too." He went into the kitchen and put his arms around her. She hugged him fiercely, then let him go. Finished now, released and blessed. He would go first to New York but then travel, like Big Sam selling Books of Knowledge, and he would meet people throughout the land, fusing his life with theirs until his voice was also their voice.

"Gawn now," said Mary. "Get fixed for supper. We got somebody coming."

"Mrs. Pentecost?" Manny teased.

"That who."

"*What!* You crazy?"

"Time somebody got crazy. She ain't got nobody."

Manny felt blood pulsing at temples. "I know about you and her. I wasn't going to say it before."

"You shut," said Mama. "Maybe she is my mama, maybe Pap knows it too, but she's an old old woman now with no peace in her heart, and she were good to me, give me my way in this world—and maybe give me something else."

"Oh?" Manny queried, recognizing a familiar tone, the stubborn caprice with which she wound up her mind like a clock.

"Maybe give me the house on Cornwallis Street where Miss Helen and Miss Kitty's Tom been living."

"So that's it," said Manny after a pause. "After all the pain, what you want for a result is some more real estate." At the back of his mind he heard the *shoo shoo shoo* of Buck McKay's propeller fan spinning destinies slowly. "Do what you want but I'm going now in a few minutes. Pap will be real late. Said he saw Ole Red-Eye again today but hasn't caught him yet. Said to tell you he may be real late."

Mary stooped to place a pie in the oven. When she straightened up, she removed her bonnet and smoothed back strands of gray hair. "Well," she sighed," all things in the Lord's time. You got to understand the old folks, Manny. The trials is over and they can't do nothing about who won or lost, they was all just standing them together. They feel good when other folks prechate how they were all standing their trials together."

Manny had not forgotten the golden fish which Stebbins had given him to use, possibly to force Mrs. Pentecost into a confession. Although he felt almost certain he would do nothing—now seeing her and everyone else as moths of destiny—he feared he might drift into passivity and end up by forgiving everybody. "What time is she coming?" he asked.

Mary wiped her hands on her apron and shook head.

"Now, if she's coming. Had my sea-feelings all day. Maybe she ain't coming."

When in the late dusk Mrs. Pentecost had not arrived, Mary went to the kiosk to telephone the Confederate Daughters Home. Presently she returned and slumped in the rockingchair, her body restricted in motion to its breathing.

Manny observed her a while before speaking. "I'll stay to supper before I hit the road, Mama."

"All right."

"She was never coming, Mama." Before Manny's inner eye flitted the jaundiced visage of Major Ball, the ancestral debauchee. "She *couldn't* come, Mama. You are the first and now the last of her daughters to be betrayed."

"Manny?"

Her voice was close to tears.

"Yessum?"

"She's done dead. Done dead."

Chapter Twenty One **Judge Babbage, Mrs. Pentecost**

Sharkfinned cars glide by schooled for home at five o'clock. Pyramid shadow of the statue of the Confederate Soldier lengthens across a stone bench. The whiterobed old woman slumps there apparently asleep like Time without an hourglass and scythe.

Overhead, helicopters go *pocka pocka pocka.*

It's an outrage, thought Judge Debnam Babbage. He was observing the police helicopters from his chambers in the Court House. His bow-string tie adjusted, his Panama straw hat in place, he was preparing to go home when he thought he knew that old woman, Pentecost's widow. He shook his head.

But ah—let them out in the glorious sunshine. Bit of old America. Made them out of whalebone and vinegar then. Tough as wheat. Then, nobody pushed them around, breathed down their necks. Faith, sir, to move mountains.

WHITE SEA UNFOLDING, SLUMPING ITS THUNDERING TORAH.

She sees the flowing manes of the waves, she hears their silent hooves approaching.

The Lord of Hosts comes riding the Chariot of His Will.

She feels her spirit stir to greet Him. Soon her heart will burst its cocoon of sleeping wings.

If the sky fall. If the sky fall, we shall catch larks: Lady Mandeville-Gordon said that.

His Chariot is nearer. Whiter the sea, louder the hooves.

There are no larks in America. Pity, said Lady Mandeville-Gordon. Who will sing at Heaven's gate?

The Lord is my shepherd, I shall not want.

And the Lord of Hosts comes riding the Chariot of His Will.

When we arrived at the Dead Sea, Mr. Pentecost rolled up his white flannel trousers and went wading according to his custom. Then we went to the little English hotel where a cup of strong tea revived me after our long voyage. In the evening Colonel and Lady Mandeville-Gordon of the Mission Aid Society undertook to dissuade Mr. Pentecost from going to the Caucasian city from which we were to set out for Kurdistan in the spring. Indeed, since our marriage that fall, Mr. Pentecost and I had been so continually on the move that we had not heard of events in that city, events that would now put our lives in danger should we proceed according to God's plan. For as the city was in revolt and Christians were being exterminated or enslaved, we might expect anything to happen, at the very least to be forced to proceed, unescorted and ill-provided-for, over the mountains in winter. To all which Mr. Pentecost replied that, as for hardship, he had lived much of his life out of doors and had been in the Great War from Chateau-Thierry to the Ardennes, and that, as for provision, the Lord would provide, and that, besides, if he did not take ship to the Caucasian city, he would miss the opportunity of rolling up his trousers and of wading in several more of the great waters of the world. On the other hand, Mr. Pentecost continued, he had reason to conjecture that I had recently been blessed with a delicate condition and was accordingly strongly advised to remain in the Holy City until such time as was fitting and safe for myself and child to follow him to the Kurdistan Mission. Nonsense, I said. I go with my husband, even unto martyrdom. Lady Mandeville-Gordon laughed and said, If the sky fall, we shall catch larks.

Hooves clatter soundlessly on the cobblestones of the dawn.

I had been in my delicate condition for six months during which time Mr. Pentecost kindly refrained from indulgence of that conjugal lust which, however acceptable in the eyes of the Lord, was yet associated in my mind with my father's unspeakable but irresistible and pitiable depravity. Mr. Pentecost's patience was rewarded by the happiness, the first I had ever known, that began to catch my spirit unawares and radiate from my countenance; and the prospect of bringing forth in joy the child of love grew every day brighter and brighter until it seemeth to me the Lord would yet forgive me my sins and save me up to His Kingdom in the Latter Days. Often in the past I had reviled myself, battered my head and clawed my breast until blood dripped from my fingernails. And when my father knew me and I had conceived an abomination within my womb, had the Lord not stayed my hand, I had dashed myself to pieces. WILT THOU ALSO DISANNUL MY JUDGMENT? WILT THOU CONDEMN ME, THAT THOU MAYEST BE RIGHTEOUS? HAST THOU AN ARM LIKE GOD? OR CANST THOU THUNDER WITH A VOICE LIKE HIM? Thus answered the Lord unto Job out of the whirlwind. And also mine own right hand could save me. And behold, I did not lift up my hand to smite me for my sin nor violate the sanctity of life. AND DID NOT ONE FASHION US IN THE WOMB?

Famines, epidemics, massacres, and tyrannies had been the immediate successors to revolution in the Caucasian city, as we learned as soon as we arrived there in the spring. Mr. Pentecost decided, that afternoon of our arrival, that we must make haste to depart that place by any means possible. By evening he had purchased a cart and pair of oxen which were to take us across the mountains to the Kurdistan Mission. Such, however, were my fatigue and nausea that we delayed our departure that night, drew the cart behind the wall of a burned-out building which afforded a view of a large deserted cobblestone square, and made shift to rest as best we could. In the middle of the night we were wakened by a strange sound that was like the cry of multitudes within an echoing basilica. Then suddenly shouts, shots, screams rang out, a riderless horse clattered across the square, and a torchlit rabble of armed men, firing on the run, swarmed before our eyes! Never, said Mr. Pentecost, in all my time in the trenches and gasgreen woods of France saw I men as pitiful as these with their ragged frocks and tattered nankeen trousers and shoes of rags and paper, and yet they too will give their lives for liberty and brotherhood, for, alas, if you but observe yon faraway shadows, my dear Mrs. Pentecost, the godless swine who murder and enslave the very people whom they profess to liberate are about to send in cavalry. And all happened as he said. The night was filled with screams of wounded and dying, and the square was soon heaped with the corpses of men, women, and children chopped to pieces by the saber-wielding devils. Whereupon Mr. Pentecost wrung his hands and cried, how can there be liberty without restraint, humanity without reason, and brotherhood without atonement? When the horsemen were gone, we ventured into the square and rendered comfort where we could.

JUDGE DEBNAM BABBAGE PAUSED at the foot of the Court House steps, adjusted his wing collar and bowstring tie, tugged the brim of his Panama, and decided to run for governor.

IT VISITED ME IN THE WILDERNESS. The oxcart creaked and jolted for many days and I was in labor and I rejoiced in my fool's heart, thinking I had put the child of my darkness from me yet was given a new babe to cherish. But it must have been strangled somewhere on the road from Tiflis. Mr. Pentecost cried out, rise, Kate, see, and I saw it towering above the clouds until we lost sight of Mt. Ararat that day. We stopped in a valley of stones. I could go no further. All that night I lay in the cart while the snow thickened its silence about me. Then it was time. I tore a strip of quilting and gagged my mouth. Sweat and the effluvia of oxdung had impregnated it, but I was glad until I pushed and pulled the dead man-child toward the incandescent dawn. Lo, I knew the Lord was in it. I tore off the quilting. With my teeth I severed the cord and tied it with my hands that would not yet believe in this death but that the Lord was angry and must have my next child as His servant or bride. Then I lay down in a swoon and listened to the doom in my blood. I prepared my heart for destroying. The sea of God drowned me until we resumed our journey.

O Lord of Hosts come riding the Chariot of Thy Will, O my Lord and Redeemer, consider for I am vile but would be saved by Thy Grace and Mercy at the Last Trumpet.

JUDGE DEBNAM BABBAGE NOTICED a brown applecore at Mother Pentecost's feet. He decided that his first act as governor, if elected, would be to build luxurious communities for the retired, old and infirm.

IN THE SWEET CAUCASIAN SPRINGTIME *I discovered that partaking of a wine cordial just before bedtime considerably improved my temper, upon which this aphrodisiac acted so well that not long after our sorrow over the loss of one child, my womb was made fruitful again, much to the mutual gratification of dear Mr. Pentecost and myself. And lo, it came to pass that in the fullness of time I was delivered of my precious daughter Katherine whose life I at once consecrated to Thy service, Lord. And it came to pass that my breasts overflowed with milk, and word went forth to the heathen that this was so; and there came a veiled woman unable to suckle her newborn with Christian milk, therefore I gave it suck, and there also came a* *score of women with nurselings, and to these also I gave suck. Then were lambs and kids and puppies brought unto me, and I had milk for these. Lord, I had great store of milk.*

And all our children were the children of Noah. After several years they came to me with their laughter and hugged me with their spiky little arms and did much to restore me in spirit.

How radiant the manes of the horses of the sea, how fiery the wheels of the dawn! Such snorting and flaring of nostrils, such trampling of hooves!

She will sing at heaven's gate when the chariot arrives. Already radiant spokes are spinning, and spinning there also are the faces of the righteous and the ungodly, the good and the damned, and she sees there her father and Kitty and Fitzhugh St. George and Pentecost and Jackson and many others, and her amazement is too wonderful for surprise.

Our journey was long, the emigrant ship crowded. On the last morning Liberty rose from the mists like a dream or prophesy and lifted her lamp. And Mr. Pentecost and I joined those thronging the decks and cheering and waving HALLELUJAH, and my darling Kitty clapped her hands for joy and clung to me. Then was my heart full of rejoicing.

He comes for me at last. Already I hear the cobbleclattering horses of the first great dawn . . .

JUDGE DEBNAM BABBAGE REMOVED HIS PANAMA, bowed, and said, "Forgive me for intruding, ma'am, but may I offer you a ride home in my car?"

A moment later he realized that his courtesy was superfluous.

Chapter Twenty Two **Squint, Boom-Boom**

They were invisible men, though they were made of blood and bone and flesh, quite a lot of flesh in fact. They were nameless men, though they had names given them by their American moms and dads, and they had code names and numbers assigned them by American commissars, by quite a lot of commissars in fact. They were unknown men, though enough was known about them to provide detailed profiles for manila folders and data-processing cards: places of birth, parents' places of birth, race, education, churches preferred, distinctions, promotions, wives, habits, thoughts, especially thoughts. Did they live now, or did they intend to live, off the proceeds of prostitution? No. Had they ever been convicted of any crime or misdemeanor, if so, state particulars? No. Did they believe in the overthrow of the government? Certainly not. Did they have psychiatric consultation? Not applicable. They were friendless men, though their former military commanders, with whom they had brownnosed and killed, had filed buddy reports and commendations, and there were encomiastic letters of reference from schoolteachers, bank presidents, ministers, and football coaches, especially football coaches. They were mindless men, though their braincells functioned and responded to all the right stimuli: big breasts, Thanksgiving turkey with all the trimmings, Mother Nature, white pigmentation, dry martinis with just that whiff of vermouth, a night on the town with the boys, law and order and the flag, especially the flag. They were rootless men, though they were at home wherever they went, and they went to motels with swimming pools and T.V., to Western movies, to skinflicks, to strip clubs where pretty girls, for an extra century, would give them round-the-world, to nightclubs and gambling casinos, to country clubs to wear their off-duty sooper-dooper maroon trousers with white belts, and to bars, to quite a lot of bars in fact. They were always moved on. It was their job to be kept on the move, always the new towns, the new stakeouts, the new raids on junkies, perverts, and commies. They liked their work because it paid well, because questions had already been decided for them, because their nation's security depended upon them, and because they could look forward, wherever they were dispatched throughout the continent, to meeting new faces, new girls, new commissars—best of all, new commissars.

Had anything been wrong, somebody would have known.

There was presumably nothing wrong with the two men who reported to a commissar in Poe's Hill sometime during the last week in May. They had been to Poe's Hill before, living it up at the Bright Leaf Hotel until the time came to arrest that crip—Brodie?—take him to the top floor and shove him out the window. Both men in their mid-twenties, they had recently been circulating among some of their contemporaries; they hadn't shaved or washed in months, they had cultivated their blanked-out expressions, and they wore filthy T-shirts and jeans patched in the correct fashion. They established surveillance of Bermuda Farm and strapped on gun-belts.

The raid was set for June the seventh. They listened to the

taped telephone conversations of the professor and his girlfriend, but nothing interesting turned up here—except the fact of the girlfriend. Otherwise things were slick.

The commissar hadn't briefed them about his girlfriend. One of the men, the squinteyed one—called Squint—could do a slick job without worrying about the women. But Squint worried about the other man, whom he nicknamed Boom-Boom because of some incidents when women had been around. Over in Haight-Ashbury, Boom-Boom had busted a female junkie so hard that she splatted out against the wall and the plaster cracked and fell around her. Boom-Boom had to be watched. Otherwise things were slick.

And stayed slick until about eight o'clock on the night of the raid and they arrived in the darkening field where they had camouflaged their truck with its electronic devices and found these so battered and smashed that for some while they walked around in a daze, their whole world turned into a blank of imbecile outrage.

"Hey, man," Squint finally muttered after a low whistle, "you don't destroy government property."

"Shit, no," said Boom-Boom.

The men looked at each other in the dark, and without further words loosened revolvers in their holsters.

When they reached the farmhouse, it gleamed in a sheen of moonlight. They had expected the place to be deserted at this hour. Nevertheless, they followed the drill, first one man darting forward, crouched, then the other man. In this manner they came to stand together, breathing heavily, in the shadow of an oak tree. Here they drew their revolvers.

Squint nodded. Boom-Boom went.

Two seconds, perhaps three.

Out of the cricketloud moonblanched field streaked a growling beast that was already sinking fangs into Boom-Boom's leg, pinching deeply the nerve, already lunging for that shrieking man's throat before the report of a pistolshot echoing had brought some logical order to an instinctive kill.

The big yellow fyce was blown away several yards by the impact of a bullet. Its carcass spun in convulsion, the spine severed, not a whimper in the spasm of death.

Squint, his pistol arm still upraised though relaxing from recoil, rushed the farmhouse door, found it, incredibly, unlocked, and bolted upstairs.

He could see to his dismay that the bed was empty.

Chapter Twenty Three **Jackson, Max**

Hearing manshriek and pistolshot, Jackson knew Pharaoh would be dead. The dog had started snarling as soon as they reached the bluffs. Then the dog sprang, running low and hard out of sight just as the old man was limping in excruciating pain from the woods into the clearing about a hundred paces from the house. He stopped. A gnarled shadow uncoiled into the house, followed by another, lurching shadow. He melted, himself, into shadows of the pinewoods. He knew what sort of men these were, men who came with guns and manacles and pieces of white paper.

His blood ran cold. He ached in every limb. His body felt feverish and exhausted from its long battle with Old Red-Eye who to his imagination had been appearing and reappearing just beneath the surface, eluding every baited hook. Finally as the light faded and just before moonrise, the old man had saluted the river and accepted defeat. Life was ebbing from him even as he broke his rod and dropped it into the waters. He was leaving the wilderness for the last time, going home for the last time and not coming to the river again.

He sank to his knees, breathed resinous pine-needles, listened to the cry of a killdeer, piercing and funereal. He had been a strong man once. Now it was as if the bullet that had killed the dog had grazed his own heart, leaving him helpless and floundering just when all his strength was needed. It seemed to him he would not be strong enough to push himself to his feet again.

Through dim eyes he watched helplessly as windows of the house came ablaze with light and revealed disheveled men moving rapidly about. After a while the lights of the house went out.

But the killers remained inside.

MAX AND FANNY, FORTIFIED WITH HIGHBALLS served in President Koontz's office, were driving home about nine-thirty. "Now," Max declared with a pretence of exasperation, "explain."

A certain down-beat to her merriment accompanied the explanation. Fanny, having discovered Hasbrouck's ruse, had simply removed the carton of cocaine from the bookshelf and returned it to the Jaguar, under the seat. Later, before the committee met, she had telephoned the police to intercept the car at the airport. "It was all stupid," said Fanny. "I'm sorry Ginny has been arrested. I doubt she stoops to Hasbrouck's skullduggery. You know something?" she asked in a rising inflection.

"What?"

"When I first met him in California, on the night he promised to establish the Trust, he made a speech about his resentment of unhappiness. He was sincere, I'm sure . . . his unhappiness so obsessional that, on that occasion, he twisted a quotation from Shakespeare about cakes and ale . . ."

Max knew that one. " 'Dost thou think, because thou art virtuous . . '?"

"Yes, yes. But he said something like 'think not because thou art *bereft*'—as if his mind dwelled upon bereavement."

"*Why?*" Max exclaimed as his thought took another tangent.

"Why did Kitty marry him, of all people?"

"Haven't you, darling, discovered Kitty's reasons yet?"

"Search me," Max said.

"For the woman, *mi corazón*, a complete man is mind, heart, and body, but she is too realistic to expect to find a man with these in balance, so she may admire the mind where no heart is, or the man's body where the mind is like a baby's."

Keeping half of his concentration on the road, Max still shook his head. "You haven't answered about Kitty's *reasons*."

"Hasbrouck was incomplete for her: one reason. There's more. From what I have learned of Kitty, especially from her letters, she was a natural, clever, good young woman—at best—but, at worst, stilted, sentimental, and ultimately selfish and loveless. With due respect to the difficulty of her circumstances, she was—I'm sorry but you've had it coming—a fixer, a manipulator, a destroyer who almost destroyed you."

"I see." Max paused to let it all sink in. "In Hasbrouck she met a fellow fixer, one like herself though hollow and corrupt . . ." His voice trailed off. Then, in any icy flash of pain at the heart, he saw the truth he had stumbled brokenly toward all along. "She never loved me or anybody. She *couldn't* love me or anybody. Instead of love, she had . . . freedom. *Freedom without love*. Kitty Pentecost, my country 'tis of thee. Jesus. I mean Santa Claus, an illusion."

After a pause to allow Max's bitterness to subside, Fanny offered her own interpretation. "Maybe she's a genetic code. Look, she tried to connect. Like all of us, she tried to find her way out of darkness. You've said yourself, there's something in us that transcends us."

"Strange," Max remarked a few minutes later as he wheeled the Chevy down his driveway and brought it to a halt beside the oak tree. Usually by this time Pharaoh would have been illuminated by the highbeams, or, if Jackson had kenneled him in the barn, the barking would have already reached a frantic pitch. For a moment's thought, this logic held and seemed sustained, portentously, by the all-possessing cry of the crickets as he listened. Max shrugged, did not explain, sighed heavily. “It’s nothing, dear.”

“You’ve been under a strain,” said Fanny. “My bag’s upstairs, I’ll give you a knock-out injection, just as if you were in labor with twins.” She half-laughed. “Thank gods Monday’s my night off, and I can be more of a wife than a mid-wife.”

When, presently, Max opened the housedoor and flicked on the lights, he had but a moment to comprehend that his home had been pillaged, furniture broken, cushions slashed, books, papers, paintings, strewn about. In that moment he had already made a deduction concerning what Fanny had revealed about Hasbrouck’s planting of cocaine: somebody expected to find it on the premises. But even as adrenaline shot through his limbs, there came a continuous explosion that struck him on the jaw and in the pit of the stomach, and then something hard like the blunt end of an ax seemed to fall upon the tendons of his neck, and all was black . . .

AFTER SPINNING THROUGH A UNIVERSE held together by spiderwebs, Max returned to half consciousness, to a barrage on his senses. He tasted blood in his mouth. His neck was bowed under a cataract’s weight. His volition oppressed him with its first thought, *Get up*. If you were going to be killed, you would be killed standing up. It didn’t seem such a hell of a bad idea. Gradually, like a hoop unbending, he separated himself from his pain and stood up. He thought he saw a bearded, squintyeyed man pointing a revolver directly at his head.

The man spoke. “Turn around. Put your hands behind your back.”

“You’ve made a mistake,” Max said. His words had a slurred quality.

“Heavy, man.” The revolver motioned. Max turned. His wrists

were grabbed, swiftly manacled. A hard object pressed against the back of his skull. "Where is it, man? Gimme right answer or that's all she wrote."

She, she . . . she. "Where is she?" Max croaked. His brain formed words but his lips were too swollen to shape words, blood and spittle drooling down his chin.

"The chick's cooperating . . . The answer."

The revolver was a gimlet at the base of his skull.

"Dr. Hasbrouck was arrested tonight in possession of the stuff you're looking for. I want to see my . . . wife."

The revolver bored in. "Hey Boom-Boom!"

"Yeah?" a voice replied from upstairs.

"She said anything about a Dr. Hasbrouck?"

"Shit no. Wait," said the voice.

Max heard floorboards creaking overhead and a woman's soft laughter rising and relaxing . . .

No, Max thought. The protest repeated itself in his mind at first feebly and then in despair.

"She don't know nothing," came the voice from upstairs. It seemed a voice without reverent attention. "You leave us alone . . ." There was a pause, after which Max was pushed toward the open front door. "Move out," was the command. "I'm gonna show you what happens to people who destroy government property."

Max felt a little fear now. The white mountain of his dream glimmered to his perception, inviting him in. Images, ideas, plans for escape swooped and landed in his mind and took flight again. Doubts lingered longer, nothing credible was happening though he knew that things happened to other people, other places. Then in the dark, in the tall grass beside the driveway, he stumbled over an object which he recognized as the stiffened corpse of Chris's dog, eyes rolled into sockets, whites pale in the moonlight. Max concentrated on his footsteps, picking his way through the dew-glistening grasses of his fields, the house well behind him, thin clouds scudding across the moon as in a time of long ago at the beach the youth going to war and the experience of blind Chance. Regularly now the prod of the revolver in his back, he experienced a compulsion to lift his feet higher, each step, because his shoes were getting wet . . .

HE WOULD NOT HAVE KNOWN WHAT A STROKE WAS, except by the sensations of numbed helplessness and of dizziness in his eyes. Scent of pine-needles arrived on each suspiration. In intervals, the killdeer was shrieking, deadly.

Shadows quavered, then the shapes of two men materialized coming toward him across the field and passing by him, not ten paces away.

The gun, the manacles.

The chains rubbing, warping, the toes frozen, yet he lifted the hammer and brought it down, *huh*, and he lifted his hammer and brought it down, *huh*, and Mr. Burgess was there watching, *huh*, and Mr Burgess fondled his sawed off shotgun—*huh!*

Jackson's fingers began to claw the earth, faster, harder. Suddenly he could support the weight of his head and shoulders, then his chest. Sweat stung his eyes. His body no longer numbed but convulsing in one pain as if immolated in a sacrificial flame, he drew in his legs and, with what seemed the last of his ebbing strength, thrust himself upright.

He stumbled, careening against trees, through the woods . . .

MAX MADE UP HIS MIND NOT TO TRY TO REASON with the agent who was a professional, an unyielding force. Professionals could justify anything. You learned in war to identify this phenomenon. You learned as a professor pledged to expose cant and moral shams of all kinds to fear it. Max said nothing but went on thinking.

He was not particularly surprised to discover what the agent had in store for him: that anvil-shaped rock that was an outcropping of the bluffs and beneath which, by several hundred feet, was the hollow roar and pale gleam of the river. Even when he was prodded onto this rock and knew that he would be allowed to turn and face his assailant—and turned and saw that shabby, hulking emissary from the Court of Saint Apathy—he was thinking quite calmly of the report that he had committed suicide.

But no! There was more to it than—Yes! Brodie! Carlos Brodie! It had to have been this way. Murder, not suicide. *Carlos Brodie was murdered!* For nothing . . . except a dialogue with scientists who were slaves yearning, as in the poem, to be free.

The man had backed a few feet off the ledge. He held his revolver with two hands.

Yet hesitated.

Riverroar in his ears, Max felt an impulse to cry out that there had been a mistake, that it wasn't fair. He heard Ginny's mockery, *He's always teaching.* And held his tongue.

It was the agent who spoke quizzically, as if he expected his victims to beg for life. "Hey, man, say something."

There had always been in Max a conviction that it was all right to laugh. Retrospectively he would remember how, just then, a redbird had darted and the underbrush had given off the sound as of some small animal scampering, and how, not reasoning from these things, he had said, for a joke in which a middle finger should have been stiffened upwards, "Ecce Homo: Santa Claus."

But then everything happened in one swoop that would be, retrospectively, a sequence: the stumbling warwhooping charge of Jackson from the woods, the agent's wheeling about and firing two shots rapidly but too late, his body grappled and, in that embrace, torn from the earth and thrust, still embraced, for several horrifying seconds, to the silence of the screaming river. That cry would haunt him for the rest of his life in whatever warm bed or dim alleyway he would make his own last farewell, but he was running now toward a future he could not know and from a past he no longer cared about . . .

He burst into the house and, there, leveling a revolver at him, stood Fanny.

Just behind her, crumpled at the foot of the stairs, lay Boom-Boom.

"My gods, I almost shot you. I thought you were the other one . . . Oh Max." She flung herself on his neck.

Little by little, Max pieced together what she had done.

Seeing him unconscious and mauled and seeing how the house had been ransacked, she had known at once how things would go with her if she lost her nerve. The first thing she had said was that she was a doctor and that she needed to get her bag upstairs in order to give Max medical attention. The big oaf, the one called Boom-Boom, said he would take her upstairs. There was a quarrel about this, but presently she did go upstairs, though cautioned to go slowly since the oaf, apparently, was in pain from a dog bite in his leg. From this information she had taken her lead. Up in the bedroom she coaxed the oaf into believing that she was ignorant of any knowledge of what the officers wanted but that she, as a doctor and ordinary citizen, always cooperated with the police. Then she pretended to be upset about the oaf's tooth-gashed leg. He would require a tetanus shot at once. There was a rabid dog in the neighborhood: anybody bitten by it would be dead of lockjaw within a short period of time unless jabbed with a tetanus shot. In case Mr. Boom-Boom didn't trust her, she would fill the hypo while he watched. He could jab himself. All this time she could see in the oaf's eyes what he really wanted. About this time Max had been marched out of the house. She had the oaf thinking he was making a conquest. The rest of the story was simplicity itself:

instead of preparing a hypo of tetanus vaccine, she had filled one with a massive dosage of pathadine, a drug she often administered to patients on the maternity ward.

Fanny hugged Max and laughed lightly against his chest. "I don't think he knew what hit him after I jabbed him. His eyes spaced out as if concentrating on events in another galaxy. His tongue protruded. He leapt off the bed, strode to the top of the stairs, and collapsed head over heels. The patient, Mr. Boom-Boom, is resting comfortably."

Chapter Twenty Four **Tom**

After a long labor, Helen was delivered of a son about one o'clock in the morning at the university hospital. As that time approached, Tom was invited into the delivery room. There Helen lay swathed in sheets while masked white figures encouraged her to push and finally from the shaven, breached perineum delivered the sleek salamander head and wizened face, presently crying, hungering in wilderness.

Helen's had been the cry of wild joy, bestowing gladness upon Tom's spirit. He felt as if he were springing on air. He no longer only lived for himself and Helen. He lived in the environment of a new world.

Helen's bed was one among many in a semi-private ward. Tom was permitted to visit with her until the first feeding some hours later. Curling up at the foot of her bed, he fell asleep.

About five o'clock he was wakened by a voice calling over a loudspeaker system, "MOTHERS, PREPARE FOR YOUR BABIES . . . MOTHERS, PREPARE FOR YOUR BABIES."

A nurse came through swinging doors pushing a four-tiered trolley full of swaddled babes like warm yeasty bread.

He kissed Helen and walked quickly down echoing corridors to a reception room where he telephoned the police. He informed them about Mason, pusher of drugs.

There had been a time in May when Tom was walking down Cornwallis Street on his way home from an art-history class. Outside Mason's store stood Widge, smirking. Widge had shown him a wad of money that was a lot of money and Widge had boasted about what he was doing with the money and then had gone, with Tom, into the store and had done it. Mason had looked glum and glowering but perhaps had believed Tom would not squeal to police and Tom had not, at that time, upheld law because Mason had befriended his mother.

Now the world was cast in a new, different light.

As he was leaving the hospital, Tom saw a coin-operated box that was riveted to the wall and inscribed:

WHILE U WAIT
START THE DAY RITE
Insert Dime
THE LORD'S PRAYER WILL PLAY.

He went outside and breathed the great morning.

Our Father.

He was alone in the great morning, alone but jubilant, and he didn't need drink to celebrate, ever again. His pace quickened until he was jogging and leaping and yelling at the top of his lungs, "Mothers, prepare for your babies!"

Biography

Alexander Blackburn was born in Durham, N.C., where his father at Duke University was a teacher of writers, including such future luminaries as William Styron, Mac Hyman, Reynolds Price, Anne Tyler and William deBuys. Blackburn carried a passion for writing across his academic training at Andover, Yale, UNC Chapel Hill, and Cambridge University (Ph.D. in English). After graduation from Yale he volunteered in the U.S. Army during the Korean War. After stints teaching creative writing at the University of Pennsylvania and world classics at the University of Maryland's European Division, he pioneered in the teaching of those subjects at the new University of Colorado at Colorado Springs, where he founded and edited *Writers' Forum*, a literary journal dedicated to discovering and publishing writers from the West. Blackburn has edited two anthologies of stories by Western writers, and recently he discovered, selected and edited *Gifts From the Heart*, memories and chronicles by the daughter of a Latino cowboy. Groundbreaking critical studies by Blackburn have also been published: *The Myth of the Picaro* (North Carolina), *A Sunrise Brighter Still: The Visionary Novels of Frank Waters* (Ohio

University Press) and *Creative Spirit: Toward a Better World* (Creative Arts). His memoir, *Meeting the Professor: Growing Up in the William Blackburn Family* (John F. Blair), identifies true educators as great-hearted artists. The main thrust of Blackburn's literary endeavors has been as author of the novels *The Cold War of Kitty Pentecost, Suddenly a Mortal Splendor, The Voice of the Children in the Apple Tree, and The Door of the Sad People.* He lives in Colorado Springs with his wife, Dr. Inés Dölz-Blackburn, Chilean-born author and professor of Spanish Language and Literature.

About the Type

The Cold War of Kitty Pentecost
is set in *Adobe Minion Pro.*

Minion is an old style serif typeface inspired by letters used during the late Renaissance-era. It was designed in 1990 by Robert Slimbach for Adobe Systems. It has proven to be a popular and adaptive type, used for everything from Stieg Larsson's Millennium Trilogy to other languages including Arabic, Cyrillic, Hebrew, Thai, and Song (Chinese). Minion is noted for its versatility, warmth and balance, making it one of the most readable and widely-used fonts available today.

Have you seen
our other
Rhyolite Press
Publications . . ?

"I am pleased to highly recommend Don's memoir, expecially of his Bureau service. I always found him to be an exceptionally capable and responsible agent. This memoir should instill and impress interest in those seeking a career in government. A career that embodies service before self and dedication to country".

—Jack Egnor, former agent-in-charge, Denver division of the FBI

The Voice of the Children in the Apple Tree

by

Alexander Blackburn

Alexander Blackburn is one of the most important writers in the American West today. —The Bloomsbury Review

This major novel offers a vision of hope for the future: Citation of Alexander Blackburn's *The Voice of the Children in the Apple Tree* for the International PeaceWriting Award.

$18.95 at bookstores everywhere, or direct from the publisher:
www.rhyolitepress.com

ISBN 978-0-9896763-2-8

The Voice of the Children in the Apple Tree

The love of a New England heiress who becomes a public nurse and of a country boy from the south and southwest who becomes an atomic physicist spans half of the twentieth century and culminates in their repudiation of the decision to use the atomic bombs against Japan in the Second World War. The shared conscience and intrepid compassion of Trinc and Aeneas reveal the inter-connectedness of life, the refuge of a new world of consciousness, and the hope for recovered innocence, one suggested by T.S. Eliot's imagery, "The voice of the children in the apple tree." This epic novel braids the lives of highly individual, brightly vivid characters into the history of their times. It is a love story for the ages that takes place in the shadow of the atomic bomb.

The atomic bomb is a turning point in world history. Both Trinc and Aeneas are closely involved in historical events, inseparable from them, and the vicissitudes they endure are those ingrained in the times they live through. They are terrific characterizations! *The Voice of the Children in the Apple Tree* is large, the event momentous, and the perspective always fitting. Here is another real triumph.

—Fred Chappell, Poet Laureate of North Carolina

The Door of the Sad People is a coming-of-age story that takes place against the background of the Colorado coalmining wars long-remembered for the Ludlow Massacre of 1914. Visionary, the novel traces the tyrannous countenance of a corporate society to its origins in humankind's "sad" limitations and flaws.

Young Tree Penhallow escapes an abusive father and an attempted murder but finds a surrogate father in "Kill Devil" Dare, a friend in Mother Jones, "the miners' angel," and a home in a loving, once-patrician Hispanic family now eking out a hardscrable life through farming and mining. When his adoptive family is almost entirely exterminated by militia during a strike, a spiritual "door" opens, confirming for Tree the eternal truth of compassion, how it holds humanity together.

Tree Penhallow matures into an artist and hero who confronts the violent and perverse powers of evil, a theme as relevant to today's world as it was to the world of yesterday.

Every once in a while a good unknown writer gets anointed, the Pulitzer committee issues a prize, and sales jump. Still, for every winner there are scores of writers who are as good but are virtually unread. To that list of unknown writers, good writers toiling in obscurity, add the name of Alexander Blackburn.

—*The Dallas Morning News*

Colorado Noir is a walk on the dark and wild side of America's most controversial city. Ten stories and one novella.

$16.95 at bookstores everywhere, or direct from the publisher:
www.rhyolitepress.com

ISBN 978-0-9896763-0-4

"This guy is the next Tom Clancy"

Bill Hill, USAF (Ret)

Colorado Noir by John Dwaine McKenna
is our first multiple award-winning publication

Praise for *The Neversink Chronicles*

"A gifted and natural born story teller with command of dialog and dialect. Congratulations!"
—Clark Secrest, Author, *Hells Bells,* San Diego, CA

"A gifted storyteller. An amazing first book. Keep writing, you have a great future ahead of you."
—Allison Auch, Copy Editor, Durango, CO

"Hated parting with the manuscript, as I knew things were changing quickly in *Neversink*. That's when you know you have a great book in your hands."
—*Leigh Daily*, Paralegal, Boulder, CO

"This is a book to read over and over. The people are real, the life is true and the author has to have been everywhere and met everyone to have captured all of these personalities so well. I'm waiting for more from him."
—Mary Lelia, Austin,Texas

" 'Just Another Day', gave me chills remembering my own Vietnam experience".
—Skip Mooney, Financial Consultant, Manitou Springs, CO

". . . and the winner, First Prize for fiction, 2012 goes to . . .
The Neversink Chronicles"

18th Annual CIPA Awards Ceremony
Denver, CO May 17, 2012

The Whim - Wham Man

A STORY THAT HAS IT ALL . . .
A CRIME YOU CAN'T FORGIVE
A PLOT YOU COULDN'T IMAGINE
AND A CHARACTER . . .
YOU'LL NEVER FORGET!

There's no sanitary way to write about murder. "The Whim-Wham Man," a gut-punching novel of a teen-aged boy whose idyllic life in rural Colorado comes crashing down when reality and adulthood rush in after the brutalization and savage killing of two young girls . . . **It's a helluva yarn.**

CIPA EVVY Award Winner, 2013
2nd prize, Best Fiction

$15 at bookstores everywhere, or direct from the publisher:
www.rhyolitepress.com

ISBN 978-0-9839952-2-7

<u>Praise for ***The Whim-Wham Man***</u>

"It's a helluva yarn."
—Dick Kreck, Author of *Murder at the Brown Palace* and *Smaldone*

"Great Job! It got my blood boiling! Then it got my mind thinking."
—Linda Comando, Publisher and Editor of *The Tri-Valley Townsman*

"It was like eating popcorn . . . I couldn't quit. Congratulations. I am looking forward to more Jake McKern novels."
—Bill Calls, Scottsdale, AZ

"This short book with the odd title is the hard-to-put-down story of a 15-year-old youth who grows up in a hurry when a grisly tragedy strikes his family."
—Mary Jean Porter, *The Pueblo Chieftain*

"Well-written, so compelling I couldn't stop reading until the last page."
—S.M. Albany, NY

"*The Whim-Wham Man* is the most thought-provoking novel I've read in a long time. Thanks for writing it."
—Kathy Hare, *The New Falcon Herald*

". . . and the silver award winner for fiction 2013 is . . .

The Whim-Wham Man."
19th Annual CIPA EVVY Awards, Denver Co
May 10, 2013

THE BOY WHO SLEPT WITH BEARS

Pulled from the pages of history, a fiction novel that tells the heart wrenching and heartwarming story of Tomas Dequine, or Sak-wa-ma-tu-ta-ci, 'Blue Hummingbird' in his native tongue, a thirteen-year-old Southern Ute boy whose family and way of life are being crushed by the onrush of white European settlers in 1880s Colorado . . . a time when the Utes were being driven off of their ancestral lands to be resettled on reservations. Told in a warm, grandfatherly voice, Douthit's novel is a past winner of a coveted golden CIPA-EVVY award for fiction. It has been read and loved by ages eight to eighty, and contains a reader's guide and bibliography.

One of our hottest novels!

CIPA EVVY Award Winner, 2005
1st prize, Best Fiction

$15 at bookstores everywhere, or direct from the publisher:
www.rhyolitepress.com

ISBN 978-0-9839952-8-9

Praise for *The Boy Who Slept with Bears*

I loved this book and didn't want it to end as I grew to understand Tomas and his relationship with the earth and brother bear. A great book for young and old alike.

—Valorie R. Hornsby

George Douthit's book *The Boy Who Slept with Bears*, is the moving story of a Southern Ute boy coming of age at a time when the Ute traditional territories were being overrun by non indians during the gold rush and the Utes removed to reservations. The author captures the boy's desire to avenge his father's murder at the hands of white soldiers. He steps from boyhood into a man's world while struggling to hold onto his traditional beliefs. Though fictional, Douthit weaves true historical details of the Southern Utes and a legendary grizzly bear named "Old Mose" into a masterful story that leaves the reader enthralled and captivated.

—Vickie Leigh Krudwig, Author, *Searching for Chipeta*

A terrific read for both young and old! Outstanding! *The Boy Who Slept with Bear* is the best book about native Americans I've ever read. Please send two more copies for my nephews.

—Leonard Foxworth

Prune Pie
And Other Moving Stories

by Victoria Ward

The heartfelt stories in *Prune Pie* are laced with humor and truth and spoken in clear, homespun language that is both compelling and entertaining. Don't miss Victoria Ward's true tales of her life on the road with the soulmate and cowboy troubadour husband she calls "Bear".

$15 at bookstores everywhere, or direct from the publisher:
www.rhyolitepress.com

ISBN 978-1-943829-00-2
eBook ISBN 978-1-943829-01-9

"Life on the road can be rather mundane for a cowboy singer. That is, unless your wife is traveling with you, and can find humor in every situation. In *Prune Pie & Other Moving Stories*, Victoria Ward not only pokes fun at her award-winning husband, Barry Ward, but she also occasionally owns up to her own blunders. You don't even have to like cowboy music to enjoy these stories. This is a fun read."

— Orin Friesen KFDI Radio, Wichita, Kansas

www.ingramcontent.com/pod-product-compliance
Lightning Source LLC
LaVergne TN
LVHW041113080826
845145LV00007B/1794
* 9 7 8 1 9 4 3 8 2 9 0 7 1 *